CITY OF DREADFUL NIGHT

First gripping mystery in the Brighton Trilogy

July 1934. A woman's torso is found in a trunk at Brighton railway station's left luggage office. Her identity is never established, her killer never caught. But someone is keeping a diary. July 2009. Ambitious radio journalist Kate Simpson hopes to solve the notorious Brighton Trunk Murder, and she enlists the help of ex-Chief Constable Robert Watts, whose role in the recent botched armed-police operation in Milldean, Brighton's notorious no-go area, cost him his job. But it's only a matter of time before past and present collide...

CITY OF DREADFUL NIGHT

Peter Guttridge

Severn House Large Print
London & New York

This first large print edition published 2011
in Great Britain and the USA by
SEVERN HOUSE PUBLISHERS LTD of
9-15 High Street, Sutton, Surrey, SM1 1DF.
First world regular print edition published 2010 by
Severn House Publishers Ltd., London and New York.

British Library Cataloguing in Publication Data

   City of dreadful night. -- (Brighton trilogy)
   1. Cold cases (Criminal investigation)--England--Fiction.
   2. Riots--England--Brighton--Fiction. 3. Police chiefs--
   England--Brighton--Fiction. 4. Radio journalists--
   Fiction. 5. Brighton (England)--Social conditions--
   Fiction. 6. Detective and mystery stories. 7. Large type
   books.
   I. Title II. Series
   823.9'2-dc22

   ISBN-13: 978-0-7278-7965-3

Severn House Publishers support The Forest Stewardship Council
[FSC], the leading international forest certification organisation. All
our titles that are printed on Greenpeace-approved FSC-certified paper
carry the FSC logo.

MIX
Paper from
responsible sources
FSC
www.fsc.org
FSC® C018575

Printed and bound in Great Britain by the
MPG Books Group, Bodmin, Cornwall.

For the late John Wynn

MAIN CHARACTERS

Sarah Gilchrist –
  Detective Sergeant, Brighton police force

John Hathaway –
  Brighton crime boss

Kate Simpson –
  Radio journalist

William Simpson –
  Government fixer and Kate Simpson's father

James Tingley –
  ex-SAS soldier and security adviser

Donald Watts –
  Novelist (writing as Victor Tempest) and
  Robert Watts's father

Molly Watts –
  Robert's wife

Robert Watts –
  Chief Constable, Brighton police force

Reg Williamson –
  Detective Sergeant, Brighton police force

'The City is of Night; perchance of Death'
The City of Dreadful Night (1874)
by James Thomson (B.V.),
not known for laughs.

'Brighton – the City Beautiful'
Sir Herbert Cordon, idealistic creator
of much that is good and
much that is bad about Brighton.
Just about balances out.

PROLOGUE

Brighton Gazette, Saturday, 23 June, 1934

GHASTLY FIND AT BRIGHTON

BODY IN TRUNK

WOMAN CUT TO PIECES

SCOTLAND YARD'S TASK

Brighton was shocked early in the week by the news of a particularly horrible crime which came to light with the finding of the nude torso of a woman in a trunk at Brighton Central Railway Station, and the discovery of the legs in the King's Cross Station Luggage Office.

The grim discovery was made on Sunday evening, 17th June. The trunk was forced open after there had been a complaint to the police that there was an offensive smell coming from it. The naked remains of the woman were found inside. The head, legs and arms had been sawn off. The trunk had been deposited on Wednesday, 6th June.

Clue of Letters

The remains were wrapped in brown paper and tied with window cord. On the edge of the paper, written in blue pencil, are the letters 'ford'.

Scotland Yard was called in to deal with the ghastly affair, in conjunction with the local police. Chief Detective Inspector Donaldson and Detective Sergeant Sorrell at once came down and set to work after a long conference with the Brighton Chief Constable, Capt. W. J. Hutchinson.

It was at first thought that the woman was about forty years of age, but later Sir Bernard Spilsbury, the country's leading forensic pathologist, gave as his opinion that she was in her twenties and certainly not more than thirty years old.

Legs found at King's Cross

There came a startling development on Monday evening, 18th June, when detectives from Scotland Yard visited King's Cross station and in the Left Luggage department found a suitcase which contained the legs missing from the Brighton body.

The suitcase at King's Cross was deposited on 7th June, the day after the trunk was deposited at Brighton. The attention of an attendant at King's Cross was drawn to the case by the odour.

The Inquest

The proceedings only lasted two minutes before Mr Charles Webb, the Deputy Coroner, adjourned the enquiry until Wednesday, 18th July, at eleven o'clock.

Mr Webb summarized the events of the past few days since the body was discovered. Referring to Sir Bernard Spilsbury's examination of the previous day, Mr Webb said there were no marks or scars on the body by which it could be identified. The cause of death was not known.

ONE

I will not screw up.

Detective Sergeant Sarah Gilchrist repeated the sentence to herself like a mantra. She was determined to do everything right. Aside from anything else, she refused to give Finch the satisfaction. He was boorish about women police officers at the best of times, but when it came to them taking part in armed response operations he was positively Neanderthal.

For the same reason she was determined not to show her fear. All the way here in the van he'd been coming on Mr Machismo whilst she'd been trying not to vomit.

John Finch was now at least out of sight around the other side of this seedy house as Gilchrist crouched in its rubbish-strewn back garden, her pistol clenched tightly in her fist. She was anxious but determined, trying to stay focused – on her breathing, on the job in hand.

Three officers were crouched beside her. Two more were poised beside the back door, the battering ram hanging from short leather loops between them. There were police marksmen in upstairs rooms of the houses immediately behind her.

They were all waiting for the word in their

13

earpieces to signal the start of the operation.

In her anxiety, Gilchrist's physical discomfort loomed large.

It was a hot, humid evening; beneath her body armour she was dripping sweat. Her knees were aching from the crouching, her thighs and calves were feeling constricted. One of the team, possibly her, had trodden in some dog shit. The stink made her want to vomit even more.

She felt heavy, weighed down, sinking into the soft earth beneath her boots. Yet in a moment or two she would have to surge forward and go through that back door at the gallop.

Her unit's job was to secure the ground floor of the house. The kitchen was the other side of the back door, then there was a passage with first the dining room and then the living room off to the right. On the left, the staircase to the first floor faced the front door. The other unit would come through that door at the same time and head for the first floor and its target.

The target had entered the house at eight p.m. carrying bottles in a plastic bag from the local off-licence. He was reported to be upstairs in the front bedroom. He was reported to be alone.

This would be Gilchrist's fourth armed home arrest but she was more anxious than she'd been on her first.

Partly, this was because of the relative inexperience of the members of this evening's task force. It was supposed to comprise the tactical firearms unit of the South East Constabulary, acting as support for an elite team from Gatwick Airport.

The airport officers were well used to armed operations but the Gatwick team couldn't leave the airport because of a terrorist alert. Her team had become the lead unit whilst a second unit from three different divisions had been hurriedly assembled. For some members it was their first operation. And none of them had worked together before.

That would have been OK had Danny Moynihan been leading the operation on the ground. Moynihan, ex-SAS, was experienced, careful, as cool as they come. She trusted him implicitly after her other three operations with him. But at the last moment he'd been stood down – she didn't know why – and replaced by Chief Superintendent Charlie Foster. Who was definitely second eleven.

The timing of the operation was unfortunate too. The other operations she'd been involved with had been dawn raids, the targets asleep in their beds. Sunrise streaking the sky as the house doors front and back had been breached, the explosion of violence rupturing the morning's calm.

But this was ten in the evening. Dusk had just fallen, but there were lots of people out in their gardens, television shows and music blaring from open windows, cars revving by. Ten in the evening, there were all sorts of problems. Especially here, in this neighbourhood.

The main reason for her anxiety.

'It's straightforward enough,' Charlie Foster had said in the briefing before they left the station thirty minutes before – but he was sweating when he said it. 'Career criminal called Bernard Grimes. Wanted in connection with a string of armed robberies and the shooting of two security guards in a payroll robbery in Willesden. Hard nut.

'He's got a place on the Cote de Crime – all the best crooks prefer Provence to the Costa Brava these days.' He got a rumble of laughter for that. 'We have a tip from a reliable source that he's heading there via tomorrow morning's New-haven–Dieppe car ferry. And that he's spending tonight in a house in Milldean.'

Several people groaned when Foster men-tioned Milldean. It was one of the toughest neighbourhoods in Brighton, ruled for genera-tions by half a dozen crime families. The closely packed housing estate was a virtual no-go area for the police.

'We're going in mob-handed, I hope, sir,' Finch said. He was a burly man with a shaved head and a little indent in his ear where once he used to wear a ring.

'On the contrary, John. We don't want a pitch-ed battle or a riot. We want it to be fast. We'll set the roadblocks, isolate the house, get the marksmen in position. Then we'll flood into the premises, close him down, get him out of there and off the estate. It's a classic Bermuda.'

Bermuda as in Bermuda Triangle. That was the name the force used for its standard armed build-ing-entry technique because it was a triangulated operation. Front, back, marksmen outside at elevated points. Not that Gilchrist was super-stitious, but she'd always wondered if the name

16

could also mean that the target might disappear without trace.

'Lean and mean,' Finch said.

It was Finch's first operation with the tactical firearms unit. Gilchrist assumed his bravado was a mask for his nerves. He couldn't really be like that – could he? If he was, she couldn't understand how he had got on the team. Sure, armed response units comprised people like him who were fit and had quick reflexes. But these people were also calm, focused and thoughtful. Well, that was the theory. How somebody as gung-ho as Finch had got through the psychological testing, Gilchrist couldn't imagine.

'This is a one-night-only offer, ladies and gentlemen,' Foster said. 'We miss him tonight and he's gone. Any questions?'

Geoff 'Harry' Potter, one of the more phlegmatic of the team, raised a hand.

'If he's being sheltered by one of the families, he's unlikely to be alone.'

'The intelligence we have indicates there's no link with any of the families. I'm confident it's one hundred per cent accurate. We've had the house under surveillance for the past two hours.'

Gilchrist shifted in her crouch to ease her legs. She'd been in the back garden about three minutes but it seemed ten times longer. She strained at the static in her ears, willing Charlie Foster's voice to come through.

She was vaguely aware of muffled music from the pub on the corner. It became louder when the pub doors opened and a raucous din spilled out.

'We're going on a count of three,' Foster said quietly, his voice unexpectedly intimate inside her ear.

A car horn blared.

'Damn!' The voice in her ear was strained. 'All units: go!'

As Gilchrist hurled herself towards the rear of the house, the two officers stationed against the back wall swung the ram and hit the door just above the lock. The door flew open, splinters flying. The two men took up positions either side of the door.

Lights came on in the house. Her three colleagues with Heckler & Koch machine pistols went into the kitchen first. She scanned left to right as she came through the door. Unwashed crockery piled in the sink. Harsh fluorescent lighting set crookedly in the ceiling.

The passage was ahead, a turn, then the staircase. She was aware of the unit that had come through the front door pounding up the stairs.

Her unit fanned into the dining room. Prints of seaside landscapes in cheap frames on the walls.

They looked behind the door, under the table. Nobody.

Down the hall to the living room. Widescreen TV and DVD player in the corner. Magazines and redtop newspapers strewn on the sofa. Toffee wrappers and cigarette stubs overflowing an ashtray.

They looked behind the sofa and the single armchair. Nobody.

From upstairs she heard shouted commands. Then, the sharp crack of a gunshot. And another.

Her three colleagues looked at each other. Ignored her. Jostled into the hall. Started up the stairs. More shots, too close together to say how many.

When Gilchrist moved to follow, the last one on the stairs waved her back. She remained in the living-room doorway, tilting her head to try to see up to the first floor. Out of the corner of her eye she saw a door under the staircase open.

None of them had spotted it when they'd come down the corridor. It opened towards her, obscuring her view of who was on the other side of it. She heard the sound of someone hoofing it towards the kitchen.

Gilchrist took two steps and barged the cupboard door closed. A skinny guy in white T-shirt, jeans and trainers headed through the kitchen to the open doorway. He was holding something away from his body in his left hand.

The thought that there was only supposed to be one person in the house flitted through her brain. Was this skinny man Grimes? If so, then what was the shooting upstairs about?

She aimed at the man's back.

'Halt, armed police officer!' she called, relieved that her voice was steady and clear. 'Drop your weapon and halt!'

The man kept moving. Adrenaline surged in her. She knew she couldn't – wouldn't – shoot him. If she did, she'd kill him. She'd been trained to take no chances, trained to aim for the biggest target with the most body mass. Don't try tricky leg, head or arm shots.

19

She'd been trained like that but even so she aimed at his left leg just above the knee. She aimed but she didn't fire. The man went through the doorway into the garden.

And almost immediately re-entered the kitchen, flung backwards, arms wide. He landed with a heavy thud flat on his back, blood spreading across his chest. As he hit the floor, whatever was in his left hand skidded away into the corner of the room.

Fuck. Gilchrist edged cautiously towards the prone man, nervous of presenting a target to the trigger-happy police marksman outside.

The man wasn't moving. Blood spread across the kitchen floor. Gilchrist swallowed. There was little doubt the man had died a split-second before he'd come flying back through the door.

She frowned when she realized she had stepped in his blood. Frowned again when she couldn't immediately see what had fallen from his hand anywhere on the floor.

Whatever it was, it could have slithered under one of the cupboards that lined the walls to her left. She was trying to puzzle out how to check without contaminating the crime scene or getting herself shot when she heard heavy boots clumping down the stairs.

Then, in her ear, intimate again despite its agitation, Foster's voice.

'Stand down. Everybody stand down.'

Finch and two officers Gilchrist didn't recognize filled the passage. Finch was white-faced, his eyes panicked. The three men crowded into the kitchen. Finch looked at the body at Gil-

20

christ's feet.

'Shit, Gilchrist – you do that?'

His voice trembled. One of the men with him pushed forward. Gestured to her.

'You're needed upstairs. We'll take care of this.'

Gilchrist bridled at his tone.

'And you are?'

The man was about six inches taller than her and broad enough to fill up most of the kitchen doorway. He smiled, revealing two missing front teeth. It made him look like a big kid.

'Just a messenger. You're needed upstairs.'

He stepped to one side, extending his hand in an invitation for her to go past. Finch was still gawping at the body on the floor. The second man was smirking at Gilchrist.

She pushed past them and headed for the first floor. There was a bedroom at the top of the stairs. Harry Potter was standing against the wall looking blankly along the landing.

Gilchrist edged past him. A second door was open to her right. A bathroom. The toilet faced the door. A man was sitting on it, hunched forward, his head over his bony knees, his trousers and a widening pool of blood eddying around his ankles.

Most of the policemen were crowded in the doorway of the front bedroom, looking in, guns dangling. She could hear a television blaring somewhere in the room.

She was tall enough to see over the shoulders of the two who were blocking her way. She saw the double bed, saw the man sitting up in it. He was bare-chested, tilted to one side. There was a spray of blood and other material on the wall behind him and a red jagged hole in the centre of his forehead. Someone hadn't been aiming at body mass.

The naked woman sitting dead beside him had no face left to speak of.

Gilchrist seemed to have a heightened sense of smell. The man and woman had been having sex, she could tell. But there was also the smell of cordite, sweat, blood and shit.

She could hear the heavy breathing of the policemen all around her. Ragged, snorting. Animal.

'I was told I was needed upstairs,' she said to the first policeman to notice her presence. He looked at her coldly. Slowly, they all turned to her. She shivered.

'Chief Superintendent Foster?' she said.

The first man she'd addressed tilted his head as if to get a better look at her. He frowned.

'Outside.'

She went back down the stairs. She glanced down the corridor to the kitchen as if she could picture tomorrow's headline there, printed in large letters on the fridge. Neatly alliterative: Massacre in Milldean.

Finch and the other two policemen had gone. The body of the skinny man was still there. The pool of blood had spread wider across the floor, thick and syrupy, though other footprints had now joined her own. Finch and the others she assumed.

She walked to the door of the kitchen and,

crouching, peered under the cupboards. She was thinking about what had fallen from the man's hand. But she could see nothing.

TWO

I was at an official dinner in the banqueting room of the Royal Pavilion when the roof fell in on my career. My beeper vibrated in my belt just as Bernard Rafferty was beginning to grate.

Rafferty was the director of the Pavilion, a pompous little man who also wrote political biographies. I saw him all the time in Brighton – for though it might be a city, it is still a small town – but I also regularly encountered him in national radio and TV studios. We were both used as pundits, although his favourite topic of conversation was himself. Tonight he was launching a fund-raising initiative to turn a run-down part of the city near the station into a cultural quarter.

I was sitting at one of a number of round tables in the ornately decorated room. They were ordered around the long central table set for a Victorian banquet. A huge dragon chandelier hung over it from the canopied ceiling decorated with fantastic animals. Around the perimeter of the room were Spode blue lampstands and rosewood sideboards and the walls were hung with large canvases of Chinese domestic scenes. The

23

room was an incredible confection. As was this gathering.

The top table was filled with local politicians and wealthy businessmen. Both the city's MPs were there with the Leader of the Council, Rupert Colley, sandwiched between them. All three looked to be texting on their phones. Winston Hart, the head of the Southern Police Authority, was gazing up at the ceiling.

I was hoping the Prince Regent had more fun when he stayed here than I'd ever had at these dinners. A young woman from the council's tourism department had been mildly flirting. She'd pressed her business card into my hand and insisted I call her if I ever wanted a private tour of the Pavilion. I'd enjoyed the attention but had not taken it seriously. I loved my wife, Molly, who was at home in the grip of another migraine.

Events like this were enough to induce migraine in anyone. Molly, however, was particularly unsuited to her role as company wife. She suffered from depression. It had come on after the birth of our second child, Tom, and had never really gone away.

Medication lifted her moods but, in common with many depressives, when her mood was lifted she chose not to take the medication, thus prompting a new bout of despair.

I whispered an excuse to the tourism officer and left the banqueting room unobtrusively, looking at the number on the beeper only when I was in the corridor.

My deputy, Philip Macklin. I frowned. I'm an obsessive by nature. I've always found it diffi-

24

cult to delegate. Once I made Chief Constable – the youngest in the country – I recognized that was neither practicable nor good management practice. I resolved that my management style would be as liberal as my policing policies – well, all but one of my policing policies.

Delegation was key, I knew, and because I was reluctant I overcompensated. I delegated too much. The difficulty I had with delegation was compounded in my deputy's case by the fact that I wasn't sure he was up to the job.

I speed-dialled him.

'Philip, it's Bob.'

'Sorry to disturb you, sir, but we have a major situation.' Macklin sounded panicked. No change there, then. 'A dynamic entry by the tactical firearms unit. Home arrest. The information was sound ... Seemed sound.'

'Terrorists?'

'No, sir.'

'You were the gold commander?'

My force operated the standard gold/silver/ bronze system of command and control for firearms operations and incidents. Gold commanders, who were at least chief inspectors or superintendents, could take responsibility for authorizing firearms issue for specific operations. They took strategic command with the help of a tactical adviser.

One of the things I intended to address was that we had far too many officers qualified to be gold commanders. There were around seventy, which meant that none of them got an opportunity to gain much experience of this most sensitive of duties.

For dynamic entry, the gold commander needed to be one of my four assistant chief constables. Macklin, as my deputy, was the most senior, though not the best.

'I'm gold commander, yes, sir.'

'Pre-planned or spontaneous?'

We divided firearms operations into those two categories.

'It falls somewhere between the two. We had about two hours' notice.'

I could hear muffled applause in the banqueting room. Rafferty had finally stopped preening.

'Any of our people hurt?'

'None, sir.'

'Good. What happened?'

'Information was received from an impeccable source. A violent criminal, wanted for two shootings and suspicion of involvement in three others, was holed up in a house in Milldean before crossing to France tomorrow. He was known to be armed and dangerous.' Macklin cleared his throat. 'I approved an operation to enter the premises forcibly and arrest him.'

'And did we arrest him?'

'No, sir.'

'He resisted arrest?'

Macklin hesitated. I could hear his strained breathing on the other end of the phone. I felt my stomach knot.

'Philip, just tell me what happened.'

Macklin reverted to formality.

'Four people have been killed in a house in Milldean.'

26

'Jesus Christ. What was this – the *Gunfight at the OK Corral*?' I looked around to see if anyone could overhear but the nearest security guard was a good thirty yards down the long corridor. 'I take it he wasn't alone, then.'

Macklin was silent. My mind racing, I continued:

'Kratos?'

There were regular rules for firearm incidents – officers should shoot to incapacitate suspects and aim at the upper body because it provided the largest target and offered the best chance of knocking out the central nervous system. Then there were Operation Kratos tactics.

These allowed police to shoot dead suspected suicide bombers without the need to issue a warning. Under Operation Kratos, a senior officer was on standby twenty-four hours a day to authorize the deployment of special armed squads to track and maybe shoot dead suspected suicide bombers. Shoot dead in any damned way they could.

'No, sir.'

'But none of our people were injured, you say. Were they fired upon?'

Another hesitation.

'That's not entirely clear at this stage, sir.'

'But these dead people *were* armed? Tell me that at least.'

'That's not entirely clear either. Sir.'

It does me no credit to say that I immediately went into containment mode. I was sorry these people were dead but I wanted to protect my force, minimize the fallout. And, if I'm honest, I

27

wanted to protect myself.

'Get hold of Jack.'

Jack Lawrence was my chief press officer. He was experienced at dealing with high-profile cases after a long stint with the Met.

'Jack's on the scene already.'

'With journalists?'

'I believe so.'

'They were bloody quick.'

'With respect, sir, you have been encouraging a more open relationship with the press. Jack thought the raid would be a good story for journalists to be in on.'

'OK. They were in the house?'

'Not in the house, no, sir.'

I found myself staring at a small porcelain figure of a Chinese man on a plinth directly in front of me. His head was slowly nodding.

'Get Jack to call a press conference for noon tomorrow. I want a full report on my desk by nine in the morning.'

'Sir, you might want to wait a little—'

'I don't want anyone to accuse us of closing ranks—' I caught Macklin's tone. 'Why might I want to wait a little?'

Macklin cleared his throat again. He was driving me nuts.

'Yes?' I said sharply. 'Tell me there isn't a way this could get any worse.'

I waited out the silence.

Finally:

'It seems we might have raided the wrong house.'

* * *

When I had taken over the Southern Police Force three months earlier I had walked into an organization in need of a major shake-up. Macklin, who had gone for my job after years as Assistant Chief Constable, was on my list of people to sack. And overhauling the ramshackle way the force's tactical firearms unit operated was one of my priorities.

However, although I hit the ground running, I'd been sidetracked by the fallout from a mishandled child murder and a load of other stuff that needed sorting. I'd also been hindered by Macklin and others on my Force Command team, as well as lower down the hierarchy.

I guess I'd hoped that we could muddle on as we had been doing until I could really get to grips with the situation. After all, Gatwick Airport Division was part of my command so I had the elite Gatwick tactical firearms unit to fall back on. Plus firearm incidents in our area were relatively rare, even with the increased threat of terrorist outrages.

Clearly I'd been unduly optimistic.

'When did this happen?' I said to Macklin.

'Thirty minutes ago.'

'I'm on my way. Give me the address.'

'I'm not sure that's a good idea, sir. There's a situation developing.'

'What kind of situation?'

'The pubs are emptying, there are a lot of people on the streets. Some stones have been thrown.'

I laughed harshly.

'Oh, great. So now we have a riot.'

29

'It's not got to that stage yet. But you know Milldean at the best of times. And with the drink...'

'Get police in riot gear down there. I want this containing before it does get out of hand.'

I was obliged to go now, although I didn't relish being doorstepped by journalists asking questions about an operation I had no fucking clue about.

Macklin seemed to read my thoughts.

'There was no need to bother you with it, sir. I have the authority and from the briefing notes I received it all seemed pretty clear cut.'

'I'm sure it did, Philip. I'm sure it did.'

My driver already had the address. En route I tried to get hold of William Simpson, the government adviser who had been my friend since childhood. He had been a spin doctor until the government had banned the term (though not the spinning). I left messages for him at home, at work and on his mobile.

The Home Secretary and PM would need to be informed. I had the ear of the current government over my sincere belief that British policemen should be armed. Indeed, the government secretly favoured this policy, keen as it was to be seen as tough on crime – the tough-on-the-causes-of-crime part of the rubric of the previous government was long forgotten.

I had consistently argued for the increased safety of the community if the police were routinely armed, even after the debacle on the London tube. I had become the government's poster boy on the issue. I knew the fact I was a

30

liberal on all other police matters made my view on this issue all the more powerful.

It was a sultry evening so, although the car was air-conditioned, I lowered my window as we drove up the London Road and out towards Milldean.

My phone rang as we passed under the high railway viaduct, which I always regarded as the boundary between the city proper and its outskirts. I recognized the number. Rupert Colley, Leader of the Council, a man who prided himself on his grass-roots politics. However near his ear was to the ground, I didn't believe he could have heard so quickly, although he would have seen me leave the dinner. Not that it would have made any difference. I would still have ignored the call.

Traffic was light so we sped past Preston Park then swung right on to the estate. We followed the labyrinth of pitted streets until I saw a large crowd of people. Milldean was a typical fifties council estate: low-rise but with many of the problems a decade later associated with high-rise.

Wide avenues, cheap houses but a lot of them. In one part of the estate there were a couple of hundred prefabs still in use. When they'd been put up at the end of the Second World War they were only meant to be a short-term solution to the housing shortage.

The mood was unpredictable. We edged by the crowd and pulled up in front of a set of steel barricades.

The divisional commander for the area came

31

over to the car as half a dozen uniformed officers cleared a way for us. He slid into the car beside me.

'We've got to disperse these people,' I said as we passed through the barricade. I could see more people milling at the far end of the street. 'I've got two dozen officers in riot gear on their way,' he said. His name was Lewis. He was a by-the-book officer, competent enough but lacking in originality. And he was rattled. He spoke in staccato sentences. 'There are a few troublemakers among this crowd. People heard the shots, of course. Mostly when that happens round here people know to stay indoors. There are wild rumours. The police have shot a pregnant woman. A ten-year-old girl.'

'And did we?' I hissed.

'No ten-year-old girl,' he said quietly. I looked at his pinched face. He looked back at me with sad eyes.

'We don't know at this stage if the woman is pregnant.'

I clenched my fists and tried to control my breathing. I have a tendency to rage. It's not something I'm proud of, although it has served me well when I've been in physical jeopardy, as I often was during my army service.

Jack approached the car, neat as ever in a lightweight blue suit. He held the door as I got out.

'Sorry about the hacks,' he said, nodding towards a middle-aged man and an attractive young woman standing in the street some twenty yards away. The man was looking nervously at the crowds gathered behind the barricades then scribbling in a notebook. The woman – bespectacled, hair twisted into a knot, vaguely familiar – was talking intently into a microphone.

'Not your fault. Bad timing. Who are they?'

'Just locals so we shouldn't have a problem. The guy from the *Argus* – Vince Proctor – is solid.'

'And the girl?'

Jack lowered his voice. 'She's fluff from the local radio station. A trainee.'

I nodded.

'Do they know how many dead at this point?'

Jack shook his head. I touched his sleeve.

'Openness is our policy, but we have to play this carefully. Organize a press conference for noon tomorrow. That should give us enough time to sort out what has happened. Everyone will expect us to close ranks, as the police always do. But we won't.' I looked around. 'Where's Danny?'

Jack looked at me oddly.

'Danny Moynihan? He's not here.'

'So who was the silver commander?'

The gold commander took strategic command of an armed response incident. The silver commander decided on the tactical response and was in charge of the actual operation. I had the same problem with the silver commanders as with the gold – there were too many of them. Given how rarely such officers fulfilled this role, how could we expect them to do it with confidence? However, I had absolute faith in Moynihan.

33

'Charlie Foster was silver, sir.'

'He's in the IR van with the guys?'

'And the girls, sir. It was a mixed team.'

'I was using guys in the American way,' I said absently. 'Do we know who the victims are? The woman?'

'We have no clear identification yet. It was a rented house. You may have heard a rumour about the woman –' I nodded – 'I don't know whether or not that's true.'

'Bad enough that we shot her in the first place,' I said quietly.

I thanked him and went into the house. A couple of people in white bunny suits were kneeling beside a man lying on his back in the kitchen. Blood had congealed around his body. I could smell its thick iron tang. A third man straightened and pointed me towards several more sets of overalls.

I suited up and climbed the stairs. At the top another man in white coveralls barred my way.

'Sorry, sir. Can't risk you contaminating the crime scene. You can see from here well enough.'

I nodded and looked past him through the bars of the landing guard. I saw a man slumped on the toilet, as if in the middle of a particularly difficult bowel movement. By pulling myself up and leaning over the top of the banister I could just see the dead couple in the front bedroom.

The divisional commander was waiting for me at the bottom of the stairs.

'Terrible business,' he said as I stripped off the overall.

'Something of an understatement,' I said, bunching the overall in my fists and tossing it in the corner. 'Call Philip Macklin, will you? We need an immediate debrief – tell him to set up a post-incident room. I also need him to call the Police Complaints Authority and alert them, then choose a force from the MSF to investigate on the PCA's behalf. Suggest Hampshire – I rate Bill Munro.'

Bloody acronyms. MSF stood for Most Similar Family. All forces in the country were grouped into 'families' on the basis of social, demographic and economic factors rather than size, proximity or regional location. Our other MSF included Avon and Somerset, Bedfordshire, Essex, Kent and Thames Valley.

'I'd like us all to get the hell out of here but the scene of crime team are going to need to be in this house for the next week or so. If we can't disperse the crowd, they're going to be doing their work under siege.'

I used to brag that I worked best under pressure. Now my mind was in overdrive, considering possibilities, predicting outcomes. A part of me stood back and contemplated what a selfish shit I was, as some of my thinking was about how it was going to play in the press.

I was determined to come through this unscathed. I had ambitions to go higher in the police service. I knew I could make a difference. I wasn't going to let this bring me down.

I left the divisional commander and went to the immediate response vehicle parked across the street. I had to be careful what I said to the officers inside because at the moment I didn't know what had happened, didn't know if they were culpable.

Even so, I wanted to support them. I know from my army days what it's like to walk into an apparently controlled situation that goes haywire.

I rapped on the back doors of the van, pulled them open and hauled myself in. It reeked of stale sweat. It was crowded with officers hunkered down in black swat team T-shirts and trousers. Two groups of four men, talking in low rumbles at the far end of the van. That loudmouth Finch among them.

By the door, two women. I recognized one as DC Franks. She was pale, tense and dry-eyed. She was being comforted by another woman, who was whispering in her ear. The other woman turned her head to look at me and my heart sank. DS Sarah Gilchrist was the last person I wanted to see there.

I left Milldean at three in the morning. The situation on the street had been tense and there had been some stand-offs but no real problems had developed. When I climbed into bed beside Molly she didn't stir. The smell of alcohol was heavy in the room, a bottle and a half-empty tumbler of whiskey by the bed.

I was up again by six. The phone rang just as I was on my way out of the house. I hurried back in to answer before it woke Molly. William Simpson's velvety voice was distinctive.

'Bob, terrible business.'

'I thought I should alert you to the situation—'

'Quite right, quite right. Well, it's a tragedy but something can be salvaged if we act quickly. The press conference at noon – announce your resignation then.'

I was too surprised to speak for a moment.

'My resignation?'

'Your position is clearly untenable.'

'William, it was an operation by one of my divisions. Responsibility—'

'Is ultimately yours. It wasn't a Kratos operation. You know that rules drawn up by the Association of Chief Police Officers says shots can only be fired to stop an imminent threat to life and, I quote: "Only when absolutely necessary after traditional methods have been tried and failed or are unlikely to succeed if tried."'

'I'm aware of that—'

'The guidelines also say that officers are not above the criminal law.'

'William, I could refer you to section thirty-seven of the 1967 Criminal Law Act, the bit that reads: "A person may use such force as is reasonable in the prevention of crime" – but what's the point? I intend to stay to find out exactly what happened and make sure it can't happen again.'

Simpson sighed, almost theatrically.

'Bob, the press are going to have a field day. Think about it.'

I had been thinking about it, trying to figure out some way I could keep the government on my side.

'I know you're going to have a hell of a time

spinning this,' I said.

'We don't spin any more, Bob – didn't you read the papers? In any case, the only spinning to be done here is out of control. The most outspoken proponent of routinely arming the police authorizes an operation involving armed police that turns into a bloodbath. Post-Menezes it's an absolute catastrophe.'

'You have excellent contacts in the press...'

'Bob, of course, unofficially I'll do what I can.' Simpson could actually purr sometimes. 'You know there was a brief period post 9/11 when gung-ho was good. But then 7/7 came along and the shooting of Menezes. And the lies...'

'I know all that—'

'You being opposed to a national force hasn't helped.'

'Jesus, William – the inefficiencies of any one force replicated at a national level.'

He wasn't purring now.

'I've been charged with damage limitation on this. The government can't be seen to appear foolish. I'm afraid your position is too exposed. It's important that you act quickly to avoid us getting drawn into this mess.'

Of course. This government, careering from disaster to disaster, was so terrified of accusations of sleaze or incompetence it readily abandoned those closest to it at the first hint of impropriety. And this was much more than that. I realized that Simpson, friend or no friend, had been ordered to cut me loose.

'I'll have to think about this, William. You've

38

taken me by surprise.'

'If that's true, then you're not as politically canny as I supposed you to be. Give it some thought but don't take too long. If you don't resign at lunchtime, the press will really go to work on you, I'm sorry to say.'

At the time I thought Simpson was merely making an observation about the workings of the press. Only with hindsight did I see it was a threat.

THREE

The debrief was a joke. It was past midnight when it started and just before one when it ended, and in between Sarah Gilchrist heard nothing of value. She sat with Philippa Franks at the far end of the conference table, Harry Potter sitting upright on the other side of Franks, and watched in appalled fascination as Charlie Foster, the silver commander, struggled with a debriefing sheet he'd clearly never seen before. She could smell his fear, rank right down the table.

Philip Macklin sat stiffly beside Foster, eyes fixed on his tightly clasped hands. Macklin had a dual role – gold commander and the main representative of Force Command. Sheena Hewitt, the Assistant Chief Constable in overall charge of operations, also represented Force Command.

Gilchrist liked Hewitt. She didn't take any shit

39

from the men but she was also determinedly feminine. Hewitt was in her forties but still wore her hair long. Gilchrist wouldn't have, but she recognized that Hewitt was pretty enough to carry it off.

Hewitt was wearing casual trousers and a silk blouse – she'd been having dinner with her husband in The Ginger Man when she'd been summoned. She'd grimaced when she entered the room, walked to the window and opened it as wide as it would go. Foster wasn't the only one who was giving off an odour.

Hewitt looked round the table from one officer to the next.

Nobody was saying much, which is why it was a joke and why Hewitt was irate. The unit had closed ranks. Nobody admitted to firing the first shot although several officers admitted to joining in after that. Their weapons had been tagged and ammunition counted. However, since no record was usually kept in the armoury of who took which weapon and how much ammunition was taken out, that wasn't going to be very useful.

Any kind of auditing to do with the armoury had long been abandoned. There hadn't even been an official armourer for the past two years. Savings.

Gilchrist watched the big man with the missing teeth she'd encountered in the kitchen in Milldean. His name was Donald Connolly and he was based at Haywards Heath. The smirking man, who was sitting diagonally across the table from her, was Darren White, also at Haywards Heath. Finch was beside him, slumped in his

40

seat, sick as a dog.

Connolly, biceps bulging, was sitting to the left of her, his body angled towards Foster and Macklin. At one point, sensing her stare, he turned and looked back with hard eyes.

She was the first to turn away. The man's apparent hostility could be put down to the same prejudice against women officers that Finch shared. Or it could be something else.

The fate of the object in the dead man's hand in the kitchen was niggling at her. She hadn't done a proper check under the cupboards but she hadn't been able to see anything. She'd checked the evidence room before she'd come here. Nothing had been deposited in connection with the man killed in the kitchen. She was wondering if, against all procedures, any of the three policemen who'd joined her in the kitchen had taken whatever the object was.

Macklin wasn't saying much of anything. Gilchrist guessed why. He'd already pulled up the drawbridge. He'd authorized this operation. He'd made a judgement on information he'd apparently received from DC Edwards, who in turn had received it from his snitch. Macklin was *responsible*. And she guessed that therefore all he was thinking was how to save himself.

As silver commander, Foster had run this woebegone operation. He too was in deep shit. Gilchrist thought him a good man, a moral man. She knew he would feel ultimately responsible. His sense of guilt was palpable. Five deaths were a heavy burden for any conscience to bear. Whilst he was clearly frustrated with everybody's reluc-

41

tance to speak, he didn't seem to have the energy to take it further.

It was left to the increasingly exasperated Hewitt to be the heavy. She brought her palms down heavily on the table.

'Jesus, we're on your side. Talk to us and maybe we can figure out what to do. When the Hampshire police arrive they're not going to be anywhere near as gentle.'

Her eyes swept the table. They stopped on Gilchrist.

'Gilchrist?'

'I was downstairs, ma'am. I heard the shots. We had checked the ground floor rooms and they were secure so my colleagues went upstairs to support the other unit.'

'But all the rooms weren't secure, were they?' Hewitt looked at the notes in front of her. 'This man appeared...'

'It was a cupboard under the stairs. The door was concealed. Ma'am, I should mention that he had something in his hand.'

'What?'

Gilchrist flicked a look at Connolly, White and Finch. They were all staring at the table.

'I thought it was a weapon at first but after I wasn't sure.'

'You didn't examine it when he had been shot?'

'It fell from his hand and – well – ma'am – I couldn't immediately locate it without contaminating the crime scene.'

'I'll make a note for the scene of crime officers. Thank you, Detective Sergeant.'

Hewitt turned to Foster.

'We don't know who *any* of these people are? Do we at least know if one of them is Bernard Grimes?'

'Not yet, ma'am,' Foster said.

'Only two of them were carrying identification,' Potter said. 'We have their names and OPS1 is having them traced. But none are known to us, that's correct, ma'am.'

OPS1 was the designated title for whichever high-ranking officer was on shift in charge of the Operations Room. The Operations Room was the focal point of police operations each day and night.

'Where's DC Edwards?' Macklin said. 'He should be here. It was his informant who started this off.'

Nobody answered. Macklin shuffled papers whilst Foster stumbled through the remaining questions on his sheet.

The 'hot debrief' petered out ten minutes later.

'All of you are off-duty as of now,' Hewitt said, rising.

'Suspended, ma'am?' Foster said.

'Pending an enquiry, it's inappropriate for any of you to continue with your duties. But hold yourself available for questioning from tomorrow by the investigating officers from the Hampshire police force.' She looked round the table. 'Ladies and gentlemen, this is about as bad as it gets. It does you no credit to avoid saying what exactly happened in that house.'

She looked at Macklin.

'Philip, perhaps we could use your room for

our meeting?'

He nodded, his face grim. He'd rather be any-where but here. Hewitt nodded at the room and followed Macklin out. Those who remained avoided each other's eyes. As Connolly, the big man, rose, Sarah leant over. She could smell his aftershave. Sweet. Noxious.

'Excuse me.'

He ignored her. She reached out and gripped his bicep.

'Excuse me.'

He looked at her hand on his arm.

'I'm spoken for but I'm sure you'll find one of the other lads willing.' He sniggered. 'Try Finch – he isn't too fussy, I hear.'

They both looked over at Finch shambling out of the room with Darren White, the other Hay-wards Heath officer, stretching up to whisper in his ear.

'Did you remove evidence from the kitchen?'

'What evidence?'

'Whatever it was he'd had in his hand. Judging from the footprints in the blood, it looked as if someone had been moving about in the kitchen.'

He picked up her hand as if it were a dead thing and removed it from his arm.

'I don't know what you're talking about,' he said, turning for the door.

'He had something in his hand.'

Connolly put his hand in his pocket and continued walking.

'So have I. D'you want to hold it?'

'I saw it,' Sarah said.

'Big, isn't it?'

'In the man's hand.'

'Well, I didn't.' He nodded at Finch's retreating back. 'And nor did Finch. Or White.' He looked back at her. 'So there's only your word for it.'

I'm not a pessimistic man, rather the reverse. My optimism used to anger my wife, Molly, especially when she herself was plumbing the depths. She would call me Pollyanna, her voice cold and jeering.

'Only people with no imaginations are optimists,' she snarled at me more than once.

Getting through the days after the shooting at Milldean tested my optimism. These were probably the worst days of my life. Worse than when Molly and I later split up – I leave you to decide what that says about me.

That night Phil, my driver, dropped off Jack Lawrence, my press officer, back in Brighton then drove me over the Downs to the little hamlet where Molly and I had settled four years before. I always liked the idea of leaving Brighton behind. Although my remit covered all Sussex, there was something about Brighton that seemed to stand for the venality and the criminality of the whole region.

Leaving it, coming over into the pure country air of the Downs, allowed me to leave the job behind more effectively than anything.When I got home Molly was already asleep. I tiptoed up the stairs, put my head round our bedroom door and listened to her heavy breathing. I could smell the alcohol.

I went back down the stairs, poured myself a brandy and went out on to the terrace. I could see the nimbus of the city's light pollution across the top of the Downs. I imagined it getting brighter and brighter as Brighton's pollutants threatened to spill over the South Downs into the countryside beyond.

I wondered if there was any way I could save my job. I thought about phoning Simpson again. I wondered how bad tomorrow would be.

The new area police headquarters were on the border between Brighton and Hove, down on the seafront. Given the traffic along the seafront, it was a ridiculous place for any kind of rapid response policing but I enjoyed the view from my window. I preferred bad weather days to good – watching the waves crashing over the groynes and spilling on to the promenade energized me.

I love Brighton. OK, I know the city is officially Brighton and Hove since the councils merged but that's just a sop to Hove civic pride. Although there are restaurants and bars springing up in Hove, Brighton is the engine that drives the city.

I love Brighton for its energy and for its odd mix of people – a mix that, frankly, is a big policing headache. The students from Brighton and Sussex Universities clubbing until dawn, and the gays and lesbians who live in the city or come to visit in droves – all prey for any local gang, mugger or rapist. The unemployed kids on the estates around the city. The druggies, a danger to themselves and others. The crooks who come down from London at the weekends to have a lavish time on a strictly cash-only basis. The prostitutes. And, of course, the local crime families. There were two main ones – the Cuthberts and the Donaldsons – although a man called John Hathaway was rumoured to be the town's crime kingpin.

There was tension in the air when I strode through reception and the open-plan ground-floor office. I clocked covert and overt glances as I passed. At the rear of the building I jogged up the stairs to my office.

Winston Hart, the chair of the Police Authority, had been phoning my mobile during my journey but I'd ignored his calls. He was a pompous prat of a local councillor from Lewes, one of many academics from the local universities involved in local politics. He'd left four messages with Rachael, my secretary.

I eased behind my desk and looked across at the painting on the opposite wall. I'd bought it ten years ago when I could little afford the expense. I loved the mystery of it – a man and a woman sitting at a table, both gazing at a flower she was holding in her hand. A pot of the same flowers behind them on the window sill. The colours were bright – a yellow wall, red chairs, the man's green coat, her black hair. But what was its story? That was the mystery.

I sighed and called Hart. Our conversation was brief.

'I have utter faith in my officers,' I said. 'Whatever happened was, I'm sure, justified.

I've asked Hampshire Police Authority to carry out a full investigation but I'm confident it will confirm my belief.'

Hart had a spindly voice and always sounded tetchy.

'Do you know exactly what happened?' he said.

'I know enough about my officers to stand by them.'

When Hart and I had finished speaking I buzzed through to Macklin.

'And?'

'We're still not clear, sir,' he said. 'The statements we took last night leave a lot unexplained. And we can't locate DC Edwards. It was his man who gave us the tip about Grimes staying in that house. We think he was also the man monitoring the house.'

As he spoke, I picked up the photo of Molly and the kids beside the phone and looked at their smiling faces. It was taken a long time ago.

'Is Foster still around?'

'They're all on suspension but he's writing up the debrief.'

'Find him. I want to talk to him today. Listen, Philip, why wasn't Danny Moynihan leading the operation? He's our most experienced silver commander.'

I put the photo back on the desk.

'He'd done the morning shift. I called him but he stood himself down. He'd been drinking after his shift. He wasn't drunk but—'

'Yes, I get it. He was complying with the rules.'

The regulations for armed operations stated that officers should have had no drink or drugs of any nature in the previous eight hours.

'Philip, why don't you have anything for me? You have responsibility for our use of firearms, for God's sake. There's a press conference this morning. People will expect me to have answers. I expect to have answers, but I don't. I'm supposed to go out on a limb and stand up for my officers when I don't in fact know what has happened.'

'Don't you think it might be a good idea to postpone the press conference?' I could hear by the tone of his voice that he thought I'd been wrong to call the press conference so soon in the first place.

'I can't do that.'

'Well, then, why not keep it low-key?'

'Were any weapons found at the house?'

'No, sir.'

'Have the people been identified yet?'

'No, sir.'

'So we don't know if Bernard Grimes was even there.'

'It seems unlikely, sir.'

'Do we know who Edwards's informant was?'

'No, sir.'

I shook my head wearily.

'Philip – give me something. *Anything.*'

At the press conference I announced that I'd asked Hampshire police to investigate under the direction of the Police Complaints Authority.

'All the officers involved in last night's inci-

49

dent have been suspended pending that investigation. That should not, however, be taken as an indication of guilt.' I looked round the room. 'In fact, I'm sure they will be vindicated.'

'How can you be so confident that your officers haven't acted badly?' It was the young woman from the radio station.

I repeated what I had said to the chair of the Police Authority:

'I have utter faith in my officers. Whatever happened was, I'm sure, justified.'

I saw Jack Lawrence's jaw clench.

'Did you actually know about this before it happened?' she asked.

The jackals pricked up their ears.

'I take full responsibility,' I said.

'Clever girl,' I muttered to Jack as I left the room five minutes later.

'She's still learning, though – you don't ask the decent questions when the pack is gathered – they just steal the answers for their own headlines.'

I nodded.

'Sir.' Jack sounded awkward. 'Do you think you should have—?'

'No – but it's done now.'

Ten minutes after the end of the conference, William Simpson was phoning my mobile.

'What was that, Bob?'

'A press conference.'

'And your resignation? I thought we had a conversation.'

'I'll be more effective if I remain in post.'

There was a silence on the other end of the

phone. Then, before he hung up:

'I hope you're ready for what's about to happen to you.'

The team from Hampshire arrived an hour or so later. I left them with Macklin. Mid-afternoon he phoned down to say that not only Edwards but also Finch and Charlie Foster were unavailable.

'Unavailable?'

'We can't find them, sir.'

When I put the phone down it immediately rang again. Catherine, my daughter, on the line from Edinburgh. She'd heard a report on the radio about the deaths.

We had a difficult conversation. But, then, when didn't we? She was appalled that I should defend my officers for such a horrendous crime without knowing the facts. I pointed out that she didn't know the facts either. The conversation went downhill after that.

The evening papers all over the country agreed with her. They questioned my 'arrogant pre-judgement' of the case.

The riot in Milldean started that night.

It was the crime families taking the piss. Reminding us who really ran the estate; punishing us for carrying out an operation in their neighbourhood without their say-so.

Those bastards could force almost anybody on the estate to do what they wanted because most of Milldean was in hock to them. The crime families between them, aside from all their other villainy, ran a big moneylending racket and had no shortage of clients too poor to get credit anywhere else. The ruinously high interest rates they charged meant people who borrowed money from them were pretty much indebted to them for life.

We kept the street blocked off as our SoC investigators trawled the house where the incident had taken place. At six in the evening, a crowd began to gather at the north end, near the pub. Most of the rioters issued out of the pub, the worse for wear after a day's drinking. Stones were thrown.

The half dozen policemen at the barrier withdrew down the street to join their colleagues in front of the house. The crowd advanced.

The men in it were stereotypes from video footage of rioting drunken English football fans. Faces distorted with primitive rage, mouths contorted in hate. Animal. Men walking from the shoulder or with arms swaying like simians. Mindless. Utterly animal roars.

Riot control officers were waiting in a van at the other end of the street. Twenty of them. They came out with shields and advanced towards the mob. More stones. At the back of the crowd, a gang of men rolled a car over. Windows of the adjoining houses were smashed. Obscenities were hurled. The car was set on fire. Then, at 6.47 p.m., the first petrol bomb.

Rioters overturned more cars at each ingress to the estate to prevent police getting through. Windows of shops were broken. There was looting. By 7.30 p.m. we had another fifty officers with riot equipment deployed on the estate.

The riot continued through the evening. Three

empty houses were torched. It wasn't safe to send fire officers in. Other houses were broken into. Later, we heard about three rapes.

I wanted to go down but thought it more sensible to stay at HQ, both for operational reasons and because I was myself a flashpoint. Chief Inspector Anderson was OPS1 for the evening so I avoided the Ops Room – he was easily alarmed.

The Hampshire police, meanwhile, were hard at work. They hadn't been able to locate Finch, Foster and Edwards, either. And the identity of Edwards's snitch was not, of course, logged into the computer system.

I phoned Molly to warn her I would be home late, if at all. She didn't answer. I left a message on the voicemail.

I don't need much sleep. I can get by for weeks at a time on four hours a night. I dislike the fact that I share a common trait with Margaret Thatcher and Winston Churchill, but there it is. I don't know about them, but my body tells me when I do need more rest – I crash for a couple of days, then, revitalized, start all over again.

I stayed up until around four a.m. The rioting had calmed down by then so I used the sofa in my office to get a couple of hours' rest.

I was up again at seven, thickheaded, in time to see the morning newspapers. They all splashed on the riot and laid the blame squarely on me and my remarks.

I spoke to Winston Hart, my chair, half an hour later. He alternated between panic and bluster. He was a long way out of his depth. Essentially he should have been a school governor and left it at that.

At eight Molly phoned. It was another difficult conversation.

At 8.15 a.m. I heard that Charlie Foster, the silver commander on the Milldean operation, was dead. A self-inflicted gunshot wound. I scarcely knew the man, so whilst I was sorry for his family's loss, I cursed him for his selfishness.

We got the riots under control during that day but they flared again in the early evening. We used tear gas. Baton charges. Rioters set more cars on fire and smashed windows. Smoke gushed up from the estate, an oily black pall drifting over the city and out to sea.

The rioting was sorted by midnight, but by then the press were baying for my blood. I'd had two more conversations with Hart from the Police Authority. He was increasingly pissed off that I'd defended my officers before the investigation had taken place.

My old pal William Simpson, government fixer, phoned again.

'Well?' He was icy.

I put the phone down.

I've struggled all my life to curb my temper, tried not to bridle when others tell me what to do. If I think you're being reasonable, I'll listen, but if I don't ... And don't ever order me. That was my undoing in the army.

By the end of that day, I told the press office not even to approach me with stuff until we had something to report.

At home I ran a gauntlet of press hyenas hanging about outside my house, then ran into a shit storm with Molly.

'What the hell are you doing?'

She was standing in the kitchen, hands on hips, almost vibrating with tension, a pulse clearly visible in her neck.

'Trying to calm a situation.'

'You know I've not been able to get out of the house today. Those bloody scavengers. They've been trying to climb over the walls. Telephoning every five minutes. How dare you put me through this?'

She looked ashen and haggard. I wanted to put my arms round her but I couldn't seem to take a step towards her. She was speaking slowly, precisely. I noted the almost empty bottle of wine on the kitchen table.

'Tom called from Bristol. Your son wanted to know what's going on. I had to tell him I had no bloody idea.'

'I spoke to Catherine today. She's OK.'

Molly stepped towards me.

'Like hell is she OK. I spoke to her too. She's having a hard time with this. With you defending murderers.'

'My officers are not murderers.'

'How do you know? Were you there – or are you God and you were watching with your all-seeing eye?' She waved a dismissive hand at me. Curled her lip as only she could. 'The arrogance of you.'

'A good leader has to stand up for his men and women.'

'Not if they've done something wrong.'

'Especially if they've done something wrong.'

It sounded pompous, even to me. She sat down at the kitchen table. 'Bollocks. So what are you going to do? You have to resign.'

'I don't and I won't. I want to see the force through this.'

'At whatever cost to your family.'

'I'm a public servant.'

'You're a bag of wind.'

I turned my back on her.

I took a glass out of the cupboard and emptied into it what wine remained in the bottle. Thinking about the way the body count was rising.

FOUR

Sarah Gilchrist didn't sleep much after the hot debrief. Her mind was flooded with images of the dead people in the house, whilst the analytical part of her was trying to work out what might have happened.

Once she'd seen Connolly and White from Haywards Heath leave HQ at the end of the meeting, she had phoned Jack Jones, a scene of crime officer she'd once had a fling with.

'You're lucky, Sarah,' he said. 'I'm just taking a fag break out in the garden, otherwise you wouldn't have got me.'

'Haven't managed to kick it, then?' Jones had been a sixty- a-day man. One of the reasons their relationship hadn't lasted longer was that she couldn't bear the cigarette smell on his breath, on his clothes, on her. Another reason was because she didn't want any kind of commitment. But that was another story entirely.

For Jones to be smoking whilst attending a scene of crime meant he was still as hooked as ever. With the new DNA-based forensic examinations of crime scenes, inadvertent contamination was a real issue. Putting your hand on any kind of surface was enough to leave your own DNA evidence.

SoC officers took special care. Having a fag part way through an investigation required a real palaver – taking the kit off then putting new kit back on.

She could tell by the tone of Jones's voice that he was up for a bit of flirting but she was too tense. She couldn't be as relaxed as he was about sudden death. She told him about the man in the kitchen, the thing in his hand that went flying. He picked up on her mood, promised he'd get back to her the next day, let her know if they found anything.

'Though if we do find something, I can't say what,' he said. 'You know that, don't you?'

She knew that.

'I just want to know you've found *something*.'

She had about four hours' sleep then got up and prowled her flat waiting for Jones to call her. Finally, she called him.

'I hadn't forgotten,' he said impatiently. 'There was nothing there.'

She put the phone down, her brain buzzing.

57

She paced the flat, stood by the window looking down into the street, paced the flat again. Twenty minutes later she called DC Philippa Franks, the other woman involved in the Milldean operation. Franks had been terribly upset on the night. Gilchrist had comforted her as best she could.

'Philippa, it's Sarah.'

There was silence on the line, although Sarah thought she could hear a man's voice in the background. The television? Then, cautiously, Philippa said:

'We're not supposed to be in contact until the enquiry is over.'

Standard procedure, so that the officers under investigation couldn't cook up a story together.

'I know. It's just that I'm stumbling around in the dark here. I have no idea what happened upstairs.'

'That makes two of us.'

'But you were there. You saw it.'

Franks's voice was harsh.

'I can't talk about it.'

'Who went up the stairs first?'

More silence. Gilchrist thought she could hear Franks's breath. Short, almost panting. Then there was a click and the sudden buzz of a phone hung up.

She tried Harry Potter next. She hadn't forgotten the sight of him leaning heavily against the wall at the top of the staircase in the house in Milldean. He had looked so defeated.

Potter's wife picked up the telephone.

'Hello?' she said cautiously.

'Hello, Mrs Potter. It's Sarah – Sarah Gilchrist.

58

I work with Harry – with DS Potter. I wonder if I could have a word?'

Mrs Potter put her hand over the mouthpiece of the telephone. Gilchrist could make out a muffled conversation then she heard Potter's voice.

'Sarah, this isn't a good idea.'

'I know – I'm sorry. I'm just so in the dark. Can you tell me anything?'

Potter cleared his throat.

'I was focusing on the back room. It was empty. The shooting started when I was in there. I went along the landing but nobody was letting me through – and, anyway, the damage had been done.'

'Were our men fired on?'

'I have no way of knowing. I just heard shots. Finch would know.'

'You looked shocked by it all when I came up the stairs.'

'Weren't you? I signed on to protect people not kill them. What happened was appalling.'

'Do you blame our men? Do you think they were trigger happy?'

Potter was silent.

'Harry?'

'Not for me to say, is it?' Potter's voice had changed. 'Let the investigation decide that. Look, Sarah, I've got to go. My wife ... you know.'

Gilchrist tried Finch next. Aside from anything else she was curious about his relationship with Connolly and White from Haywards Heath. Judging by his appearance at the hot debrief, the cocky bastard had had the stuffing knocked out of him by the events in Milldean.

Finch's phone rang and rang and then voice-mail clicked in, inviting her to leave a message. She declined the offer. The moment she put her own phone down, it rang. She jumped. It was an officer from the Hampshire police service asking her to come in for an interview later that morning.

Bill Munro from the Hampshire force came to see me on Wednesday lunchtime.

'Sorry to be talking to you in these circumstances, Bob.'

Bill and I had served together for three years. We were of an age, though I'd risen higher. He was a stolid, methodical copper. Not much flair but then, except in novels, policing isn't about flair. It's about methodology and luck, in about equal measure.

He was one of the few happily married policemen I knew. I put his girth – he was a couple of stone overweight – down to love of his domestic life. And love, more specifically, of his wife Alice's cooking.

Molly and I had been round to dinner once, years earlier, and Alice had produced a four-course blow-out that must have been from some fifties French cookbook – heavy on cream, butter and virtually every other fat-forming food.

I was pleased to see Bill, despite the circumstances. My high regard for him was the reason I had chosen to bring in the Hampshire force rather than any of the others in our family.

'I have to say, Bob, this is a bloody mess.'

'Five people killed – I can see why you would think that.'

'Five? Oh, you mean your officer, too. Yes, it's especially bad when one of ours go down – though I'm not sure what I think about suicide. But you're in deep shit for more than that. This riot. And I have to say you're utterly exposed. The procedures you have in place here for armed response operations – or rather the procedures you don't have in place – frankly, the whole thing is a disgrace.'

'I was about to address it.'

'About to? Given current international circumstances, it should have had absolute priority.'

I was terse. 'Tell me something I don't know.'

And I did know. Even so, I resented him saying it. My conceit, I suppose. When I was brought in, the Southern Force was in decline after years of liberal posturing and neglect. I'd put off doing something because I had vested interests to contend with and I was drowning in other procedures.

'There is so little audit stuff in place that anyone can go in to the armoury and take whatever the hell they want. They can use it to shoot at anything or anyone they damned well please, then drop it back without the force being any the wiser.

'And this particular operation is a total botch. Your officers are doing no one any favours by remaining silent. Nobody knows where the tip came from. The policeman who received it is unavailable. Your gold commander is watching his back and your silver commander – who should

61

never have been in operational charge – has killed himself.'

'The procedures in place are standard around the country.'

'I well know that,' Bill snapped. 'It's the way those procedures are carried out that matters.'

I nodded, looked down at my desk.

'Is everybody covering up?'

'Except for Gilchrist. But she's got a fixation on the man shot in the kitchen. She claims he had something in his hand but it wasn't entered into evidence. She claims someone took it.'

'Another officer?'

'That's the implication.'

I looked up at him.

'Who is the man in the kitchen?'

'Still unidentified.'

'Who shot him?'

'None of your snipers are admitting to firing the fatal shot. We're running tests on the rifles in the armoury to see which one has been fired. But we won't know who checked it out because there's no signing in and out of weapons. Any forensic evidence we get will be contaminated as everybody seemed to be handling everyone else's weapons.'

He shook his head then leant back.

'You're being pretty squarely blamed for the rioting too. What are you going to do?'

'Find out what went wrong.'

Munro shook his head again. Put his hand on his paunch.

'I can't let you near it, Bob. You're part of the investigation now – and you've shot yourself in the foot by that damned stupid announcement.'

I sat up straighter.

'Supporting my team, you mean?'

'Anticipating the results of my enquiry. I can understand why you were tempted to do it. But I wish you'd resisted the temptation. Especially as, on the evidence I've been able to gather, you may well end up with egg on your face.'

'I assume they didn't just go in guns blazing – they fired because they thought they were about to be fired upon.'

He shifted in his seat.

'Don't be so sure. At least one of the killings looks horribly like an execution. The man on the toilet...' He shifted in his seat again. 'How's Molly handling all this?'

'Not well. She's not good under pressure.'

He eased himself up in his chair.

'Give her my best.' He looked down at me. 'So will you resign?'

'Everybody and his dog wants or expects me to.'

He gave a small smile.

'That'll be a "no", then.'

'I came here to make a difference. I haven't had a chance to do that yet. And it would be cowardly of me to resign. I want to be here to see this through.'

'It's not going to be pretty.'

'Bill, I know I'm part of the investigation. But if you could keep me informed—'

He put up his hand, then got to his feet. He nodded and left the room without another word. But at least he hadn't said 'No'.

* * *

Sarah Gilchrist couldn't recall a worse time in her life. The fucking insulting interrogation she'd endured from the two Hampshire policemen had been bad enough. Were they trained to act in a way guaranteed *not* to get information from people they questioned?

She'd told them about the evidence going missing. They didn't seem interested. They thought, in fact, that she was using it as a plausible reason for discharging her firearm.

'But I didn't discharge it,' she said. 'The man in the kitchen was shot by a police sniper stationed outside the house.'

They didn't respond. She decided there and then she'd rather stick needles in her eyeballs than give these assholes any help.

She kept mostly indoors for the next few days. From her flat near Seven Dials she emerged only to go to the gym, then get the papers and food from the local deli.

In her flat she would wait for the phone to ring, trying to figure out what was going on, trying to figure out what to do.

She knew something bad had happened. Not just that people had been killed, although that was bad enough. She couldn't find out who was in the wrong place at the wrong time. Was it the police or the people in the house? Had the police raided the wrong house? Nobody was saying.

Then there was the bastard with the missing teeth – Connolly. And the dead man on the kitchen floor.

At the end of that terrible evening, as they were

64

all cooped up in the armed response vehicle, she'd got nowhere when – out of curiosity and because she was involved – she'd tried to find out exactly what had happened upstairs. And, more to the point, who had shot whom. She couldn't decide if they were stonewalling or simply being patronizing. Either way, it pissed her off.

Now, three days later, she'd still been unable to get hold of Finch. She'd been told about Foster's suicide. And, courtesy of the radio and TV, she'd heard about the riot. God, what a fuck-up.

The missing evidence was difficult for her. Automatically, she felt loyalty to her fellow officers. In such a situation, ranks closed. And if ranks closed, did she want to be the one on the outside of them?

Staying home was driving her nuts. She liked her own company well enough but she also liked to keep active. The gym helped. It was a women's-only place up near the station. She tried to choose times when she was unlikely to run into people she knew. She hit the machines for an hour, used the sauna and the Turkish; tried to sweat the emotion out.

Occasionally she got hit on but she was used to that in Brighton. She didn't mind, she just wasn't that way inclined.

She jogged there and back. There was easy – it was all downhill. Coming back up was something else again. She took another shower when she got back to her flat.

She prepared her food, taking more time than she ever had. Marinating meat overnight, chop-

65

ping the vegetables finer and finer, cleaning the skillet and pans. Again and again. Cooking slowly, adding herbs, really getting the timings right.

Then throwing the result in the bin. Instead, scarfing lumps of cheese, olives from the jar, rice cakes from the packet, spoonfuls of yoghurt from the pot.

On Thursday, the fourth day of her suspension, she became front page news.

On Thursday my home life ended. I'd been hoping things were quietening down. I didn't see the papers until I got into work. As I walked through the ground floor office, I wondered why people avoided looking at me.

Then I saw the newspapers my secretary had left folded on my desk. The headlines.

The tabloids had gone for the jugular. 'Top Cop's Sex Romp With Massacre Shooter,' said one headline. The story that followed suggested that perhaps the reason I was so eager to defend the probity of my officers at the Milldean murder was because I'd had a one-night stand at a conference with one of the female officers. Sarah Gilchrist.

I groaned. She'd sold her story to the papers.

My first thought was to phone her. Except that I didn't know her number. Human Resources would have it, but I could hardly phone up and ask for it. Or ask Rachael, my secretary, to do so. I tried directory enquiries on my mobile. Nothing. Some detective I was.

Perhaps it was just as well. I was furious with

66

her. Furious at myself, too. And sick of the thought of Molly hearing of my infidelity in such a humiliating, public way.

I phoned her. There was no answer. I left a message on the answerphone. I wondered whether I should go home but there was so much work to do.

Winston Hart, my Police Authority chair, phoned at eleven.

'I think your position has become, if possible, even more untenable,' he said crisply. 'I must also inform you that I have received a letter from the Home Secretary stating that he has lost faith in you and asking us to press for your resignation.'

Typical of the Home Secretary, the most right-wing one we'd had since World War Two, and one with an eye on the *Today* programme. He was too quick to give the sound bite and regularly had to back down.

'It will blow over,' I said. 'I'm not quitting.'

'It seems to me that you don't care about your force – you're making it into a laughing stock. You just care about yourself.'

I hung up on him.

I left for home at lunchtime. Molly was sitting in a chair by the French windows, looking out at the green and velvety Downs. She didn't stir when I came in.

'I came to see if you were all right. After the newspaper report today...'

She stood up and walked towards me. I looked at her, obviously for a beat too long. She swung at me.

67

'You bastard!'

She whacked me just below my left eye, came in with her other fist and whacked my right ear. I held her off. She was shaking with rage.

'I want you out of this house.' She was bellowing. 'Today. You did this to us? You did this to us?'

I took a room at The Ship on the seafront in Brighton. I was worried the manager would recognize me as I'd been to lots of functions here, but he wasn't around and the blank-faced receptionists had no clue who I was.

That evening I stayed in my room, sipping a whisky from the minibar and gazing blankly out to sea and across at the Palace Pier in its blaze of white light. I refused to think of it as Brighton Pier, although that's what its sign proclaimed. That honour rested with the ruined West Pier. From time to time I phoned my son and daughter but I couldn't reach either of them. I went back to the minibar.

The next morning my mobile phone rang just after nine.

'Bob, it's William.' William Simpson, my erstwhile friend. 'Can't tell you how sorry I am about what's happening in the press.'

'And?'

'You'll be resigning now, I assume.'

'Like hell.'

'Bob.'

'William.'

'You must resign. They've only just started.'

'What do you mean?'

'The press. They'll move in on your family.

Your wife, your kids.'

'There's nothing there. How dare they?'

'The press dare, believe me. Then they'll root – *really* root – for anything. Anything. If you've something in your background, they'll find it. Your family, your parents—'

I must have clicked my tongue.

'Bob – I'm telling you as a friend. This could get very, very much worse.'

This time he hung up.

I was summoned to an emergency meeting of the Police Authority. Winston Hart was at his pontificating worst. He kept lifting his chin to ease his neck from the too-tight collar of his shirt and touching his moustache as if checking it was still there.

'We've had a letter from the Home Office stating that the Home Secretary no longer has faith in you. We've had another letter from the Police Federation stating that they are unhappy with your conduct. I don't, to be honest, understand why you haven't already resigned.'

I forced a smile. 'I feel I can best meet my responsibilities by staying in post until I can find out what has happened.'

'Had you not, by your public declaration, already prejudged the investigation, that might have been possible. However, your position is now clearly untenable.'

Hart had a mobile phone on the desk in front of him. It rang. He picked it up without apology and looked at the number on the screen. He put the phone to his ear then wordlessly passed it across to me.

It was Simpson. There was no preamble.

'They're authorized to give you a generous settlement. It won't be leaked to the press. You can walk away with it. But you have to resign before you leave that room. If not, the Home Secretary's letter will be leaked and worse will follow. Take your life back, Bob, I beg you.'

I handed the phone back to Hart. He started to smirk but stopped when he saw my face. He seemed to rear back in his chair as if he thought I was about to launch myself over the table at him.

I was tempted. I did want to hit him but I never would. Well, not never, just not now.

I was seething.

I didn't want to go, was stunned by the speed with which the media had turned against me. My every instinct was to stay and fight. But what concerned me was the thought of reporters dragging my immediate family into it. What family doesn't have its skeletons hidden in the closet? My mother was dead, but I couldn't put Molly, the children and my father through that.

I stared at Hart but I think he could see in my eyes that he had the upper hand. I dropped my gaze.

'I'll resign.'

The press discovered I was staying at The Ship. They besieged me. I was wondering where to go next when family friends phoned to invite me to house-sit their farmhouse near Lewes whilst they went off to Spain for a month. I was touched by their thoughtfulness and accepted with alacrity.

70

I spirited myself out of The Ship and disappeared from view. Except that after two days I resumed my habit of early morning swims at the sports club I used in Falmer, on the Brighton University campus. Nobody else I knew was a member and I always kept to myself, so I had no worry about being tracked down there.

However, I reckoned without Sarah Gilchrist. At the start of the next week she doorstepped me in the club car park.

I was halfway from the club entrance to my car when I heard her call out. She was standing beside her dark blue Volkswagen Polo. She was in jeans and a fleece. Her hair was down. I have to say, she looked beautiful. However, my immediate response was anger.

'What the hell are you doing here?'

'There's no press,' she said, twisting her mouth into a grimace, giving a little shrug. She'd guessed what I was thinking: that this was some kind of photo set-up.

I looked round at the other parked cars. She started to walk towards me. Usually she had a rangy, easy lope. Today she moved stiffly, awkwardly.

'I hope they paid you well. Have you any idea what you've done to my wife?'

She stopped ten yards or so away from me.

'What *I've* done? She's not *my* bloody wife.'

I shook my head, exasperated with her, with me, with the whole mess.

'I shouldn't be talking to you. The investigation.'

I was aware of movement to my left. I glanced

71

over at a woman walking up from the club, her wet blonde hair plastered to her skull, her gym bag over her shoulder.

'It wasn't me.'

'They quoted you,' I said.

'Hardly. You know I don't talk like that.'

'I don't know you at all.'

Gilchrist walked over to me and looked down.

'Sir, I'm truly sorry it got in the newspapers – but it wasn't me.'

I took a deep breath. I realized my fists were clenched. I flexed my hands.

'You can call me by my name,' I said quietly. 'In the circumstances.'

She nodded.

'How did you know I'd be here?'

She shrugged.

'I didn't really. I just took a chance.'

'You must have told somebody,' I said.

I was watching the woman unlock her car and sling her bag in the back seat. She was a swimmer too. We often shared a lane but never acknowledged each other, in the water or out of it.

Gilchrist cleared her throat, perhaps to draw my attention back.

'Somebody I thought I could trust,' she said.

I could smell her musky perfume.

'On the force?'

She sighed.

'Doesn't matter. He betrayed me.'

She had kind eyes. I'd always felt they would be a problem when she had to deal with hard cases. They'd see her eyes and think they saw weakness. I didn't know her well enough to

72

know if she was weak. Hell, I'd only spent one drunken night with her.

'They made up your quote?'

She sighed again.

'That first time. Then they phoned me, said they'd got the story, said they'd do a real number on us unless I spoke to them. I panicked.'

The woman was in her car, moving out of her space.

I put my arms around Gilchrist.

'It's OK.'

She was stiff inside my embrace. I released her.

'It's not OK,' she said, pulling back. 'It's fucking awful. You're screwed and, frankly, I'm screwed.' She looked fiercely at me. 'Again.'

My turn to step back.

'Are they giving you a hard time in the office?'

Police officers are essentially tribal.

'I'm suspended, remember? The shootings...'

'What the hell happened in there, Sarah?'

She dropped her eyes.

'Sarah, I really need to find out.'

'Why bother?' Her voice was harsh.

'So many reasons.' I gripped her arms. I felt her muscles bunch. 'Please.'

She shrugged me off.

'What about this thing you thought you saw in the dead man's hand in the kitchen.'

She looked furious.

'I thought I saw? I imagined it, you mean?'

Her head was thrust aggressively towards me.

'You tell me.'

'No.'

'What was it – a gun?'

73

She shook her head, stepped back. I heard the metal door of the gym clang closed.

'Leave it. You need to focus on what's happening to you and not worry about the rest of this.'

'What's happening to me has already happened.'

She smiled faintly as she turned away and started walking back to her car, lithe again.

'I somehow don't think that's the end of it,' she called back. 'Sir.'

A couple of days later I went to see my father, Victor Tempest. His real name was Donald Watts but he'd used his nom de plume for years. I thought I should tell him first-hand what had happened.

He lived in a cramped-fronted house across the road from the Thames in west London. On the big Georgian house to his right, a blue plaque commemorated Gustav Holt's stay there when he was in London at the turn of the twentieth century. Another plaque on the house to his left commemorated dancer Nanette de Valois's time living there. My dad probably hoped there would be a plaque for him when he passed on.

You could almost miss his house as it was set back from the road. The narrow courtyard at the front was dominated by a huge, low-hanging tree that all but hid the doorway. The flagstones were littered with empty fast-food packages, crisp packets and a crushed beer can. He kept his downstairs front room shuttered. The windows were grimy.

He kept it like this deliberately. Deters burglars, he used to say.

Inside was a different story. From the first floor there was a lovely view over the Thames and across the graceful iron bridge. His walled garden at the back was secluded and tranquil.

My dad had made a good living as a thriller writer and although his books were not so much in demand these days he still got feted when people remembered he was alive.

He'd bought this house with his first big lump of money after he'd divorced my mother. I never lived here, nor even stayed over. My father never remarried. He was a womanizer until late into life. Even now, probably, if he could get away with it.

He was expecting me but there was no answer when I rang the bell. I stepped back into the street and looked towards the pub a few hundred yards away on the riverbank. He'd probably be there.

I waited for a break in the traffic then hurried across the road. I walked under the bridge, on to the towpath and headed for the pub. I inhaled the sour smell of the river. I liked it almost as much as the briny tang of the sea in Brighton.

Ye Olde White Hart had a long balcony overlooking the river and, below them, long tables with benches attached set in concrete right at the river's edge on the towpath. When the river was high, the towpath flooded and the concrete was the only way to ensure the tables didn't float away. I'd always thought it would be a pleasantly surreal experience to drift down the river

75

sipping your drink at your table.

My father was inside the pub. It was big, Victorian with a high ceiling and a circular bar in the middle. A boat was suspended from the ceiling – this was a popular venue for watching the boat race.

He was in conversation with a young barmaid who was standing by his table. He was leering at her and when she moved off he turned his head to watch her backside. Ninety-five and still a lecherous bastard.

He had a live-in nurse/factotum/cook. He'd had a series of them. He usually made a pass, so they either laughed it off and stayed on, or took offence and left. At the moment it was a Polish girl, Anna, who coped with him very well. She'd been with him a couple of years.

'Did you forget I was coming?' I said, putting my hand on his shoulder. He tilted his head back. 'I knew you'd find me. Smart copper like you.'

In his youth, my dad had been a robust, broad-shouldered man. With age he was shrunken but his shoulders were still broad and he held himself erect. His neck had shrunk, though, so his shirts always looked too big and his jackets hung oddly, almost up around his ears.

My father had always been charming. Turned it on and off. Could charm anyone. Especially women.

He was remarkable. He'd run his last marathon on his ninetieth birthday. But I wasn't sure what he did to fill his days, except ogle women in pubs, I suppose.

We weren't close. Indeed, we'd had a lot of

76

problems over the years, mostly because of the way he'd treated my mum. I was pretty sure I had half-brothers and sisters somewhere and that they would come out of the woodwork when he died.

I got him another beer and sat down with a glass of wine. He watched me for a moment.

'You've come a cropper, I gather.'

'I wanted to let you know the full story – didn't want you getting the wrong idea.'

'There's no such thing as a full story. As I understand it, you shot your mouth off about how innocent your officers were after you'd got your leg over one of them. You being in Brighton, I suppose we should be grateful it was a gal, not a bloke.'

'Finished?'

'Pride's taken a bit of a bashing, then?'

'It's not over yet.'

'Looks like game, set and match to the other side from where I'm sitting.' He took a drink of his beer and I saw his eyes follow another woman across the room.

'Is yon government bloke going to help? Billy Simpson? Or has he put the boot in, too?'

Good question, I thought, but didn't say. My father looked at me.

'Like father like son, eh? Billy's father were always watching out for himself. Anything I can do to help?'

This was typical of my dad. He'd always given me a rough ride but once he'd had his say and given me grief he'd be there if he could. Well, sometimes.

77

'Not really. Got to stick it out, I guess.'

'What are you going to do to make a living? Write your memoirs?'

He smiled as he said it. It was a thin smile. My father had a mean face. I'd often wondered about that. Does physiognomy reflect character? In the nineteenth century, police forces throughout Europe had built a whole system on that assumption. And some people did look cruel or sour. It was usually to do with the set of the mouth. My dad had a tight mouth drawn down. Eyes protuberant, unblinking. And he was cruel. When I was growing up, praise had been grudging. He'd always been demanding, always lorded it over the household. He was a bully, sharp with his words, contemptuous of what he saw as weakness.

I think he was missing an empathy gene. He could feign kindness. He was regarded as a charming fellow. But underneath he'd always been cold, hard.

'A bit young for a memoir. Consultancy. Lecturing – I don't really know.'

'Crusading? Not that the word has the right connotations in these days of warring religions. Son, I have no idea where you have got this crusading thing from.'

'What's your point?'

'My point is – there's nothing good about any of us. We're all in the gutter—'

I started to finish the quote but he interrupted.

'I know the bollocks you're going to say. Oscar Wilde – the man who invented sound bites. Some of us like to think we're looking up at the stars, but whilst we're doing so someone is nicking our wallet, someone else is shitting on our shoes and that other bloke is fucking us up the arse.'

He leant forward to take a sup of his beer, his Adam's apple bobbing. He caught my look.

'What – you're shocked to hear your dad talk like this? Bit late for finickiness, isn't it, after what you've done? You've spent your life taking the moral high-ground about me and your mother but now you see how it can happen. You know what I thought when I read about your leg-over? Thank bloody Christ he's actually got blood in his veins – because I often wondered.'

'There's nothing wrong with fidelity and having a moral code.'

'Fidelity is for my old hi-fi system and don't get me going on morality.'

His eyes were burning fiercely, his jaw jutting at me.

'Dad, you've always been ice – there's no give in you.'

'Your mother was fire. Fire and ice is a good combination, don't you think? Anyway, I'm a writer. We're all less than human.'

'You're not exactly James Joyce,' I said in exasperation. 'You write thrillers.'

My father looked at me for a moment then continued:

'Graham Greene said every writer should have a sliver of ice in his heart.'

'You quote that approvingly. How does that work with family?'

He shrugged.

79

'You seemed to have survived OK. Aside from your daft antics, and I don't see how I can be held responsible for that.'

'Did you know Graham Greene?'

'I met him a couple of times.'

'At some authors' do?'

'The second time.'

'Is there an anecdote?'

'I don't do anecdotes.'

This was true. He was notoriously close-mouthed.

'What was he like?'

'The first time he was arrogant; the second time better.'

'When was the first time?'

'1934. Then in the sixties at a Foyles literary lunch.' He sat back in his chair. 'So what *are* you going to do?'

'Visit you to get your blood circulating.'

He barked a laugh.

'Aye. It's not exactly aerobic but it's better than nothing.'

As the sky started to lighten, the two hooded men left the car. When they opened its doors, no interior light came on. The taller of the two men unlocked the boot and swung the lid open.

The other man looked along the deserted road then up at the dark house, perched on the edge of the cliff some quarter of a mile away. He nodded.

The two men lifted a long, bulky bundle from the boot. The bundle squirmed. Hoisting it between them, the two men walked up the steep grassy sward to the cliff edge.

The taller man looked along the line of the cliff, the brilliant white chalk pale in the dim light. He looked down to the sea some four hundred feet below. The tide was full. He could hear the slap of the waves against the rocks, the undertow sucking at the beach.

The bundle squirmed more vigorously.

The taller man gestured to his partner. Together they swung the bundle back and forth. Once, twice, three times. On the fourth swing they released the bundle. It rose in an arc up and beyond the cliff edge. For a moment it hung in the air, silhouetted against the brightening sky. Then plummeted to the sea below.

FIVE

I was on the mobile arguing with Molly when I hit the deer. I clipped it as it lunged suddenly out of the black night. My headlights caught the panic flaring in its eye as we collided.

I should have anticipated it. I take pride in thinking ahead and I knew this lane well, every blind bend of it. But it had been a long day, Molly was raging in my ear and I was distracted by the sight of a car in flames in the middle of a meadow to my right.

My reactions in any case were slower than they

used to be. Months of chauffeur-driven travel had had a deleterious effect – and on more than just my driving.

I gripped the steering wheel with both hands and skidded to a halt. The phone slid off the passenger seat on to the floor. Through my open window I heard the deer's hooves skitter on the hard surface of the road. Then it cleared the gate into the meadow and was gone.

I became dimly aware of Molly's voice from the phone in the well of the passenger seat. I reached down and switched the phone off.

I took a torch from the glove compartment and got out of the car. The torch's beam was feeble in the darkness of the meadow and I could make nothing out. I guessed the deer was far away by now. I was relieved I didn't seem to have done it serious harm.

I turned to watch the burning car. Five years ago, burnt-out cars were confined to the other side of the Downs. I'd pass them on the outer edge of Brighton, near the golf course and on the wide grassy verges above the Hollingbury estate.

A couple of years ago, the first two or three appeared on the Downs themselves. Only last week, a stolen car was set on fire in the car park of the Ditchling Beacon, two miles from the outskirts of Brighton and on a lip hanging over this deep countryside. Centuries before, the warning beacons lit in this Iron Age fort were visible for miles around. So too was this conflagration.

I saw the trail of burnt-out cars as further evidence of the creeping approach of Brighton crime into the country beyond the Downs. And now it was here.

I climbed over the gate and walked across the uneven ground towards the burning car. It had probably been abandoned after a joyride or a robbery but I wanted to be certain nobody had been injured.

I approached gingerly. I was pretty sure the petrol tanks had already blown, judging by the way the flames had a hold, but I wasn't experienced enough at this kind of thing to know for sure.

I got within ten yards before the heat from the fire stopped me. Flames were consuming the whole car. The windows had blown out and burning fragments were scattered all around me. I felt the heat on my face but I stayed where I was. For from here I could see that there was a human form in the passenger seat, the head wreathed in fire. The person was clearly dead.

I backed away then turned to go back to my car and my phone. I swept the ground around me with my torch beam as I hurried to the gate, suddenly fearful that I might, after all, not be alone.

'It's Bob Watts, Ronnie,' I said when I got through.

Ronnie was the neighbourhood policeman. He was surprised to get a call from me.

'Hello, sir,' he said after a moment. 'How can I help you?'

'You've got a possible homicide on your patch.' I filled him in on the details.

'I'll be right down. Will you wait?'

'The truth is, Ronnie, my involvement will just

cause unnecessary complication. Once you've called it in to Division, everybody will be down here. If it's all the same to you, I'll go on home – you know where to get me when you need me.'

'Fair enough, sir.'

I never could get him to call me by my first name. After my disgrace some people cold-shouldered me and others sneered. A minority, like Ronnie, however, thought I'd been treated shabbily, made a scapegoat. They still called me sir because they felt I'd done a good job in the brief time I'd been Chief Constable here.

Molly was standing in our kitchen as I drove by. I gave her a wave I knew she couldn't see and carried on my way. Two miles further along the road I pulled through the first set of gates into the long gravelled drive of Harlingden Manor.

Whenever I took taxis, the drivers got excited around now, thinking they would be getting a good tip when they caught sight of the big manor house. I drove towards the second set of ornate gates at the entrance to the house then, as usual, turned left and followed the gravel drive round the back to the servants' quarters.

This bungalow – it used to be the chauffeur's in the old days – had become vacant just as Molly and I were separating. After my month in my friends' farmhouse was up I'd moved straight in. It was by no means ideal. Boxes of my things were piled in the hallway, not because I hadn't got round to emptying them, but because there was nowhere for the contents to go. However, it was all I would allow myself. And it was near Molly if she needed me.

The light was flashing on the phone. Probably Molly, angry that I'd hung up on her. Unsurprisingly, she was angry whenever we spoke these days, masking her hurt with rage. This evening she'd been angry because I'd made the mistake of telling her the truth. I'm a trustworthy man, on the whole, but I still believe truth is sometimes overrated.

'What do you mean you're going to go back into the case?' she had said as I was driving over the Downs after a tense meeting in Brighton.

'I'm even more convinced now that I was set up. I can't allow that kind of corruption to flourish.'

'Can you hear yourself, Mr Knight in Shining Armour? I'm as sorry as you your glittering career ended so abruptly but, Christ, you presided over a massacre that caused two nights of rioting.'

Her voice was venomous.

'And are you really so arrogant, so egotistical, as to believe that the botched operation and everything that followed was just aimed at ruining you? Get a life, Robert.'

'I had one. It was taken away from me.'

'With not a little help from you. Nobody asked you to shag that little tart and wreck your marriage.'

She was right about my one-night stand, but I was convinced that I was briefed against by someone near the top of the political food chain, that the story of my affair was leaked to the papers. And the set-up was real, I was certain of that too.

I do hate corruption. And I do belief in truth in the large sense. I couldn't bear the thought that there was corruption at the heart of the police force that I had led. But I had to be honest. Sure enough, I wanted to find out what had happened so that the truth would be known.

But most of all I wanted revenge.

I'd been to Chief Superintendent Charlie Foster's funeral the previous day. It was a small affair. Perhaps the fact of his suicide put some people off. I'd driven over to the crematorium early but had held back until the last minute, then slipped in at the back. Sheena Hewitt was in the front row representing Southern Police and there were a handful of familiar faces from the station. Sheena was now Acting Chief Constable. It should have been my deputy, Philip Macklin, but since his role in the Milldean incident was under investigation, the police authority preferred to go with someone uninvolved in – untainted by – that investigation.

Foster's son, a well-dressed man in his mid-twenties, gave a sombre valediction, although he did give a wan smile as he recalled his father's passion for trad jazz. I left as the coffin went through the doors and into the flames to the jaunty sound of Acker Bilk playing some New Orleans strut.

A man called after me as I crunched over the gravel back to my car. I turned. Bill Munro was hurrying towards me, puffing as he came. I hadn't noticed him in the chapel.

'Didn't expect to see you here,' I said as we

shook hands.

'Nor me you,' he said. 'But you've saved me a trip. Have you time for a drink in half an hour or so?'

We met in the Fortunes of War on the beachront. It was a pub dating back to the twenties, set in the arches, cramped and with a low ceiling. I figured nobody would see us there. It was quiet – no people, no piped music.

We sat upstairs by an open window and looked out to sea as we talked in low voices.

'Did Foster leave a note?' I said.

'None that we've found. You know what happened? His wife didn't know where he was and couldn't get him on his mobile so she went down to their beach hut. It was locked from the inside but she could see blood coming under the door so she called us and an ambulance.' He shook his head. 'Poor woman.'

'You're assuming it was guilt over his responsibility for the raid going wrong.'

Munro sighed.

'He did more than that. He buggered up the return of the guns to the armoury after the incident. He immediately got the weapons handed back, right enough, but he didn't tag which weapon had been in the keeping of which officer. That went for the snipers' rifles too. Everyone's DNA will be over everything. He compromised the investigation before it even got started.'

'Stupidity or cunning?'

Munro shrugged and reached for his beer.

'Did you have more to tell me?'

He looked into his glass a moment.

'This would go down better with a couple of bags of crisps. Hang on a jiffy.'

I watched the people wandering by below until he sat heavily down, dropping two packets of crisps on the table.

'Cheese and onion and salt and vinegar.' He tore both packets open. 'Help yourself.'

Then, through a mouthful of crisps, he told me the investigation had stalled.

'Nobody who was upstairs will say what happened. Nobody. Not Connolly, White, Philippa Franks or Potter. None of the snipers will admit to firing the shot that killed the man coming out of the back door.

'We have the rifle that was used for that but we don't know who signed it out and checked it back in. Same goes for the other weapons. Since they were all discharged, we don't know who did what to whom.'

'And John Finch?'

'Finch has disappeared. No sign of him packing at his flat, no movement on his credit cards or his bank account since he went AWOL.'

I sipped my wine.

'Do you think he's harmed himself?'

'Or somebody has harmed him,' Munro said, scooping up crisps with his fat fingers. He shook his head. 'But why would anybody?'

'This is a murky business, Bill, I've said that from the start. Nothing really makes sense. Is DC Edwards, whose grass started all this, still on the missing list?'

'He's done a runner, looks like. He was due leave starting the next day, true enough, but he's not answering his mobile and it's turned off so we can't track him through it. Credit card used in Dieppe the day after the incident, then points south – petrol and cheap restaurants – all the way to the Pyrenees. After that, nothing.'

'His snitch?'

Munro shook his head again then took a long gulp of his beer. I waited for more. Munro hid a belch.

'The word that Grimes was on his own came via Edwards from his snitch, so that's our starting point. But since we can't locate either of them, we can't actually start.'

'What's the deal with Bernard Grimes – is he one of the victims?'

'No.'

'Was he ever in Brighton or was the whole story cock and bull?'

'No, he was here but not in that house. The tip from London was firm. The confusion comes with what happened to it at this end.'

'So did Grimes get to Provence?'

'We're still checking. We don't exactly know where he has his place in France and, of course, he's living under another name. There's an arrest warrant out for him. The French police are on the job.'

I raised an eyebrow.

'Now, now – your lot have got nothing to boast about here.'

'Do you think it odd that Edwards and Grimes are both in France?'

He shook his head again.

'I don't think Grimes is involved in this in any

89

way at all. He was a beard. Just a way to get the guns out.'

'But what's the thinking? Everybody in the task force was complicit in this?'

'Well, they're certainly being complicit now.'

I rubbed my chin.

'Can you not start with the victims?'

'When we find out who they are, most certainly. They are not on any of our databases, nor, as far as we know at this stage, on any continental European databases. We're going down the DNA route, of course, but that takes time.

'According to the pathologist, the woman's dentition suggests she's from Eastern Europe. Something to do with the composition of her fillings.'

'The others are Eastern European, then?'

He shrugged.

'How much longer are you going to spend on this?'

He looked at me for a long moment.

'You know how these things go, Bob. Your team isn't denying people got shot, they're just saying they don't know who shot them. Unless someone comes forward, there's nothing we can do except discipline them – and you know how that will pan out.'

A young couple, heavily tattooed, came to sit at the next table. Munro leant forward – not easy with his belly.

'Thing is, there's a significant amount of pressure from higher up to let this one slide.'

I leant in close and hissed:

'How high up and how in hell can you let such

a massive thing slide? The press will go bananas.'

He sat back.

'We'll see. You know that in a couple of weeks' time, before they can be disciplined, the shooters will resign on health grounds and then it's over.'

Retiring on health grounds is the standard get-out for coppers wanting to avoid disciplinary procedures. They do a deal – if they agree to go, the force doesn't have to face public disgrace. It's the police looking after their own.

'What about a private prosecution?'

'By who? Since nobody knows who the victims are, there is nobody to yell for justice.'

Munro looked at the empty crisp packets and his empty glass.

'Another?'

'My shout,' I said.

I squeezed past the tattooed couple, who were hunched over their table, rolling cigarettes in readiness for a fag break. I didn't know why I was so surprised or angry at what Munro was telling me. I knew how the system worked and I knew that the police, like any established profession, closed ranks to protect its own.

When I got back to the table, Munro wanted to talk to me about my situation. His concern, I guess, was the reason he'd taken the trouble to see me.

He rubbed his cheek, leaving a red weal.

'You've been a bloody fool in more than one way but you've also had a raw deal.'

'I've been set up.'

91

'Well, I wouldn't go that far—'

'I would.'

He sighed and tilted his glass. The tattooed couple went outside to light up.

'Sorry about you and Molly. Do you think you'll get back together?'

'Eventually, maybe. To be honest, I'm focusing on sorting this out first.'

He put his glass back on the table.

'I didn't give you an update so you could start messing, Bob. I felt I owed you. But there's nothing you can do, however unfair it might be. Family comes first – you focus on getting back home. You hear?'

'I hear, Bill. Thanks – for all this.'

We stayed another ten minutes, talking about anything but my situation. The tattooed couple came back in, bringing with them a group of boisterous friends. We finished our drinks and went down the narrow stairs out into the sunshine. Munro gestured at the pebble beach.

'I've always been fond of that Acker Bilk tune *Strangers on the Shore*. Heard it on Wogan's radio show years ago.' He shook his head. 'Funny, Foster being a trad jazz man – you don't hear that much these days.'

We looked up and down the boardwalk at the throng of young people going by. He held out his hand.

'Good luck to you, Bob. And mind what I said – focus on sorting your marriage out. The most important thing.' He grinned. 'Though we don't always recognize it when they're giving us grief.'

I watched him make his careful way through the holidaymakers. He was a decent man, a contented man. I liked to think I was the former. I'd never be the latter.

On the day after Charlie Foster's funeral, Sarah Gilchrist almost begged Sheena Hewitt to be taken off suspension. She didn't care: inactivity was driving her mad. She had sat in her flat and suffered, waiting for a phone call that didn't come. Once, she'd driven out to Haywards Heath and parked opposite the police station. It was stupid. Connolly and White were suspended too, so weren't even there. Then she'd driven aimlessly round the town thinking she might see them but having no clue what to do if she did.

Inactivity engendered a familiar feeling, one she tried to keep away from. Old stuff welling up. Stuff she hoped she'd dealt with long ago.

Finch's disappearance had made her paranoid. She roamed the streets of Brighton and Hove, keeping her head down. Once she saw Philippa Franks in a restaurant she'd been intending to eat in. Philippa was in heated discussion at the back of the restaurant with an older man. It looked like relationship stuff so Sarah walked briskly away.

She phoned the Acting Chief Constable and on the sixth attempt was put through.

'What do you want, Sarah?' Hewitt said sharply.

'I want to get back to work, ma'am.'

'Do you indeed?'

'You must have seen all the statements from

that night in Milldean. You know I wasn't any-where near all the bad things going on.'

'I don't know because I don't believe anyone is telling the truth.'

'I am.'

'You say.' Hewitt sighed. 'You know you'll never be a firearms officer again?'

'I know that when the enquiry apportions blame it will probably tar everybody with the same brush.'

Hewitt was silent for a moment, then:

'I'll see what I can do.'

Ronnie, the community policeman, came round the afternoon after I'd hit the deer. I was having lunch when I looked out of the window and saw him standing in the gravel outside the bungalow.

'Sorry – the bell's kaput,' I said when I opened the door. I stood to one side. 'Come in.'

'It's about the body in the car, sir.'

Ronnie seemed to duck his head as he walked past me. He hesitated at the end of the corridor.

'Door on the left.'

He was a tall, broad-shouldered man and the ceilings weren't high. When I entered the room as well, also stooping, it suddenly seemed very crowded. He glanced around. I guessed he was thinking it was a bit of a rabbit hutch for an ex-Chief Constable but he made no comment. I gestured to the sofa under the window.

'Want a coffee?'

'Nothing at all, thanks, sir.'

I sat behind my desk, not because I wanted it to be a barrier – my management experience clicking in – but because it was the only other seat in the room.

'No identification possible yet, I assume.'

'The SoCs are on it but the fire was intense. I just have to get a statement from you for the record. Oh, and I need the shoes you were wearing to identify your footprints in the field.'

'Sure. The locals must be in shock.'

'I'm in shock,' he said with a grimace. 'The most violent stuff I usually have to deal with are drunken youths on the weekend, the badger-baiters and the Countryside Alliance going rabid.'

I gave him my statement, such as it was. When I had finished he got up to go, then stood awkwardly for a moment.

'How's the enquiry going, sir, if you don't mind my asking?'

'It's not getting anywhere, as best I can tell,' I said with a shrug.

'Truth will out, sir, I'm sure of it.'

I smiled and patted his shoulder.

'I wish I shared your optimism.'

SIX

The severed arm was found in the children's paddling pool at about the time Sarah Gilchrist took the call from Australia. She'd been back at her desk a week, her suspension lifted, though the enquiry had not yet issued its final report. Since her return she'd been lumbered with the most menial jobs and the worst shifts – which is how come, tonight, she was alone in the office.

The phone rang as she was standing by the window. She was watching the waves roll in. It was dusk but the sky was still bright blue.

'DS Gilchrist,' she said.

'Look, I'm phoning from Sydney.' The man's voice was urgent and shaky. 'I want you to listen to something.'

'Oh yes?' Gilchrist said, immediately on her guard, especially as the man didn't sound Australian. 'Who are you, sir?'

'I got this message on my answerphone waiting for me when I got home. Fucking freaked me out, excuse my French.'

'What's your name, sir?' Gilchrist reached for a pen and pulled a pad towards her.

'It's from a bloke I know lives in Hove. You'll have to listen closely – the tape isn't very good.'

'Sir—'

She heard the muffled beep of an answerphone then this drunken voice, refracted by the phone line. What the man said sent a chill through her.

'I just fucking took a fucking hammer and smashed John's brains all over the wall, mate. Then I got one of my swords. He's all over the fucking wall, all over the floor, all over the ceiling. John's like lying on the floor in ... loads of bits. I don't know why I did that, man.'

Gilchrist blanched. The voice was gleeful.

'Is this a real recording?' she said to the caller. 'Wasting police time is—'

'I'm not wasting your time. It's a guy called Gary Parker. He's always been a bit of a nutter. His best mate is John Douglas. They live in this flat in Hove.'

'Give me your details.'

She scribbled down his name and address.

'And the address in Hove?'

It was a house almost diagonally across from Hove railway station.

'Your local police will be visiting you shortly to collect the tape and interview you,' she said.

On her way out she stopped at the desk and asked the duty sergeant to phone the police in Sydney and to send out a call for back-up at Parker's address. It still might be a hoax, but she wasn't taking any chances.

The sergeant gazed blankly at her.

'You got that?'

He gave a little start.

'Sorry, Detective Sergeant. Had a bit of a shock. A man has just phoned in to say that he's found an arm in the kiddies' paddling pool on the seafront. I've sent a couple of constables down there.'

Maybe not a hoax, then. Gilchrist nodded and headed for the door.

'I've a horrible feeling I know where the rest of the body is,' she called back to him.

Two squad cars, lights flashing, were parked outside the shabby, three-storey Edwardian building. Commuters looked over as they came from the station and drinkers in the bar opposite were standing at the windows watching the action.

Gilchrist and four constables walked up to the front door. The curtains of the ground-floor flat were drawn. She rang the bell. No answer. Rang the bells of all the other flats to get through the house door. They crowded into the hallway, littered with flyers and free newspapers. She rapped on the cheap-looking door of the ground-floor flat.

No answer.

She looked at the constables. Caught one of them eyeing her up. Ignored that.

They were hefty-looking boys.

'Break it down,' she said.

It took two attempts, then the door burst open with a splinter of wood and a screech of hinges. The constables started in but came to an abrupt halt when they caught sight of the interior. They stepped aside to let Gilchrist see.

The living room was drenched in blood. It was sprayed across the walls and looked as if it had been poured on the furniture from a paint pot. It was pooled around the gruesome object in the

98

centre of the room. A naked male, without head, arms or genitalia, spindly legs stretched out on the carpet. A bayonet sticking out of his chest.

The sickly stench of the blood hit Gilchrist as she looked around the room and down at what remained of the young man. Dispassionately, she reminded herself she was always surprised to see that a body could hold so much blood. Then she threw up.

Gilchrist was still at the station at nine the next morning. She was light-headed, nauseous and exhausted. She sipped at a bottle of water. She was standing at the window again, watching the waves roll in, when the phone rang.

It took her a moment to respond. She'd been thinking about last night's crime scene. All the officers threw up at pretty much the same time.

When she'd calmed herself Gilchrist had moved in and looked more closely at the torso. It had been hacked about pretty badly. There was a yawning red-black hole where the penis and scrotal sack had been.

In the bedroom she'd found a large plastic bag stuffed with what, after a moment, she realized were body parts. In the kitchen a pale, thin arm and hand lay on the electric hob. A hammer, a Gurkha knife and a Samurai sword, all matted with blood and hair, lay on the kitchen table.

She picked up the phone. It was Sheena Hewitt's secretary.

'Sheena thought you'd be the best person to handle this call,' she said.

'Is it to do with last night's case?' Gilchrist

99

asked.

'I believe so.'

The killer, Gary Parker, had been picked up on the beach in the middle of the night. A scrawny man of about twenty-five with a beer gut and scarred knuckles, lost on drink and drugs. His face was puffy, his eyes slitted, mouth a sour line. He'd been sitting cross-legged beneath the Palace Pier. He had his friend's mutilated head balanced between his thighs.

Later, in a holding cell back at the station, Gilchrist had asked him about the arm on the hob.

'Was going to cook chickenburger sandwiches.' He bared yellow teeth. 'The only way I could see of getting rid of him. Bits of him kept falling out of the plastic bag.'

Gilchrist had managed to get through the rest of the night without throwing up, but remembering his words now she felt another wave of nausea.

'Shall I put the call through?' Hewitt's secretary said.

Gilchrist gulped down air.

'OK.'

'Hello,' a man said in a strangled voice, 'I'm Brian Rafferty, director of the Royal Pavilion, and I must say I'm a little tired of being shunted from pillar to post. I hope you're not going to pass me on to somebody else.'

The Royal Pavilion was the city's chief tourist attraction but she'd never cared for it. The paint on the outside was drab and its garish interior looked like something out of Disneyworld.

'I hope so too,' she said without enthusiasm. 'You're speaking to DS Gilchrist, Mr Rafferty. How can I help?'

'DS Gilchrist – that name sounds familiar.'

'The reason for your call?'

'We've found some files here that belong to you.'

'Files?'

'About the Trunk Murder.'

Gilchrist tightened her grip on the phone. What files, when Gary Parker had only dismembered his friend the previous night?

'What do you know about the Trunk Murder, Mr Rafferty?'

'Only what everybody knows from books – and, to be honest, I'd got the two mixed up.'

'Two?' Gilchrist was lost.

'You know. They got the man for Violette Kay but there was this other one—'

Tiredness washed over Gilchrist.

'Are you taking the piss?' she said. She regretted the words as soon as she uttered them.

'I beg your pardon?' Rafferty sounded indignant.

'Why have you called, sir?'

Rafferty hung up.

Kate Simpson was bored silly. It was James Bond Week and Tim, the presenter, had gone off at a tangent to babble about toupees, running his words together to stave off the fear of silence that dwells in every radio presenter's heart. Kate found listening to him exhausting. Mind-numbing too, but then she had only herself to blame

101

for taking a job at Brighton's local commercial radio station.

She had wanted a job in broadcasting. She hadn't wanted her father – William Simpson, government fixer – to use his influence to get her one. In consequence, here she was, the trainee and general dogsbody, the lowest of the low.

'That's the hot question of the day, then,' Tim blathered. 'Forget Daniel Craig. Forget Piers Brosnan. We're talking Roger Moore: real or rug? The lines are open, let me hear your views.'

Tim cued up a record and Kate gazed out of the window at the flow of people heading to and from nearby Brighton station.

The phone rang.

'The toupee hotline at Southern Shores Radio,' she said, trying to hold back the sarcasm. 'What's your opinion about Roger Moore: real or rug?'

She realized nobody had spoken at the other end of the line.

'Hello?' she said.

'I wanted to talk to someone at Southern Shores Radio.'

It sounded like a man trying to do an impersonation of Brian Sewell, the art critic.

'You are,' Kate said.

'You seemed to be saying you were some kind of hairdresser.'

Kate didn't try to explain.

'How can I help?'

'We've found something that might form the basis of an interesting radio slot.'

Kate withheld a groan. In the few months she'd

been here she'd grown to dread people phoning in with 'interesting' ideas. The topics the station actually covered were banal but seemed inspired compared to the ideas the public phoned in.

'Perhaps if you would write—'

'It's about the Trunk Murder.'

'Trunk Murder?'

'It's coming up to eighty years since it happened, you know.'

Actually, Kate did know. She had come down to Brighton to do her doctorate three years earlier. For a laugh during her first Brighton Festival, she'd gone with a couple of new friends on one of those moonlit murder walks. A procession of giggly, tipsy people touring the town and hearing about the gruesome murders, real and literary, that had taken place in this street or that arcade. The Brighton Trunk Murders were a main attraction.

'I thought there was more than one,' she said.

'Strictly speaking, yes,' the man said. 'Two separate investigations often get confused, as indeed they did at the time. I believe these files relate to the first Trunk Murder. The one that remains unsolved.'

'And you are?' Kate said, conscious from the lights flashing on the mini-switchboard that people were calling in on the other two lines.

'Brian Rafferty. Director of the Royal Pavilion.'

Kate put him on hold whilst she answered the other calls. It was running two to one in favour of the wig. She patched the callers through to Mingus, the producer, for on-air discussion.

'Most of the files relating to the case were presumed destroyed years ago,' Rafferty continued. 'But we've found some of them.'

'In the Pavilion?'

'It was the HQ for part of the original investigation.'

Kate's interest was piqued.

'You've looked through these files?'

'Cursorily.'

There's a posh word, Kate noted.

'Do you agree there's a story here?'

Kate did – and it was one she wanted to handle herself. It wasn't the hard news she yearned to do but it was a cut above the ditzy fare she usually had to deal with.

'Of course there's a story. But what about the police? Don't these files belong to them?'

'I phoned the police.' Rafferty spoke with asperity. 'They kept me hanging on for an age, trying to work out what to do with me. Then they were very rude.'

'I'm sorry to hear that,' Kate said, trying to keep her amusement at his irritation out of her voice.

'But it doesn't matter,' he went on. 'It was only a courtesy call, after all. They aren't interested in decades old files. Isn't there some kind of thirty-year rule in the police force where they either destroy stuff or pass it on to the county records office?'

'I believe so,' Kate said, fiddling with a plastic beaker of tepid water. She didn't like Rafferty.

'I believe so, too.'

An anniversary of the unsolved murder would

be a good peg. She was already imagining getting one of the many crime writers who lived locally to go over the files. And perhaps a policeman. In fact, she knew exactly which policeman to ask. The ex-Chief Constable, Robert Watts.

I went back into Brighton late the next morning to meet my friend James Tingley in The Cricketers pub.

What can I say about this man, who matches that clumsy Churchillian construction about a riddle wrapped in an enigma wrapped in a mystery?

I've known him for twenty years yet don't really know him at all. I don't know his sexual preferences, for instance. I've never seen him with a woman, never seen him with a man. Never heard him talk about either in a sexual way.

He seems to be that type beloved of crime novelists – a genuine loner. And that's strange because he has an ease with people, can fit into most social situations. But he remains watchful, always, taking everything in.

I had invited him to dinner many a time with Molly and me but he'd declined. 'Not much for small talk,' he'd said. And he was right. Not that he got uncomfortable about it.

He was happy not to talk, didn't bother him. I've never met a more self-contained man. Yet there was nothing chilly about him. He was warm, caring, but always controlled.

You wouldn't notice him in the street, wouldn't look twice at him in the pub. But if you did, you'd see something that would warn you at some primitive level not to mess with him.

He was quite the deadliest man I knew, an expert in unarmed and armed combat. To my certain knowledge he'd killed five men with his bare hands. Well, hands, feet and elbows. I'd seen him do it.

We were in the army together before he moved on to the SAS and got involved in all sorts of hairy and lethal operations. Often he was in corners of the world where the SAS weren't supposed to be. And I know he spent some time with the Israeli security forces.

I assumed he'd be in the service for life, though his distaste for authority meant he would never rise to a high rank. They kept trying to promote him, but he wasn't having any of it.

I don't know why he left the service. When I asked him once, he changed the subject. Artfully. I thought he'd tell me when he was ready but he never did. Yet we were friends. I knew I could trust my life to him – and had. I believe he knew the same about me – though whether I now would be able to fulfil that trust as effectively as he, I somehow doubted.

I expected him at least to stay in government service after he left the army – become a spook of some sort – but he moved to Brighton and set up a security business. It wasn't quite clear what some of the work was. Deep checks on companies and individuals, a little bit of industrial espionage, perhaps. He might still have been working for the intelligence services for all I knew.

We didn't see each other much. He was away a lot – had been away during the Milldean mess. He'd called me when he got back and suggested we meet.

It was a bright morning. I left my car in the car park beneath the old Town Hall and walked up the steps, which as usual smelled of piss. I strolled across the road to look at the sea. Seagulls squawked, there was a salt tang in the air and the sun glittered on the shifting surface of the water.

I stood by the railings on the promenade and looked over at the West Pier, little more than a grey skeleton since the arson attacks a couple of years earlier.

Joggers and rollerbladers weaved their way through the people walking past me. The pebble beach was already crowded with sunbathers, although no one was foolhardy enough either to be in the water or to be windsurfing on it. It wasn't by accident that Surfers Against Sewage was based in Brighton.

I was thinking about my father, who used to tell entertaining stories about what went on in Brighton on the seafront – and particularly on the West Pier – back in the thirties. But then entertaining stories were my father's stock-in-trade. Truth was something else again.

I walked up Ship Street and past the Hotel du Vin, glancing through the windows to see if there was anyone inside that I knew. That would have been my preferred venue. The Cricketers, however, was one of Tingley's regular watering holes. He liked his pubs cosy and a little gloomy.

I found him sitting – alone, naturally – in the

covered courtyard of the pub. It was a sunny day and the warm light filtering through the tacky corrugated plastic above our heads made the scuffed yellow walls glow like honey.

It was over a year since I'd seen him but he looked the same – so neat as to be nondescript. He had regular features with well-cut black hair combed back from his forehead. As usual he wore an understated dark suit, white shirt and plain tie.

He was of medium height and slim, despite the amount of drink he seemed to consume. I could think of many occasions when I had been start-led by the quantity he had put away, although I had never seen him act in a drunken way. Even overseas, in the forces, where there was little else to do off-duty but drink.

Tingley drank a disgusting concoction – rum and peppermint – that he called rum and pep.

He was sitting in the courtyard, his rum and pep, packet of cigarettes and lighter lined up in front of him. It wasn't yet noon so I'd bought a cup of coffee. I pointed at his drink. He shook his head.

I sat down opposite him, held out my hand. He took it, gave it a little squeeze.

'You've been better, I warrant,' he said, inspecting my face. 'You should have got hold of me. Let me help.'

'I'd heard you were out of the country.' It was an unspoken agreement that I never asked him where he'd been. Never pried at all, in fact. 'Besides, I fight my own battles.'

'But now...?'

108

I laughed.

'Now I need your help.'

He nodded.

'What exactly are you doing these days?' I said.

He took a sip of his rum and pep.

'Does it have to be exact?'

I smiled.

'I hope you're not risking your neck doing security in Iraq or Afghanistan.'

'I'm mad but not that mad.'

'Good money.'

'If you live to spend it ... Tell me,' he said, putting his drink down. 'Why'd you put your neck on the block?'

'I did what I felt was right.'

Tingley laughed. For some little while. He saw my discomfort – OK, my mounting anger – and laughed some more. Then he pointed at me.

'Your ego is your blessing and your curse. Gets you places because you can't imagine you can't get there. Fucks you because you don't know when to stop.'

'Thanks for the analysis, Dr Tingley,' I said, smiling again. Or, at least, attempting to.

He tilted his head.

'Actually, ego and obstinacy – are they the same thing? Because when you think you're right, you're outrageously obstinate.'

'You think I was wrong?'

Tingley caught the heat in my voice, reared back, hands out.

'Whoah, Bobby. I'm on your side, remember.' He looked hard at me. 'Remember?'

I remembered. The Gulf War – the first one. Pretty much of a turkey shoot, except my squadron had been sent out on reconnaissance with the wrong grid references. We'd strayed into friendly fire from the Yanks, who preferred to be sure rather than safe when it came to obliterating everything that got in their way.

Then we'd hit some Iraqis who were up for a fight and knew what they were doing.

A dozen of us survived but only with the weapons we had in our hands and what we stood up in. Our communications were buggered, we didn't have so much as a compass and a map between us. We didn't know where the hell we were.

Nothing but sand and blistering sunshine. We slept during the day in sweltering sand scoops, moved at night when the heat was only slightly less, navigating by the stars as best we could.

And then we stumbled across this man. One minute we were trudging across the dunes, sinking up to our thighs in the soft sand, the next a sandman was standing in front of us. We should have shot him but our reflexes were buggered. He peeled his balaclava off. Spoke to us in English.

He laughed like a drain when I told him where we were supposed to be.

'I'll take you there,' he said.

As we waded through the sand, I asked him how long he'd been out here. He told me a couple of months, living off the land. Jesus – what was there to live off? We'd been out a week and were suffering big time. My respect for him was established there and then.

He got us to our destination. He got down and dirty with us when we met opposition on the way. He pointed us in the right direction then disappeared into the night.

That was the first of many encounters all over the world. He saved my neck more than once and, I modestly submit, I did the same for him on a couple of occasions. We kept in touch, met up pretty regularly when we were both in the same country and off-duty.

He was one of the few men I trusted absolutely.

I'd tried to get him talking many a time but he always turned the conversation back on me. And, well, like he said, I had an ego.

'I want to find out what really happened in Milldean and what was behind it.'

'What about the enquiry?'

'They've got nowhere fast, as far as I can tell.' I fiddled with my empty coffee cup. 'And nobody in the police service is willing to talk to me. I'm outside the tent as far as my old associates are concerned.'

'I don't have an in there,' Tingley said, looking past me and lowering his voice as a young couple came through from the public bar and sat at the far end of the courtyard.

'No, but you're well connected locally – and nationally.'

'Locally is fair enough but – what? – you think there was some kind of conspiracy at a national level?'

I drained my coffee.

'All I know is that the government and the

media turned against me pretty damned quickly.'

'Bobby, Bobby – surely you can see why? You shot your mouth off in support of your officers when you shouldn't have done. Plus you were the poster boy for arming the police and oversaw a bloodbath. You had to go.'

I'd been hearing this from everybody I spoke to. Intellectually, I understood it but, emotionally, I was having a tough time accepting it.

'What do you want, Bobby?'

'Revenge.' There it was again, out on the table.

'It doesn't help.'

I sighed.

'Oh, I think it will. Me, anyway.'

'Revenge against whom?'

'Against anyone involved with what happened.'

'Will it get you your job back?'

'Probably not.' He arched an eyebrow. 'No.'

'Sometimes you've just got to accept they're bigger than you. Remember donkeys years ago that Manchester copper went over to Northern Ireland and did a report nobody liked? He resigned and resigned himself to his fate, made the most of his reputation as an honest copper. That innocent Liverpool lassie – all the mud they sprayed on her, they knew some would appear to stick. The gay cop who was soft on drugs – stitched up.' He shook his head. 'If they want to get you, they'll get you.'

'I don't want a new career advertising double-glazing or house security systems, thanks very much.' I rubbed the scars on the knuckles of my left fist. 'And I don't give up.'

I pointed at his glass. He nodded. When I came back with his drink and a glass of red wine for me, he leant forward intently and started speaking before I sat down.

'And you still don't know who the people are who were killed in the house?'

'There may be an Eastern European connection but nothing solid.'

'And Milldean – nobody's talking there, right?'

'Nobody ever does,' I said. 'But I'm out of the loop, remember.'

'Know what the Israelis would do with that estate?'

'Flatten it and kill everybody they could?'

'Nah. They've got unrivalled intelligence. Maybe the Jordanians are better. Maybe. You go through that estate house by house. You find out who lives there, what they do for a living, what school they went to, who their friends are, which of their friends' sisters or brothers they've shagged. Once you know everybody's interrelationships, that's when you know how things really are there. Grasses just aren't enough. You've got to get the detailed picture.'

I shrugged. He touched my arm.

'So you want my help?'

'Please,' I said. 'It is, as you say, essentially an intelligence gathering exercise.'

'Know what would make the police job easier? Get everybody in the land DNA'd and finger-printed.' He caught my look. 'What's wrong with that?'

'They're talking about it. Civil liberties might be a problem.'

113

I looked at him sitting opposite me. I was thinking about him in Israel. I knew he'd killed Palestinian terrorists – freedom fighters, if you will. I think he'd been in Lebanon for the last shindig against Hamas. I hoped he hadn't been in Gaza.

'OK, as I understand it, this is what you need to know for starters, outside of what actually happened in that house.' He tilted his glass, examined the viscous liquid inside it. 'Who was the informer who said Grimes was in the house in the first place? Who was watching the house to give the false information about him coming back from the off-licence alone at eight o'clock? Who the hell *were* the people in the house? Oh, and what happened to the disappeared policemen – Finch and Edwards?'

I nodded.

'That's a start.'

Tingley downed his drink in one, gently replaced the glass on the table and spread his hands.

'Easy-peasy.'

SEVEN

Gilchrist's treat for the day was to investigate a body found in a secluded cove at Black Rock. The drift patterns for bodies at the whim of the tides suggested it was probably a suicide from Beachy Head, the high chalk cliff that vied with the Clifton Suspension Bridge in Bristol for the most popular place in Britain for people to off themselves.

She was accompanied by Reg Williamson, a policeman she already knew. He was a dour, cynical old stager who had been her boss briefly before her promotion to detective sergeant.

There was little human to see in the bloated body crammed between rocks and wrapped in seaweed. It doesn't take long for dead bodies in water to deteriorate. Undersea scavengers get to work almost immediately, waves and rocks buffet them, water mixes with gases to pump them up to twice their actual size.

Gilchrist didn't get nearer than five yards. Sometimes, she knew, bodies exploded, letting out foul and noxious fumes. She talked with the medical team who were getting the body on a stretcher to take back to the lab, spoke to the local coastguard about tides, then scrambled back over the rock to where Reg Williamson stood, belly out, fag in his mouth, his face tilted towards the sun.

'Beachy Head?' he said when she came up to him. He was still taking in the sun's rays.

She nodded and moved past him.

Kate Simpson was a meticulous researcher. Before she went to her meeting with Brian Rafferty at the Royal Pavilion she went into the local history library in the Brighton Museum to see what it had on the Trunk Murder.

There were a handful of people sitting at desks or in front of the microfiche readers. Kate went to the card index and found a dozen or so entries for the Trunk Murders. She was hoping for a quick in-and-out, but the books and pamphlets were in the basement and would take ten to fifteen minutes to deliver to her. She asked about using the fiche machine to look at newspaper reports from 1934.

'You've got to book in advance,' the stocky guy behind the enquiry counter said. 'And there's nothing free for a couple of days.'

He looked down at the list she'd compiled.

'The Trunk Murder? Hang on.'

He came out from behind the counter and walked over to a filing cabinet. A couple of seconds later he pulled from it a see-through folder and proffered it to her.

'We've made files of newspaper cuttings and other stuff that we're always asked for. This is the one for the Trunk Murder.'

'It's that popular?'

'Sure.' He smiled shyly. 'This should get you

started.'

There were some thirty cuttings in the file. They were from the *Brighton and Hove Herald* or the *Brighton Gazette*. The *Gazette* for Saturday 23rd June had the headline 'Ghastly Find At Brighton: Body In Trunk: Woman Cut To Pieces.'

Kate read the article and scanned the rest of the cuttings quickly. She hadn't realized quite what big news the Trunk Murder had been at the time. It had attracted both national and international coverage.

A woman's torso had been found packed in a trunk in the left luggage office on 17th June 1934. The next day her legs and feet had been found in a suitcase at King's Cross station's left luggage office.

The famous pathologist, Sir Bernard Spilsbury, had examined the remains and provided a profile of the victim that concluded she was a well-nourished young woman, aged around twenty-five, who was pregnant for the first time. There were no body scars, no poison in the stomach, no sign of violence on the body (except, of course, its dismembering), no sign of death from natural causes.

For twelve months Scotland Yard led the murder hunt throughout Sussex, much of Britain and other parts of the world. The investigating officers were swamped by information – thousands of letters, hundreds of written statements and over one thousand telephone messages.

Eight hundred missing women were reported to Scotland Yard. Impressively, 730 were traced and accounted for. The case histories of the others were examined but none revealed a link with the dead woman.

In the event she was never identified. The cause of death was never established. And her killer was never caught.

As they drove along the coast road, Williamson went on and on about Beachy Head.

'Don't know why they don't fence the whole of the Seven Sisters off.' He was chewing a nail as he spoke. 'It's not safe at the best of times, lumps of chalk falling off. It's not long ago they had to move that converted lighthouse back a hundred yards so it didn't fall into the sea.'

'You think it might have been accidental death?' she said, for something to say.

'Fuck knows. Beachy Head has won Suicide Spot of the Year twice running. Sometimes I think we should station somebody up there permanently just to make sure the suicidal form an orderly bloody queue.'

He chewed at his nail some more then, when Gilchrist didn't say anything: 'Or two queues – one for jumpers and the other for people in cars. I don't mind so much if they do it when the tides in. I fucking hate it when you've got a fifteen-year-old Ford scattered across the beach.'

'Not to mention the driver.'

'Yeah, right,' he said, laughing until he realized from her expression she wasn't joking. He scratched the stubble on his chin. 'Listen, Sarah. Anybody selfish enough to top themselves I ain't got time for – they can drop dead as far as I'm

118

concerned.'

'They do.'

'Yeah, well.' His face was flushed.

'Well, what?'

He glared at her.

'I see the pain they cause for the people they leave behind,' he said vehemently. 'Children without mothers...'

Gilchrist glanced across at him. He was working his jaw and looking out across the sea.

Kate Simpson was ten minutes early for her meeting with Brian Rafferty so spent the time mooching along the corridors of the Royal Pavilion. She'd always regarded the Prince of Wales's early-nineteenth-century Indo-Chinese confection as the height of kitsch. Her favourite story about it was that during the First World War it was used as a hospital for wounded Indian soldiers, presumably on the assumption that they would feel at home there.

She imagined them waking up, looking round at the gaudy decorations, the dragons and the other mock-Chinese and Indian decorations and thinking: 'Where *am* I?'

She ambled into the banqueting room and looked up at the giant chandelier suspended from a dragon's maw. She'd dined here a few times. Usually it was during Labour Party Conferences when her father invited her to be his guest so he could kill two birds with one stone – seeing to business and seeing her.

Rafferty's secretary was waiting when she walked back down the corridor. She was a dumpy woman of indeterminate age who gave Kate the once over then led the way up the stair-case, leaning heavily on the bamboo banister. Rafferty's office was at the end of a meandering series of narrow corridors.

'Delighted, delighted,' he said, gathering her hand unctuously between his.

He was a curious little fellow. Probably in his late forties, with floppy hair and narrow shoulders. His manner made Kate think he must be gay, despite the photograph of his wife and children on his desk that he was keen to show to her.

He insisted on signing then presenting Kate with one of his books, a turgid-looking guide to *Brighton: Past and Present*. She flicked through it whilst he scurried around sorting out coffee. The book didn't feature any kind of present Brighton she was familiar with.

'So you have some files from the police investigation of the Trunk Murder,' she said. 'You don't have the trunk itself, I suppose?'

'I so like words with multiple meanings, don't you?' he said.

Kate looked quizzical.

'Well, a torso is a trunk – the victim was found in a trunk.' He smiled an awful, coy smile. 'And, of course, if we were American, the trunk would be the boot of a car. Why, I wonder?'

'You don't have the trunk, then?' Kate repeated. She took a sip of her coffee. It was good.

'Alas, no. I have files. Lots of files.'

'Which categories?' Kate said, remembering how punctilious the Scotland Yard detectives had been about separating things out.

Rafferty steepled his fingers.

'Do you know, I think I might risk a sherry. Will you join me?'

Kate glanced down at her watch. It was eleven a.m.

'No, thank you.'

'Ah – you're thinking it's a bit early. It's all right – I won't tell.'

He jumped up and scurried for a cabinet in the corner beside a replica of a large antique rocking horse that she'd also seen on sale in the Pavilion's shop.

'No – really,' she said as he took out two glasses and a bottle. 'I'm fine with coffee.'

He looked peeved but poured himself a glass and brought it back to his desk.

'Most of the files don't seem to be categorized,' he said. 'I've been reading up and, as far as I can gather, after some months, when the police hadn't in reality got anywhere, the two Scotland Yard detectives heading the investigation moved back to London to oversee the investigation from there.

'One would assume that all the files would have gone up with them but that was not the case. In 1964 the then Chief Constable of the South East Constabulary ordered all the files relating to the case held in Brighton Police station destroyed. Under, I presume, some thirty-year rule.'

He stood again and beckoned her over to another desk beneath a large window. When she approached she saw that the window led out on to a balcony. There were three cardboard boxes, each filled with brown and green files. Kate looked down at them, excitement stirring in her.

'But these had been left here?' she said.

'In error, of course. There may be others.'

'In the Pavilion?'

'No, no. But the Scotland Yard detectives continued to take statements and carry out their investigations for a further year in London. They would have had their own files. I don't know if they were destroyed.'

Kate nodded. She pointed at the nearest box.

'May I look?'

'By all means.'

She was aware that Rafferty was standing uncomfortably close. He smelt of something fusty, as if he slept in mothballs. His waxy cheeks, she noticed, had little points of red on them. She glanced at the empty sherry glass on his desk.

She lifted out an unmarked brown pocket file. Opening it, she saw a sheaf of foolscap pages, lined, each page headed 'Brighton Police'. She looked at the first sheet. Beneath the heading someone had typed 'Witness Statement of Andrea Stewart'. The statement itself was hand-written in neat, sloping letters decorated with loops and curlicues.

'Ah, yes,' Rafferty pointed at the page with a stubby finger. 'She saw a man burning something foul-smelling when she was out for a walk with some friends over at Pyecombe. He told them he was burning fish but he wouldn't let them near enough to see for themselves.'

Kate flicked through the sheets aimlessly. She felt excitement stirring as she wondered if within these files there might be some clue to the identity of the Trunk Murderer. What a coup that would be.

'I don't have time to work with you on this,' Rafferty said. 'But I expect the Pavilion's discovery to be part of the story.'

'Oh, of course. And for the programme I thought I might invite a policeman to comment on the evidence we have.'

'Indeed? Do you have someone in mind?'

'I was thinking about Robert Watts.'

Rafferty's mouth twisted into a grimace.

'That odious man.'

'Is he? Do you say that because of what happened?'

'Not at all. Simply because of who he is. I don't think I would be able to work with him.'

'You probably won't need to,' Kate said.

Rafferty smiled and giggled.

'Ah – that snippy policewoman – I've just realized who she is.'

Gilchrist and Williamson parked at the lay-by just below the lip of Beachy Head. The converted lighthouse was some hundred yards up a steep incline behind them. Williamson didn't say anything but Gilchrist could tell he was pissed off at having to walk up the hill.

He trailed behind as she strode ahead. She was enjoying the view: in one direction the sea and in the other the rich green folds of the Downs.

The wind was fierce, blowing in sharp gusts

from the sea, sending clouds scudding across the vast arc of sky.

When Gilchrist reached the door, Williamson was still clumping along some fifty yards behind. The door opened before she had even located a bell.

'Another suicide?'

The speaker was a woman somewhere in her fifties, dressed in a loose linen top and matching trousers, her hair drawn back from her sculpted face. She introduced herself as Lesley White.

She looked like a retired dancer, an impression reinforced when she moved back to usher Gilchrist into the house then led her down three steps into a spacious living room.

'Possibly,' Gilchrist said when the woman turned back towards her. 'This is just routine.' She looked around the thirties modernist room. 'Lovely. And it must be lovely living here.'

'It is and it isn't. This stretch of cliff is very popular among tourists. And among suicides.'

There was a heavy rapping on the door.

'Sorry,' Gilchrist said. 'My colleague.'

Williamson was sweating as the woman led him into the living room.

'This is Sergeant Williamson,' Gilchrist said. 'We've found a body, as you surmised, down the coast a little way. At the moment we don't know whether this is suicide. However, our visit is strictly routine.'

White gestured for them to sit down on a cream sofa. Gilchrist worried Williamson would somehow mark it, perhaps with nicotine-stained fingers. In consequence she sat particularly gingerly herself on the edge of the sofa, her hands clasped between her thighs

'How long has it been in the water?' White said, casually familiar with the procedure.

Gilchrist looked at Williamson, giving him an opportunity to join in the conversation.

'We don't know for certain yet,' he said gruffly. 'Probably a couple of weeks, judging from the deterioration. I don't suppose you remember anything from back then?'

'Well, we don't keep a suicide watch here, if that's what you mean.'

She sat so neatly, so straight-backed, that Gilchrist immediately felt lumpen and heavy. Looking at her face again she thought she might be early sixties – but looking very good on it. Gilchrist pushed her shoulders back.

'Is there anything unusual you can recall?'

'All I can recall is that we lost our cat.'

'What was his name?'

Gilchrist blurted out her question without thinking. She was a sucker for animals. Williamson caught the soppiness in her voice and gave her a disgusted look. She flushed but ignored him.

'Phoebe,' the woman said. 'But Phoebe was a boy.' She smiled quickly, showing small, even teeth. 'We got muddled when he was a kitten.'

'No wonder he ran away,' Williamson said.

White smiled again but her eyes didn't. Gilchrist could tell she didn't like Williamson, especially sweating on her pristine sofa in his sports jacket and greasy trousers.

'He's chipped by the way,' White said to

Gilchrist. It took a moment for Gilchrist to realize that White was hoping she would try to find her cat.

She stood.

'OK, well, that will be all for now.' She handed White her card. 'If you can think of anything else.'

Walking back down to the car Williamson kept pace with her. She felt awkward with most of her colleagues. First because of the shooting, second because of the splash the papers had done on her one-night stand with Watts. So she was surprised and touched when Williamson said:

'Sorry you've been going through all this shit, Sarah.'

'Oh, Reg, you know how it goes...' Her voice trailed away.

'Sorry if I've been a bit tricky today.'

Williamson apologizing too? Gilchrist gave him a sharp look as they neared the car.

'Fact is, these suicides don't agree with me—'

'So you've made clear,' she said quickly.

He looked at her, seeming to want to say more.

'Ay, well. Let's see what forensics come up with, eh?'

I was sitting in what passed for my back garden, pen and pad on my lap, when the bell of my bungalow rang out harshly. I was tempted to ignore it, as I had the telephone that had been ringing throughout the afternoon, but I felt vulnerable. I was pretty sure the front door was unlocked and whoever it was could just waltz in and find me sitting here.

I was punishing myself by living in this horrible place, sure enough. The thing about our old home was the view. Here there was no view. I had thought of renting somewhere in Brighton by the sea – another view I loved. Instead I'd chosen this place where the only view was of the big house that straddled the space between me and the Downs. A travel agent owned it. He and his wife acted like seigneurs, tramping by each day to walk their estate.

Fired up by the meeting with Tingley, I'd been mapping out a plan of action. What the hell else was I going to do? I had no job and no immediate prospect of one.

The past weeks had given me plenty of time to think. Seethe, too. I had been thinking about me, about what I am. I find it so unlikely that I got where I did. I was just a kid with wacko parents.

My dad, the writer, Victor Tempest, churning out these gung-ho thrillers. He was most successful when I was growing up. To meet his deadlines – he was writing three a year – he scarcely left his study, never mind the house. He was in his fifties before I came along and I guess he was set in his ways.

My mother was giddy, excitable – OK, mad as a hatter. Her mood swings, from the heights of joy to the depths of despair, made a big dipper seem like a sensible mode of transport. When my wife, Molly, proved depressive – post-natal depression – it didn't need a shrink to tell me that maybe I was looking for my mother in my wife. But a shrink did, unable to believe my wife hadn't shown some propensity for depression

127

earlier in our marriage. Actually, rack my brains though I did, I didn't think she had.

What did I get from my parents? From my dad, my ambition and my toughness. From my mum, something more theatrical. The drive to succeed I got, of course, from my desire to leave these two people behind. Not that you ever can, however far you go.

I was a driven man. People could see that in me. They couldn't see that I was also a fearful one. My ambition hiding my insecurity. Often before big meetings, like an actor before a first night, I was physically sick. When I first came into the police at quite a senior rank I forced myself to speak within the first two minutes of a meeting, otherwise I feared I would not speak at all. I had difficulty addressing the troops. I was conscious that I didn't have their experience, hadn't worked my way up through the ranks.

The doorbell rang again, more insistently. I left the pad and pen on my chair and padded through the back door, down the corridor to the front. When I opened it, Sarah Gilchrist was standing there, an embarrassed look on her face. I flushed and glanced at the other houses around me.

'It's an official visit,' she said hastily. 'I have to take a further statement about that burning car you came across.'

I wondered whose tactful idea that had been. I stepped aside.

'Come in,' I said, acutely conscious of my rumpled appearance, in chinos and unironed linen shirt.

Gilchrist was not in uniform, but from the little

I knew of her, this was her unofficial uniform: jeans and white T-shirt. She was big on the hips but long-legged and tall enough to carry it off.

I ushered her into my cramped sitting room.

'You know I've already given a statement to Ronnie?'

Gilchrist was standing in the middle of the room. The space seemed unnaturally confined. She nodded.

'Just a follow-up.'

'They're giving you the shit jobs, then,' I said.

'At least I'm back on duty.' She laughed. 'Although the thought of investigating the disappearance of a cat this morning did test my patience.'

'A cat?'

She told me of her visit to Beachy Head. I unscrewed the top on an expensive bottle of New Zealand Sauvignon Blanc and poured us both a glass. I laughed when she came to the end of her story.

'But you know there's this whole thing about cats being stolen around here, either to make into fur rugs and stuff or for black magic purposes,' I said.

'Black magic – the Lewes loonies, you mean?'

Whereas Brighton was everything wacky and New Age, Lewes, the market town four miles inland, was more superstition and Old Religion. Its residents still burnt the Pope in effigy every Bonfire Night because some Protestants were martyred in the town five hundred years earlier.

'Who knows?' I handed her the glass of wine. I told her my theory about burning cars as a sign

129

that big city corruption was creeping into the pristine countryside.

'Hardly pristine, sir,' she said with a laugh. 'You know how many white collar crooks live out here. I don't think anyone can be a millionaire without cutting a few corners.'

'I suppose,' I said. 'The burning car reminded me of that burnt-out car up at the Ditchling Beacon just about the time the roof fell in.'

'The roof fell in? I'm not following.'

'On my career.' I shrugged. 'Might be worth seeing if there's any link.'

Gilchrist frowned.

'Doesn't seem likely, sir.'

'Call me Bob,' I said gently. 'Please.'

She held my look, gave a little nod.

'So have they identified who was in last night's car yet?'

She shook her head. 'Folsom is working on the human remains, such as they are. We may never identify the person.'

'Dentition should help.'

'That's always a bit hit and miss.'

I nodded.

'What do you need from me?'

'Just the usual. What you saw, what you did, where you'd been. Did you pass any other vehicles or anybody acting suspiciously?'

'I saw no other vehicles on the lane. I may have passed a couple of cars coming across the Downs. I didn't really notice.'

I described what had happened with the deer and how I'd walked across the field.

'And why were you passing that way at that

130

time of night?' She saw my look. 'I have to ask.'

'I was on my way back from a meeting in Brighton.'

'What kind of meeting?'

'The private kind.'

She flushed again and seemed to tense.

'I have to know, I'm sorry.'

'Not that kind,' I said, smiling. 'I had a drink with Sheena Hewitt.'

'Oh,' Gilchrist said, not sure whether she should be writing that down or not.

'About the Milldean investigation.' I looked at her intently. 'I thought our successful professional relationship whilst I was Chief Constable might count for something.'

Gilchrist looked down at her pad but didn't say anything.

'I'm going to find out exactly what happened,' I continued. 'I can't believe the investigation so far has been so badly handled. Foster's suicide, Finch and Edwards disappearing without trace, nobody knowing who the grass was. And not a single victim identified.'

Gilchrist met my stare.

'I wish I knew what happened,' she said. 'Because it has fucked my career.'

'I know the feeling,' I said shortly.

She looked embarrassed again. Closing her pad, she started to rise.

'Please, stay a little longer. You haven't touched your drink.'

She looked embarrassed.

'I'm on duty.'

'Sorry,' I said, feeling foolish.

Gilchrist's mobile phone rang. She glanced at the number. Excusing herself, she walked over to the window. She listened but scarcely spoke. She finished the call and looked off into space for a moment.

'You OK?' I said.

'Reg Williamson just phoned. The body on the beach has been identified.'

'That was bloody quick.'

'It was Detective Constable Finch.'

'Christ – another suicide? But where's he been – he can't have been in the water all this time.' She shook her head.

'Apparently, he's only been in the water a few days. And they don't think it was suicide.' She looked up at me with her clear blue eyes. 'They think he was murdered.'

EIGHT

Kate Simpson drove carefully over the series of speed bumps on the long drive that circled the big mansion. She parked in a small car park at the edge of the cluster of houses at the back of the mansion and walked across to ring the bell on the bright blue door of the bungalow.

She was nervous. Just as she was about to ring again, the door swung open. She looked up at the tall, broad-shouldered man standing in the doorway. He had a broken nose, generous mouth and bags under his eyes. His blond hair was swept straight back from his forehead.

'Mr Watts, I'm from Southern City Radio. I wondered if you might like to help with a review of an old murder case.'

'You doorstep me for that?'

She flushed.

'I wasn't really doorstepping you,' she said quickly. 'I've been telephoning but there was no answer and you don't seem to have an answering machine.' She showed him an envelope addressed to him.

'I was going to leave you a note.'

Watts peered at her.

'I know you, don't I?'

'I was at the press conferences you gave at the time of the Milldean incident.'

'And you were there the night it happened. Yes, I know that.' He sounded impatient.

She held his look. Had he been the kind of boss who didn't suffer fools gladly? How had his staff regarded him?

'I mean you're familiar to me aside from that,' he said.

'My name's Kate Simpson.'

It only took him a moment.

'William's daughter.' Watts smiled. 'My God – I'm sorry I didn't recognize you straight away.'

'That's OK – you haven't seen me for a couple of years.'

Watts smiled.

'Local radio is a bit small beer, isn't it? Couldn't he get you a better job?'

Anger flared in her eyes. Tight-lipped, she said:

'I didn't want and don't need his help.'

He studied her for a moment then stepped aside.

'I'm sorry – I'm a bit distracted by some news I've just received. Do you drink wine?'

She followed him down a narrow corridor made narrower by piles of boxes neatly stacked along one wall.

'Books,' he said over his shoulder as he turned left into a small sitting room. 'Nowhere else to put them.'

The sitting room had a sofa and a desk. Bookshelves lined every wall, filling any available space, making the room even smaller.

She sat sideways on the sofa as he collected wine and glasses from the kitchen. She gestured at the books.

'I didn't expect you to be such a reader.'

'Maybe you have the wrong stereotype of a policeman. Maybe you're reading the wrong crime fiction.'

'Is that what these are?' she waved at the bookcases. 'Crime novels?'

He shook his head.

'I'm not a great fiction reader.'

'You have some thrillers here, though. Victor Tempest.'

She pointed.

'They're my father's, actually.'

He handed her a glass of pale white wine and sat down beside her. It was a two-seat sofa and awkwardly intimate. He didn't seem to notice.

'About this project—'

'About the money?'

'It's local radio...'

'So no money.'

She flushed.

'But being on the radio...'

He looked into his wine. She flushed again. He had done so much national radio and TV that there was nothing at all in it for him. She was aware she was out of her depth.

'What's the case?' he said in a kindly voice.

'The Brighton Trunk Murder of 1934. The unsolved one.'

He put down his glass.

'I don't think so.'

Kate put her glass down too.

'I think you were a scapegoat.' He seemed startled by the sudden change of topic. 'And I assume my father railroaded you.'

'That's not over yet.'

'Why won't you help me?' she said, leaning forward over her knees.

'It's not what I'm good at.'

She knew she wasn't hiding her disappointment. Her face always showed her emotions, however much she tried to mask them. But if he noticed, he didn't respond.

'Do you miss being a policeman?'

He nodded slowly.

'It's what I always wanted to be.'

'Family tradition?'

He hesitated, she assumed because he couldn't decide whether he wanted to share personal things with her.

'Crime is.' He smiled faintly at her bemused expression. 'My father wrote crime novels. Still writes them, though his type is rather out of fashion now. No serial killers or pathologists in them.'

'I think my grandfather was in the police.'

'He was. He made chief constable, like me.'

'I never knew him – he'd died long before I was born.'

Watts nodded.

'Does your father live round here?' Kate asked.

'Why do you ask?'

'I was just wondering if he might want to get involved with this – I was going to get a crime writer – and a father and son working on the case together...'

He shook his head and took another sip of his wine.

'He lives in London, but we wouldn't work well together. Even supposing he were interested – which I know he wouldn't be.'

'I've got all these files that were thought lost or destroyed. I've photocopied a set. Please say you'll help.'

He stood and walked to the window, looked out at the back of the Elizabethan house across the courtyard.

'Aren't they police property?'

'Apparently the police aren't interested in them.'

'Drop the documents off and I'll have a look. I'm making no promises, though.'

'The photocopies are in my car – shall I get them now?'

I watched Kate Simpson drive off, then hefted the box of photocopied documents back into the bungalow. Sarah was standing in my bedroom doorway.

'I didn't realize you were going to invite her in.' There was irritation in her tone. 'I felt weird skulking in your bedroom'

'Sorry – I recognized her. A family friend. Kind of. It was strange seeing her again.'

I looked down at the box I was holding.

'Could you hear what we were talking about?'

'Those files – somebody phoned me about them the other day.'

'You're the one who wasn't interested?'

'It was a misunderstanding.'

She indicated her half-empty wine glass.

'Do you think she noticed the presence of a third glass?'

I shrugged.

'She's a radio journalist, not Sherlock Holmes. Bright, though.'

I put the box down.

'Do you want to help with this?'

'I think that's what I was supposed to do when the call came through to me. I was out of line responding as I did.' She shrugged. 'My first cold case. Sure. As if I haven't enough else on my plate.'

There was a tension between us and we both knew why. We'd enjoyed our night together all those months ago. And not just the sex. We'd enjoyed talking, joking. It had been hard to leave it at that one night. For both of us, I suspected.

And now, here she'd been, hiding in my bedroom. We were alone and my circumstances had changed. Except that I was hoping Molly and I could find a way to get back together.

I suddenly got embarrassed, wondering if I'd left dirty clothes lying around. I put the box on my desk and turned back to her. She'd resumed her seat on the sofa.

'But what about Finch?' I said. 'If he has been murdered, then he must have been involved in some kind of set-up. What do you know about him?'

'Only that he was an asshole.'

'Did he have a girlfriend? A close friend we should talk to?'

Gilchrist shrugged.

'I don't know and we can't talk to them anyway. I'm not on this case.'

'I need to talk to Munro, see where he's got to in his investigation.'

'I wasn't impressed by his officers when they interviewed me.'

'He's a good man,' I said.

She looked at the floor.

'I thought at first that night in Milldean was shades of Operation Rambo.'

I must have looked puzzled.

'Before your time, sir ... Bob. It was part of a high-profile drugs operation. Seven officers smashed their way into a listed cottage and ransacked it. Overturned furniture, emptied cupboards, poured the contents of bathroom and kitchen cabinets into sinks and baths.'

'Looking for drugs.'

138

'Yes, but unfortunately we'd got the wrong house.'

I groaned.

'We've done it before?'

'Dozens of times, I'm sure. On that occasion we should have been battering our way into the house next door. ACC Macklin handled the house-owner's claim for compensation. He decided the man was taking the piss, the amount of compensation he was asking for. Ten grand, I think. Replacement front door in a listed building, damage to antique furniture in the house. The distress caused: the raid had taken place in broad daylight in full view of passers-by and neighbours. The local press described it as a successful drug raid. The man lost his job.

'Macklin offered two grand. The man went to court. He spent ten grand on legal fees then came up against an unsympathetic judge. He warned him to settle or risk paying police costs as well. Macklin reduced his offer to five hundred pounds.'

I shook my head.

'No wonder we get a bad press for being arrogant and out of touch.'

Sarah spread her hands.

'Look, there's something I'm not happy about,' she said. 'That night in Milldean.'

'The thing in the man's hand?'

'Nobody is interested. Command has gone to shit since you resigned. All the senior people are desperately trying to cover their backs, so nobody is doing any proper managing or policing. The crime rate is rising...'

She was getting heated.

'What was in his hand? A weapon?'

'I thought it might be when I first saw him. But I don't think so.'

'What, then?'

'I think it was a mobile phone.'

'And it never made it to the evidence box?'

'I think either Finch or one of those blokes from Haywards Heath took it. Which was odd, but I thought it would be entered into evidence. It wasn't.'

'Did you ask them about it?'

'Yes. Except for Finch. I didn't get a chance to talk to him. The Haywards Heath men denied removing anything.'

'But you're sure it was a phone.' I sat back. 'And you're thinking that the man was in communication with someone outside.'

'Not just anyone outside. A policeman, perhaps.'

'Why would you think that?'

'Just a feeling. And, if nothing else, there was a trigger- happy colleague on the outside.'

'Why couldn't he be in touch with whoever sounded that car horn?'

'Yes – what was that about? An associate of the people in the house?'

'Could it have been random?'

She shook her head and crossed her legs. I couldn't help glancing. She noticed but continued:

'The timing was too neat. It was a warning.' She paused and tilted her head. 'But I wonder who the warning was intended for? There's no one I can talk to about it. If it was a set-up, I don't know who I can trust. I've been waiting for the investigation but, as you know, it hasn't really happened. I need to get more information.'

I walked behind the desk then looked back at her.

'Are you saying that we didn't raid the wrong house by mistake? That some person or persons unknown made sure we raided that particular house and that those people were the intended victims?'

'Whoever was behind it wanted those people dead and he used the police to do it.'

'I don't buy it. Everyone in the armed response unit was in on it?'

'Not everybody – just a couple – including Finch.'

'But Foster was running the show – if what you suggest is true, he must have been in on it too. Why the suicide?'

'If it was.'

'You think someone has been going round knocking off the people who know exactly what happened that night?'

She nodded.

'You think Edwards is dead, too?'

'Or in hiding. And the same goes for the nark.'

'He's not been found yet?'

She shook her head.

'Where can we take this?' I said, coming round the desk. I moved over to her. I sensed her shrink back.

'We need to talk to the Haywards Heath men but I don't see how we can.'

141

'I've got this friend – Jimmy Tingley. He can do it. He's very good.'

'You've mentioned him before.'

She looked at her watch and abruptly stood.

'OK, then. I'd better go.'

'I'll call you when he's got back to me,' I said.

'I'll call you if I can find out anything more at work,' she said, her hand already on the door knob.

'Do,' I said, before she fled from me.

Gilchrist felt like a teenager leaving like that. Watts confused her. She was determined there wouldn't be a repeat of their one-night stand but she was drawn to him.

On a whim she decided to drive back into Brighton via the Milldean estate. She parked outside the pub and looked down the street to the house that had been the scene of the massacre. It seemed both an age ago and a matter of hours since she'd been crouching in the back garden.

She locked her car and went into the pub. A few heads turned as she entered but she ignored them. She approached the bar at the same time as a slender, unassuming man of middle height. He gestured for her to go first.

'It's OK,' she said, 'I haven't decided what I want yet.'

The barman was burly with a big beer gut and forearms like hams.

'Another rum and peppermint, please,' the slender man said.

The barman looked him up and down.

'Sure you're in the right pub, love? This isn't

Kemp Town.'

'A double.'

'Big boy,' the barman said with a grotesque pout.

There were two unshaven men standing at the bar. They sniggered. The man smiled but didn't say anything. The barman made the drink and plopped the glass down heavily on the bar. The liquid shivered but didn't spill. The man placed the exact amount of money on the bar, turned and went to sit by the window.

Gilchrist ordered a glass of wine, ignored the leering men and went to sit a few yards from the man. She wasn't quite sure what she was doing here but she knew it was the local for at least one of the crime families.

A stocky, crop-headed man in his forties came in with a posse of four noisy youngsters. They all scoped the room.

'All right, Mr Cuthbert,' the barman said. The crop-headed man nodded and got into a huddle over the bar with him. The man who'd ordered the rum and peppermint went back up to the bar and put his glass down.

'Another double when you have a minute.'

The man called Cuthbert glanced over. The barman straightened up.

'Think you've had enough, don't you, mate?'

'I think I'll take one more.'

'You live here?' Cuthbert said, staring straight ahead of him.

'Near enough to walk.'

'I was wondering why you'd come in here.' He swept his arm out to take in the room. 'It's a pub

143

for locals. Everybody knows everybody. That's the way we like it.'

The man nodded.

'That was a double, mind, not a single.'

The barman had stepped back and was standing in front of the rack of spirits and glasses. He flicked a look at Cuthbert.

'As I was explaining,' Cuthbert said, still not looking at the man, 'everybody knows everybody. We're like a family here.'

'But this is a public house, not a club. And I am the public.'

He pushed the glass across the bar.

'You can use the same glass.'

Cuthbert finally turned and as he did so the youngsters gathered in a loose semicircle around the mild-mannered man.

Shit. Gilchrist didn't want to flash her warrant card in here, but if this turned out the way it looked like it was going to turn out, she would have to intervene. And probably get a good kicking in the process. She recognized Cuthbert's name. He was a major Brighton villain. She cursed herself for coming in here, cursed the man for ordering such a ludicrous drink in a rough pub.

'Are you dim?' Cuthbert said, taking a step forward. 'We don't want you here. I don't know what you're looking for but, believe me, you ain't going to find it here.'

'I just want my drink for the road.'

Cuthbert looked at the barman and gave a quick nod.

'On the house,' he said.

144

'You're either the landlord or a leader of the community,' the man said. 'Did I hear your name is Cuthbert?'

'Not that it's any of your fucking business but, yes, it's Cuthbert.'

'I'm Jimmy Tingley.' Tingley stuck out his hand. 'And I've already heard all the jokes about my name.'

Gilchrist sat back in her chair. Jimmy Tingley. The man Bob Watts had mentioned. The way Watts had built Tingley up she was expecting Arnold Schwarzenegger, not this unassuming individual.

Cuthbert looked at Tingley's hand, then at Tingley. Didn't offer his own hand.

'You're one of the big three on the estate,' Tingley said, withdrawing his hand.

'I am?'

'You are.'

Tingley looked at the youths, who had stepped in closer.

'It would be great to talk to you privately.'

'About?'

'What goes on here.'

'And why would you be interested.'

Tingley moved closer.

'I need your help.'

Cuthbert tilted his head.

'Get his bag, Russell.'

A young man with a pockmarked face loped over to the table Tingley had been sitting at and picked up a slender bag. As he took it back over to Cuthbert, he rooted in it and came out with a newspaper and a collapsible umbrella. He peered

145

in the bag and passed it to Cuthbert.

'That's it.'

Gilchrist was back on the edge of her seat. Tingley remained impassive.

'What's this?' the pockmarked youth said, fiddling with the umbrella. Suddenly it sprang open. The youths laughed as he waved it around.

'Fucking neat, isn't it?'

'Fucking is,' one of the other youths said.

'Fucking neat.'

Tingley laughed along with them for a moment or two. Then:

'It's bad luck opening an umbrella indoors.' He nodded at the mirror behind the bar. 'If that goes as well, we're all fucked.'

He held out his open hand out for his bag.

'If you please.'

Gilchrist was thinking that in a movie, silence would have fallen at this point. Here it was a change in the atmosphere, a drop in pressure.

'If I please,' Cuthbert said. 'If I please.'

Tingley kept his hand out but looked across at Gilchrist. As she started to rise, he gave an infinitesimal shake of his head. Then he reached over and took hold of his bag. Tingley and Cuthbert exchanged looks.

'Check me out,' Tingley said. 'Name's James Tingley. I'll come back in a couple of days so we can talk.'

Cuthbert frowned but released the bag. Tingley turned to Cuthbert's posse.

'Gentlemen.'

He turned and walked to the door. Gilchrist was on her feet a moment later. Trying not to hurry, she strolled out of the pub after him.

Tingley was standing about twenty yards down the road looking back at her. She walked towards him.

'Bet you're glad you didn't have to pull your warrant card,' he said when she reached him.

'Is it that obvious?'

'To me.'

'I know of you, Mr Tingley.'

'I know of you too, Ms Gilchrist. That was very foolhardy of you to go in that pub. Had you been recognized—'

'You know who I am?'

'Your photo has been in all the papers – that's why you were taking a risk going there.'

Tingley looked beyond Gilchrist and quickly took her arm.

'Get in your car and follow me – I'm parked down at the end of the street.'

Gilchrist crossed to her car, head down, ignoring the two men who were standing outside the pub watching her. One of them called to her but she slid into her car and drove down the street.

Tingley led her to the Marina.

Driving home, Kate couldn't concentrate. She was thinking about the Trunk Murder but she was also thinking about Watts. Although she didn't really go for older men, he was a bit of a hunk. He was a quiet man, but there was something about him that suggested he could take care of himself. And others?

She wondered about the third glass – whether Watts had been entertaining somebody who had hidden. Who might that have been?

She let herself into her flat. She lived in a first-floor flat in Sussex Gardens in Kemp Town, overlooking the sea. Kemp Town was the fashionable place to live in Brighton. Rows of Georgian terraces and brightly coloured cottages interspersed with restaurants and New Age shops.

Her flat in Sussex Gardens was her one concession to her parents. When she had moved to Brighton to do her doctorate, her father had bought the flat. As an investment, he said, but for her to live in whilst she was there.

She hated being beholden to her father but her mother pleaded with her. Kate selfishly didn't want to share with other people – the last time had been a disaster – but she couldn't afford the rent on anywhere decent in Brighton. Prices were the same as London. And this was more than decent.

She agreed. It was a two-bedroom flat and her parents came down sometimes to stay in the second bedroom over a weekend. It didn't happen very often since it was awkward. She had worried at first that her father would want to stay when he came down for the Party Conference or when he had meetings with Labour politicians in town. But he chose to stay around the seafront in the Grand or the Hotel du Vin.

Kate went to the box in her living room. She moved the vase of lilies from the dining table and started to empty the box on to it. There was a box file labelled 'Witness statements' and a dozen or so cardboard files, all empty. Some had

148

odd titles neatly printed on the covers: 'Smells', 'Missing Women', 'Paper', 'Empty Houses'.

She took out the loose sheaves of papers from the cardboard box, papers that had at one time presumably belonged in these files. They were in no discernible order. A number were headed 'County Borough of Brighton' then 'Statement of Witness'. Most were typed on manual typewriters, the occasional red letter coming through in the black type. Others were handwritten in blue or black ink by many different hands.

She turned one sheet over and found something strange typed on the reverse.

'This isn't a diary as such. It's a memoir if you like. A reminiscence. A slice of autobiography. Call it what you will – just don't call it a confession.'

Her interest piqued, she turned other sheets over and soon had a stack of what were clearly entries from a diary.

Excited, Kate settled down on her balcony. She looked around the square and smiled or nodded at those people in other flats who were on their balconies. Music drifted across the square. Coldplay and Bach and Miles Davis.

The sea was calm. As the sky darkened, the white lights that strung the length of the stubby finger of the Palace Pier grew brighter.

She had gathered the pages of the anonymous diary into some kind of date order. She was sure there were more pages in the files, but since the entries were typed up on the back of other documents, or on witness statement sheets, it was difficult on cursory examination to distinguish them from other typed material.

There were fragments that didn't have dates attached. She put these aside. She started to read the entry for 6th June, the day the trunk was deposited at Brighton station.

NINE

Wednesday 6th June 1934

I *remember 6th June. I don't remember it because it was Derby Day. I'm not a betting man. I remember it because of the platinum blonde.*

It had been a difficult week for me. Frenchie had been over on the Monday for her visit to Dr M. I met her off the ferry at the West Pier and she was alternately weepy and angry. She'd said she didn't want to see me after, so I took her over to Hove and asked the receptionist to be sure she got a taxi back to the pier in plenty of time for the ferry back to France. I left more than enough money.

I was working that afternoon but I felt sorry for her – yes, me – so I nipped down to see her off. However, I got waylaid by a shopkeeper complaining about kids throwing stones at his shop window. By the time I got to the pier the ferry was already chugging towards the horizon. It was too far away to make out anybody on deck, if she was on deck.

I never saw her again.

That Wednesday was hot and sticky and I was relieved to be out of the office. Brighton's main police station is in the basement of the Town Hall, two floors below the magistrates' court. It was no place to be on a sunny day.

I'd been out since noon. First I'd been up at the railway station. It had been mobbed. The trains clattered in at the rate of 500 a day at this time of year. From London alone, a train every five minutes from Victoria, every fifteen from London Bridge. Half a million people over a weekend, five million a week in a couple of months' time during the wakes holidays.

I stood at the end of platform three and watched people getting off their trains, then swarming across to the single track inset between platforms three and four. There they boarded the special train that took holidaymakers up to the Devil's Dyke, the pleasure park set in a deep gorge on the Downs.

When I came out of the station I was jostled by more arrivals spilling into the sunlight. Some queued for the little trams that ran from the station to the two piers. Others set off to walk the quarter of a mile down the Queens Road to the sea glittering at its far end.

Many families had come from the dark slums of London and you could see them dazzled by the light, looking up at the expanse of blue sky and down towards the bright sea.

I'd observed before that usually the women and children reached the seafront first. The men would find an excuse to stop off in one of the public houses that lay between the station and their family day ahead.

A day spent on the beach, on the silver painted piers, splashing in the sea, racing in miniature motors, listening to the bands playing. Idly watching small aeroplanes out of Shoreham airport write their advertisements for all kinds of products in languid trails of smoke across the sky.

Don't tell me I can't be poetical.

No sooner did I walk in the police station than the desk sergeant sent me straight back out to deal with an incident in the Winter Gardens on the terrace above the aquarium. A drunken man claiming to be Lobby Ludd had been pestering the young women using the deck chairs.

'How do we know it isn't Lobby Ludd?' I said. 'He's due down here today.'

Lobby Ludd was sent by the Westminster Gazette to tour the south coast resorts during the summer. When he was in Brighton, his photo and approximate whereabouts were given in that day's copy of the newspaper. If you thought you recognized him, you went up to him with a copy of the newspaper and said: 'You are Lobby Ludd and I claim my Westminster Gazette prize.'

I'd heard he was so popular that special excursion trains ran to resorts where he was due to appear. His popularity was to do with the fact that the main prize was £50 – more if no one had won the previous day. There were also prizes of ten bob a go if anyone found one of the Lobby Ludd cards he hid in various places about the town.

The man claiming to be Lobby Ludd had scarpered by the time I got to the deckchairs. But the platinum blonde was there. She was pretty, with freckles and a cheeky smile.

She didn't have much to say, except with her eyes.

'Lobby Ludd? He tried to get fresh. Sat down next to me and invited me to lunch. I said no, so he said, "Well, what about a drink?" He said he wasn't after anything –' she gave me a look – 'but then you all say that, don't you?'

'You weren't tempted?' I said, giving her a look back.

'He stank of gin and he was too desperate – kept saying all he wanted was for me to "stick close".'

'Too desperate, eh? I'll make a note of that.'

A few yards along, a fat spotty girl in pink was plonked in a deckchair. Her feet hardly touched the ground. A pale, bloodless girl sat beside her. She watched me avidly.

'Was it Lobby Ludd?' I said to the spotty girl.

'He waved some cards but I don't know if they were real. He said if I went with him for a drink, he'd let me have one of his cards so I could claim the ten bob.'

'What did you say?'

'I said give me the fifty pounds and I might be interested.'

She and her friend squealed.

'Then what happened?'

'I said I couldn't leave my friend and didn't he have one – to make a foursome like? He said no, then a young friend of his turned up.'

'A young friend?'

'He looked a bit of a bad sort.'

'Did he now?'

Behind the Regency terraces and the glamour of the seafront there was another Brighton of dark alleyways and festering slums. From here violence and crime had begun to spread.

In particular we'd been having trouble with razor gangs of young criminals marauding around town. They carried cut-throat razors and weren't afraid to use them when they caused trouble in the dance halls, on the piers and up at the racetrack.

'They had a bit of a to-do,' the spotty girl said. 'Fred – that's what Lobby Ludd said his real name was – left then.'

'This young man he had an altercation with...?'

'Well, he obviously knew Fred. But Fred denied it. Even said his name wasn't Fred. Then he ran off.'

The platinum blonde was looking out across Madeira Drive to the Palace Pier. I walked back to her.

I was at the railway station twice that day. But had I been there some time between six and seven in the evening, would it have made any difference? All those people flooding off the trains – would I have noticed a man lugging a brown trunk with a woman's naked torso in it? A man who, some time in that hour, deposited it in the left parcels office, receiving in return the deposit ticket CT1945?

I returned to the station at about ten that

154

evening to see the platinum blonde safely on her train back to whichever London slum she'd come from. It was the least I could do.

Kate paused for a moment and looked across at the Pier. She wondered who Frenchie was and Dr M. She couldn't quite get the tone of his remarks about the platinum blonde. That last paragraph sounded harsh, callous.

The next entry she found was eleven days later.

Sunday 17th June
They found the woman in the trunk today in the left parcels office at Brighton station. I was the one who opened the trunk the second time. At the inquest my sergeant, Percy Stacey, stated that he'd opened it. He didn't. He wasn't even in the room. He was heaving up in the Gents because of the stench.

Old Billy Vinnicombe, the cloakroom attendant, had been aware of a bad smell for a few days. The hot weather wasn't helping. He'd narrowed it down to this trunk he'd taken in on 6th June, Derby Day. He summoned Detective Bishop of the railway police who opened the trunk. He found it contained human remains. Bishop called us at 8.30 p.m.

Percy and me had got there ten minutes later. When we'd stepped in the office with the station manager, Percy had taken one whiff and headed for the latrines.

I'd had a good day until then. I'd been up on Devil's Dyke and met a willing girl. I was still thinking about her, to be honest, when I dealt

155

with the trunk.

Bloke called Henry George Rout was on duty when the trunk had been deposited. We got him in later but he couldn't remember the man who had deposited the trunk at all: it was rush hour and the station was extra busy because of people coming back from the Derby.

I undid the straps and tugged the lid up. The stink was bad enough when the trunk was closed but as the lid fell back it was overpowering.

The station manager, Vinnicombe and I reared back and reached for our hankies. I remember Vinnicombe had a red-spotted one as if he fancied himself as Dick Whittington.

I looked into the trunk. There was a lot of cotton wool padding. I took the cotton wool out, keeping my head turned away, trying not to gag. Near the hinges the cotton wool was soaked in what looked like blood. Then I took out several layers of cheap brown paper to expose a brown paper parcel that almost completely filled the trunk. There was a thin sash cord, tied once lengthwise and three times across. I cut the cord with my clasp knife then parted the sheaves of paper.

I was looking at a naked woman's torso, her teats small, her rib cage pronounced. It took me a few seconds to realize that in such a small trunk her torso was all there was to see. No head, arms, legs, hands or feet.

I did gag then. We all did. We had to clear it up before I could do any more with the trunk, though Percy Scales kept that out of his inquest statement too. As we mopped up we tried to joke about who'd been eating what. But we were all glancing over at the open trunk. I'm a bit of a reader so I kept thinking of it as Pandora's Box. What had we let out?

Scales and I moved the trunk to the police station where Dr Pilling, the police surgeon, examined the woman's remains then had us take them to the mortuary. He thought the woman was about forty. We compiled a description, such as it was, and circulated it to all stations.

Then we told our Chief Constable. Captain W. J. 'Hutch' Hutchinson was, like many of the senior officers, a veteran of the Great War. He'd been gassed at Mons but didn't seem to have come out of it too badly. He had the occasional coughing fit but he was nowhere as bad as some of the men I'd come across, coughing up the lining of their lungs every morning. I was glad I'd been too young for that racket.

Hutch was a good enough boss, but the few times I'd had dealings with him I'd seen little evidence of his detection skills. He must have recognized this himself because the next day he called in Scotland Yard.

Monday 18th June
I had my feet up on my desk smoking a Woodbine and getting stirrings thinking about the girl at Devil's Dyke when the news came through that more of the woman's body had been found.

'You're working hard, I see,' Percy said as he barged into the office. I slid my feet hurriedly off the desk and sat up straight in my chair. 'Maybe you should be out trying to trace the shop that

157

sold the trunk.'

Not bloody likely.

We'd released a photo and description of the trunk. It was made of brown canvas and ply-wood, battened with four hoops. It was small – two foot three inches long, by one foot five inches wide, by a foot deep. It made me sad that some-one could be callous enough to pack a human being – or part of one – into such a confined space.

It was a cheap trunk you could buy almost anywhere for about 12s 6d. We'd got about fifty policemen doing the rounds of drapers, ironmongers and chemists to find out who'd sold it.

The cord I'd cut when I discovered the torso in the trunk was for a Venetian blind. One piece of the brown paper had the end of a word scrawled in blue pencil. The rest of the word had been obliterated by dried blood. The part of the word that could still be read was '—ford'.

These were all the clues we had.

There hadn't been much blood in the trunk, considering, so the thinking was she'd been dead a while before she was put in there.

'They've found the legs,' Percy said.

We'd sent out an instruction for railway officials everywhere in the Southern Railway system to search all suspicious luggage and parcels. We'd already heard there was a case at Wimbledon containing women's clothing, but as that's what luggage is for we weren't getting excited.

'King's Cross Station left parcels office,' Percy

said. 'A brown leatherette suitcase – the smell had alerted them again. Her legs and feet were inside.'

'King's Cross – he was a busy boy. No head or hands?'

'Not yet. Hutch is calling in Scotland Yard.'

Chief Detective Inspector Donaldson and Detective Sergeant Sorrell of Scotland Yard were already on their way down to Brighton. When they arrived they went into close conference with Hutch and Detective Inspector Pelling, our head of CID. The Scotland Yard blokes took over the case.

Tuesday 19th June

About fifty press men representing London and provincial newspapers were rushed to Brighton yesterday. They hang around in groups outside the police station day and night. For these first few days, they constantly invaded the station, pestering officers for information about the en-quiry.

Sir Bernard Spilsbury came down today. The best-known forensic pathologist in the country. The top man. He spent three hours examining the woman's remains. He confirmed immediately that the legs belonged to the torso – it was easy to see because the bones had been sawn through about two inches from the joints rather than at the joint. The flesh had first been cut with some-thing sharp.

She'd been dismembered several hours after death and almost certainly after rigor mortis was well established. No anatomical knowledge *or skill had been shown in the dismembering. Somebody who knew how to cut up carcasses would have known how to cut through the knee joints without needing a saw.*

Spilsbury took the body's internal organs back to London to try to establish cause of death. He announced the results of his examination before he went. I'm quoting here:

Putrefaction was advancing. The skin was moist and was peeling off, the surface discoloured. The abdomen was distended with putre-factive gas, also present under skin in other parts of the body.

There was no blood in the veins. The stomach had a small amount of partly digested food but no fluid. A little food was found in the lower part of the oesophagus. The intestines and its contents were healthy.

The uterus was enlarged and the cavity blown up. It contained a foetus that weighed six ounces. The vagina was rather large – the kind of thing you'd expect after full-term labour – but there were no other signs she'd already had a child (no pigmentation of the nipples, for instance). The size of the vagina could probably be accounted for by post-mortem softening of the tissues.

Nine long hairs were found. Some had been subjected to permanent wave, but not recently. Five hairs had light brown colour. The other four were shorter and devoid of any colour, being flaxen or grey. Probably bleached by exposure to sun in sunbathing. Her pubic hair was brown. The armpits were shaved a few days before death.

The fact there was no blood in the torso or legs and scarcely any in the trunk and case suggests the woman had been dismembered and then either subjected to pressure or movement – being carried for some distance? – before her remains were put in the boxes in which they were found.

Spilsbury made the deduction that she came from a reasonable income group partly because her size four-and-a-half feet lacked calluses – she was used to wearing good-quality, well-fitting shoes.

He put her age at between 21 and 28, not the 40 the police surgeon had suggested.

Spilsbury noted that the limbs in the suitcase were wrapped in paper that had been soaked in olive oil. There was also a face flannel and two copies of the Daily Mail, dated 31st May and 2nd June 1934. The case was new.

'Doctors and surgeons use olive oil to stop bleeding,' Percy said, showing off his know-ledge.

'Italian restaurants cook with it,' I said, showing off mine.

'We're lost without the head,' Percy said. He scratched the dry skin that runs all round his hairline. 'We've been assigned to help the Scotland Yard chappies. Council's given up some space in the Royal Pavilion for the incident room so we'll be shifting over there later today.'

Kate's phone rang, jerking her back to the present day. She realized night had fallen and that she had unconsciously brought the pages of the diary nearer and nearer to her face so that she could read it by the light spilling out of her sitting room.

Her answerphone clicked in. After the beep her father's voice came on. 'Babe,' he said. Kate winced. 'I need to talk to you. Call me on my mobile.'

In your dreams, Kate mouthed. She wondered whether to phone Bob Watts tomorrow, to let him know about this diary she'd discovered and the things in it. When she'd photocopied the documents she hadn't thought to turn them over so they weren't among his material.

She looked back at the pages she had just read. The poor woman. What Kate found most upsetting was the thought of Spilsbury examining the feet, which had been detached from the legs. She couldn't help but think of him handling them as if they were a pair of shoes, turning them in his hands, this way and that.

The woman was pregnant. She wondered if that was the motive for her murder.

She went inside, replenished her glass and switched on her balcony light. She grabbed a throw from her sofa and wrapped it round her before returning to the balcony. She took a swig of her wine and picked up the pages again. The diary jumped a day.

Wednesday 20th June
We had the inquest today. It didn't last long. Percy Scales gave evidence that we were called to the railway station to witness the opening of the trunk. The coroner announced that the dead

162

woman had been expecting her first baby. He also stated that cause of death had not been ascertained. So much for Spilsbury's talents. The inquest was adjourned until 18th July.

Brighton was full of reporters from all over the country. Those from the big papers in London stayed at the Grand. They seemed to have money to burn. They hung around in the pubs when they were open. When the pubs were closed the little café across the square from the Town Hall became the unofficial press headquarters.

They were very free with their hospitality with any policeman they saw in the pubs or the café. Hutch, the Chief Constable, was being a bit tight-mouthed – hardly ever had a press conference – so the reporters were trying to find out whatever they could on the QT.

'It's like making bricks without straw,' one of the London blokes complained to me in the pub this lunchtime, eyeing me furtively over his double whiskey. His name was Lindon Laing and I'd given him a few titbits before now, ever since he'd told me that his expenses were more than £3 a day.

'Don't suppose the cloakroom attendant has remembered what the man who left the trunk looks like?'

I shook my head. Poor Henry George Rout. The evening the trunk was deposited had been a busy one and he's obviously not the most observant of men at the best of times. But he'd been cudgelling his brains ever since we opened the trunk trying to remember what the bloke who deposited it looked like. With no success.

I wanted to give the reporter something but I didn't have anything of use. I told him about the bungalows.

'Big conference of Sussex Chief Constables yesterday. Decided to make a rigorous inspection of empty bungalows.'

'Looking for the scene of the crime?' When he grinned the reporter showed big teeth stained yellow from tobacco. He had long hairs curling from his nostrils.

'We need to know where the body was dismembered.'

Ordinarily that would have done him for the day but my news was eclipsed by the fact that Hutch made a frank statement in the council chambers to around thirty newspapermen about Spilsbury's findings. Particularly the bit about her being pregnant. He also appealed for help in identifying the young woman. This was the start of twice-daily press briefings.

Even so, press men continued to hang about outside the station. People coming to the station to make statements were intercepted and questioned. We had complaints, so usually we had to escort witnesses from the building by the back exits.

Taxicabs and press cars were kept in constant readiness outside the police station and when officers were despatched in motor cars to make enquiries, the press followed. We ended up going round the houses to reach our destinations.

Once the late evening's papers were printed there was a sensation throughout the country. Within minutes of the publication of the appeal we were besieged with callers offering information. We all worked overtime that night but Hutch also got in a relay of clerks to take statements over the telephone.

Within about an hour of the appeal we had our first possible sighting of the torso murderer. I took the call from a Territorial Army Captain – R. T. Simmons of the 57th Home Counties Field Brigade. Posh spoken, a bit querulous.

'I live in Portslade and use the Worthing to Brighton train regularly to go to either of these towns,' he said. 'On Derby Day I came into Brighton in a rather crowded compartment. There was a man in the compartment carrying a trunk which I'm sure is similar to the one I have seen in the newspapers.'

'Did you notice anything particularly about this man?' I said, the phone tucked between my shoulder and ear as I scribbled down his words.

'He kept the trunk beside him on the seat, even though the rest of us were crowded together and had little room. And when the train reached Brighton this man jumped out quickly and carried the trunk along the platform. It was clearly heavy but he ignored porters who offered to help.'

Simmons described this man as being about 35, medium height and dressed in a dark suit.

I thanked him then went to find Scales. The statement looked promising, although the timing wasn't quite right – the sighting had happened earlier in the day.

I've not been a policeman long. Perhaps that's why I was startled by the number of suspicious

165

characters that populate our town, revealed by the calls we had.

A lodging house proprietor, breathless with excitement, told me that on 4th June a man carrying a brown paper parcel and a small suitcase booked a room for three weeks.

'He seemed very worried,' my caller said. 'For the first fortnight he didn't leave his room during the day, always going out at night.'

'Did you ever see him with a woman?'

'No, no, I didn't. But he suddenly left town two days before the trunk was discovered.'

'Before his three weeks was up, you mean?'

'That's right.'

'Did you find anything unusual in his room after he'd gone?'

'Not a thing,' he said. 'Not a thing.'

I thanked him and put the phone down. A constable would follow the call up but I doubted it would come to anything. I looked at my watch and stretched. My shift was over and I had a date.

I didn't hear until the next morning that poor old Vinnicombe, sniffing around his left parcels office this evening, had found another body in a suitcase: that of a newborn baby.

Thursday 21st June

I was late into work after a long night. Everybody was talking about Vinnicombe's discovery and making jokes in doubtful taste about the contents in general of the railway station's left parcels office.

We'd had some kind of tip-off – I couldn't find

166

out what as it was very hush-hush – about visitors to the town on or about 21st May. Plainclothes police were visiting boarding houses to see who'd come to town that day.

Late in the morning Donaldson went up to London to follow clues to a missing Hove girl. We heard later in the day he'd found her alive and well in Finchley.

In the afternoon we heard from the woman who'd written the word ending in '—ford' on the brown paper we'd found in the trunk. A Sheffield woman, Mrs Ford, said that from the photo she'd seen in the paper she was sure it was her handwriting. She said it wasn't the end of the word, it was her last name – she always wrote it with a small letter 'f'.

She thought the paper was part of a parcel taken to London by her daughter, Mrs Morley. Mrs Morley had been using her maiden name, Phoebe Ford. She'd been staying at a hostel in Folkestone where she had given the piece of brown paper to a German woman.

One of Donaldson's theories was that the murder victim had come from abroad. Boats go to and fro between the pier at Brighton and France every day, as I knew full well from Frenchy's regular visits. We'd already been in touch with Interpol. He wondered if here, with word of this German woman, he had his continental link.

Then the knives turned up in Hove.

Kate's father had rung twice more from his mobile phone, each message more impatient.

She still ignored him. By now she was sprawled on her sofa, the windows to the balcony closed, utterly absorbed in the narrative she was reading. Absorbed but also repelled by the author's callous way of talking about the women he met.

Kate's doorbell rang. She jumped. She had paused in her reading to think how many human stories were hidden between the lines of every statement the police took down. Why was the man who booked in to the lodging house so troubled? Why did he only go out at night? Why did he leave before his three weeks was up?

And Phoebe Ford – had she parted from her husband? Is that why she'd gone to a hostel in Folkestone and used her maiden name?

Kate looked at her watch. It was past midnight. She frowned and padded to the door. Perhaps it was Bob Watts. In your dreams, girl. She put the chain on, then opened the door a couple of inches.

'What do you want?' Kate said.

'That's not exactly the "Pater, how delightful to see you" I was hoping for,' her father said.

She led the way into her sitting room, and waved at the sofa under the window. Her father had a small smile on his face and tired eyes. His hair was too long and absurdly floppy, as usual. He wore an expensive navy suit, although he had taken off his tie. His shoes were buffed to a brilliant shine.

'That may be because I never see you unless it happens to fit into your schedule.'

'I might say the same.'

He stood at the window looking out then he

turned round, taking in the pile of folders on the dining table.

'Homework?'

'Something I'm working on, yes.'

'Anything I can help with?'

'Not unless you want to confess to a murder.'

He nodded as if what she'd said made sense to him.

'I'm staying at the Grand.'

'Good.' She'd remained standing, feeling awkward.

'I phoned earlier.'

'I was working—'

'Several times.'

'Meaning two or three.'

'More.'

'I was working.'

Kate had a sudden urge to laugh. They were sounding as if they were scripted by Pinter, with an awful lot of subtext.

'I wondered if I could buy you dinner.'

'At this hour?'

'Then. I was worried when you didn't answer.'

'I could have been doing anything. Been out on the town. Actually, I was with Bob Watts.'

'Bob Watts?'

He turned towards the piles of folders on the table.

'The friend you railroaded out of office.'

He pursed his lips.

'He did it to himself. He could have left with dignity. He was stubborn. Stupid.'

'He was your friend.'

'Why on earth were you with him?'

169

Kate indicated the files.

'We're working on this together.'

Her father looked puzzled for a moment.

'He was your friend, Dad,' Kate repeated.

'Simply a consequence of the friendship between our fathers. And he was wrong.'

'Did you leak stuff about his one-night stand?'

He looked her in the face and smiled in an odd, intense way.

'How would I know about his one-night stand? But he would never have gone. He is the most obstinate man I've ever met.'

'So what made him?'

'Pressure points. It's knowing where to bring the pressure to bear.'

'And?'

Simpson rested his hand lightly on her shoulder, ignoring her flinch.

'Ask him about his father.'

TEN

I kept in shape. Swam or ran every day, worked out five days a week. But even so, some nights I just couldn't sleep. Maybe living alone didn't suit me. More often than not, on such nights I'd drive up to the Ditchling Beacon.

I'd been living in the area a couple of years before I realized that the Beacon had been an Iron Age fort, now pretty much obliterated. I

170

used to be interested in stuff like that, and the site of this car park was such an obvious one for defence, I don't know why I hadn't realized it before.

Tonight, I'd been sitting dozing for a couple of hours when two cars of gangbangers had come up with some girls from Brighton. It was around three. They had noisy sex to booming music. One car took the girls home. The other stayed, and I was aware of three young guys standing smoking about ten yards away, discussing whether to smash my window and steal whatever was in my car or just set fire to it. I didn't know if they realized I was in it, or whether that was the point.

I was in the passenger seat, reclined, so maybe they hadn't seen me. Then again. I switched on the headlights and turned the stereo up high. I probably should have gone but I figured the Art Ensemble of Chicago at its most dissonant would do the trick.

I watched them watching the car – I was still in darkness. Eventually they wandered back to their car, pumped up the volume of their own stereo and screeched out of the car park.

I switched to a CD on which there were actual tunes. More or less. Tom Waits at his most industrial. Molly always said I had a tin ear so liked avant-garde stuff because I couldn't tell the difference between music and noise. I don't know where I'd got my taste for such stuff. When I was growing up, my dad was firmly stuck in the big band era, my mother liked only romantic classics.

I slept but woke at five when a man in a bright yellow jacket arrived and parked his estate car next to me. He sat for ten minutes, ignoring me, his diesel engine shuddering, before he drove away again.

It was a clear morning, the sky blue and pink, wisps of cloud hanging in the still air. I could see the line of the North Downs some thirty miles away. I fancied I could make out Box Hill. I could certainly see our home from here. I looked down at my past life laid out below me and thought about how I'd fucked up.

Maybe I came here so often because I felt an estrangement from where I longed to be. An outsider looking in – something I've always felt. Peering in through the window at my own life.

Two hours later, dog walkers, runners and cyclists turned up and parked around me. The cyclists brought out frames then wheels and handlebars and put their bikes together, tugging on them, aligning them, bouncing on them and testing the brakes. A woman on horseback suddenly reared up from the path below, hidden by the parked cars until her horse trotted between them.

Another woman got out of her car, walked over to the edge to look down at the plain, her hands tucked in her back pockets. She wore sunglasses. Her hair was roughly tied back. She walked along the shallow embankment and stopped to stare at the Burling Gap in the distance. She stood there for half an hour or so. Then she reversed out and drove away.

The Burling Gap. Something Sarah had said

about her visit to the lighthouse pricked at me. I got out of my car and climbed up the shallow embankment.

I crossed the road and walked over to the dew pond. I looked south to Brighton and the sea. I kept my face from any dog walkers passing by – Molly always said I looked menacing when I was deep in thought.

I was thinking about Finch's death and what it meant about the botched raid. Was it a revenge attack? Somebody tidying up loose ends? I smiled. It was a bit late in the day, given the position I'd achieved in the police force, but I was trying to learn how to investigate this crime that no one seemed able to make sense of.

When I went back into the car park a young couple nodded at me as a black flat-coat bounded out of their jeep. I nodded back and looked across at burn marks in the asphalt. A car had been torched there not long before I came upon my own burning car on the night I ran into the deer.

And then I realized what was nagging at me and I grinned. My God. Maybe I could be a real detective.

Tim was blathering as usual: 'So collagen lip implants – luscious or loopy? And do they pass the kiss test or does it feel like kissing a pair of car tyres? If you know, or think you know, phone in now. And later we'll be discussing *Big Brother*: is Too Far the new How Far?'

Kate thought about that for a moment then decided DJ blather was a discourse all of its own, in which the meaning- less did not even attempt to masquerade as meaningful.

She'd gone to bed after her father had left. His visits always left her bothered. She thought he was probably trying to reach out to her but that he was simply inept where emotions were concerned.

When she was growing up, her father was a parliamentary correspondent for the *Observer*. He was politically committed. When she was a teenager, all her friends fancied him. She wasn't quite sure how to deal with that.

Kate had hero-worshipped her father. That was probably why at university she'd had a long affair with her professor, a much older man. There was nothing she didn't know about father figures and how bad they could be for a girl. Her professor shagged her and liked her to be around when his friends came by. However, the problem with the older man is that his friends are also older and usually uninteresting and staid.

Kate didn't get on with her mother. It was one of those things. Well, actually, it wasn't. Her mother was another journalist. It was all she did. She was obsessive – obsessed. (Kate never quite knew the difference.) She went into her newspaper every day, worked relentlessly. She had a sister who was a TV producer and both were seriously competitive.

Kate's mother was not loving. For years Kate thought that was just the way mothers were. Only when she was older did she realize it was specific to her mother. She was remote, had a coldness that combined with excessive self-absorption to exclude Kate almost entirely.

Kate eventually came to realize that her mother wasn't a particularly good writer but that that wasn't the criterion for success in newspapers. All the editors cared about was getting copy of a reasonable standard to length, on time.

She sighed. She'd brought the next portion of the diary into work. It had jumped again. In between fielding phone calls she scanned through it.

Friday 22nd June
We abandoned the boarding house search today. The new theory is that for the killer to do his dastardly work he must have used an empty house. So we're out and about searching every empty house in the area hoping we'll discover bloodstains. Or a head.

Of course, there's another theory that we're wasting time in Brighton, that this bloke came down from London and the murder was committed up there – maybe King's Cross way, where the legs were found.

Oh, we're big on theories.

We're following up the clue about 'ford' with Mrs Ford in Sheffield, then in Folkestone with her daughter and the mysterious German woman.

The inquest on the baby found in the parcel office revealed no connection to the trunk crime. Hardly a surprise.

These two knives were handed in by the dustbin people. One was a ham slicer, about fifteen inches long. The other, thirteen inches long, was a butcher's cutting knife. They'd been left in an ash-bin somewhere in Hove. They would have been collected in the rubbish on either Tuesday or Wednesday. The council bin people found them in the refuse destructor on Wednesday and handed them in today.

The Chief Constable got very excited – had them photographed to put in tomorrow's Brighton and Hove Herald *with an appeal. I had a drink with that London journalist when I came off shift, just before closing time. I told him about the knives.*

'So that's it, then – you've found the murder weapons,' he said gleefully. 'The killer is in Hove – probably did it in Hove.' He tilted his head to look at the smoke-blackened ceiling of the pub. 'The Hove Horror.' He chinked his glass to mine. 'Lovely stuff.'

'Hove detectives have whisked some bloke off in a car to look at an empty house down there.'

'A man whose identity has not been revealed,' the reporter said, his intonation putting quotation marks around the statement. 'Arrest imminent.'

'I wouldn't say that. It's just the landlord of the property, I think.'

He beckoned the barman over and bought me another round. Well, why not? I was seeing a young lady this evening and the drink would get me in the mood. Although I don't need drink for that. I'm always in the mood. Sometimes I worry I've got it on the brain.

'Who cares?' he said. 'It's a good story. So are the knives.'

176

'They probably aren't relevant – he used a saw to get the limbs off.'

'We'll worry about that when the saw turns up. Until then, the police have found the murder weapons.' He flashed his awful yellow teeth in a cold smile.

Monday 25th June
What a difference three days make. By now we've got thousands of statements. We're overwhelmed by the mass of material the public is offering us. Most of it is bound to be tripe but it's working out what isn't that's the difficult part.

The number of people who have told us about mysterious noises and smells coming from their neighbours' houses has been quite remarkable.

But we're no further forward with the brown paper with the word '—ford' on it. Turns out it's got nothing to do with the Sheffield woman, her daughter and the German woman, after all.

It would help if the Chief Superintendent could decide about the trunk. First he said it was a cheap one. Then on Friday he sent out a new statement. The trunk has clasps and fittings that you only find on certain manufacturer's trunks.

Also on Friday, after I'd gone off shift, CDI Donaldson followed up a statement that a girl's screams had been heard on a pleasure boat leaving Brighton. How do you distinguish between a scream of glee when a girl is being tickled or is overexcited and a scream of terror? The woman was alive and well.

Those knives have been bothering me. You could argue that the murderer would want to get

177

rid of the murder weapons with all this fuss in the press about the murder. On the other hand, the murder was committed weeks ago. If the murderer had any 'nous', he'd have got rid of them then, before everybody was looking for such things. And this murderer must have 'nous' – or at least bravado. I mean, what would it take for him to transport human remains in a trunk then deposit them at Brighton's left luggage office without giving himself away? Guts, that's what.

Tuesday 26th June

I took a statement from a shop assistant this morning. Pretty young thing. Flirtatious. She'd been out on the Downs in Patcham with a party of girlfriends on Saturday when they'd seen a man in a blue suit and straw hat setting fire to a pile of rubbish.

'We told him it was dangerous as it was near a wooden fence.'

'Proper little Girl Guide, aren't you?' She just looked at me. 'What did he say?'

She looked indignant.

'He told us to clear off.'

She was a buxom girl. She caught me glancing at her breasts but didn't seem to mind. I'm sure she arched her back a little.

'So we asked him what he was burning. He said fish. The smell was something peculiar but we couldn't see properly because he wouldn't let us get any nearer.'

'You like going up on the Downs?' I said.

She looked me straight in the eye.

'Are you asking in your...' she seemed to be searching for the right phrase, '...official capacity?'

Wednesday 27th June
Today we had a Southern Railway porter telling us about his experience with a man arriving at London Bridge station at 2.25 p.m. on Derby Day. He got off a train from Dartford en route to Brighton. He had a trunk that looked like the one pictured in the newspapers.

This porter – Edward Todd was his name – offered to carry the trunk. Unwillingly the man let him. Todd had difficulty lifting it – it weighed something like 60 pounds. And when he got the trunk to his shoulder he heard a dull thud inside it.

That train would have arrived in Brighton at 4.05 p.m. A bit early for the time we'd established, but this man could have been the killer.

Kate was really curious about the identity of the memoirist. She'd flicked ahead and through some of the files but couldn't find any indication. She wondered where the rest of the records might be. She was sure that there must be some official account of who attended the opening of the trunk – she could find his name that way.

She phoned the library. A cheerful young woman gave her the number for the County Records Office in Lewes. Yes, they had the files that had belonged to the Central Division of the South East Police Authority. She could make an appointment to see them. And the autopsy photographs. That last threw her.

She knew Lewes. It was a pretty town, its streets clustered about the ruins of the castle keep. It was Islington-by-the-sea for fashionable Londoners who wanted to start a family in a place where there was a better quality of life.

She'd been brought up in Hampstead, just off Southend Green. When she was a teenager and taking her first alcoholic drinks, the pub she used was the one outside which Ruth Ellis had shot her lover. A bullet hole could still be seen on the outside wall of the pub – well, they said it was a bullet hole.

Sarah Gilchrist was talking to Reg Williamson when her mobile rang. They'd moved away from finding Finch's body to the recent raid on the rotten meat store in a rat-infested warehouse in Newhaven.

The raid was the conclusion of Operation Dinner Out, in conjunction with local environmental health officers. The warehouse had been stacked to the rafters with rotten meat. Around a hundred tonnes of it. The stench had been incredible. Rancid chicken that had turned yellow through putrefaction had been bleached with chemicals to make it look healthy.

Then they'd found the 'specialty' meat. Decomposing lambs' brains and cows' feet, cows' muzzles, smoked cattle-hide, gizzards and goat carcasses in two huge freezers. It was supposed to be sold as pet food but somebody cute – and they were thinking Steve Cuthbert – had decided to buy it from abattoirs, process it, package it and reintroduce it into the human food chain.

'You know, all I see is the shit in life at the moment,' she said. 'It's really getting me down. People acting as low as they can.'

'I'm impressed by the ingenuity of criminals,' Williamson said, rolling his ever-present, ever-unlit cigarette between his chubby fingers. 'The way they can figure out how to make a buck in the gaps between. Jesus, if they applied that entrepreneurial spirit to legitimate business, they'd be captains of industry.'

'What, you think captains of industry are legitimate?'

'True enough,' he said. 'But when do they have the time to think up this stuff? Who would think Steve Cuthbert, if it is him, would say to himself: "Hello, there's a gap in the market for reusing rotten meat." How would they have the chemical knowledge to know what to do to make it at least look edible? And then to set up the production line, the transport infrastructure. And these are guys who were kicked out of school at twelve.'

Gilchrist stood and walked over to the window.

'I don't eat meat in ethnic restaurants any more,' she said. 'I'm sorry, I just don't. Most of that rotten meat ends up in halal butchers and specialist outlets. I'm not being racist but I do want to know where my food has come from.'

'It's no worse than fast food,' Williamson said, 'big greasy burgers.'

'I don't eat them either. Or sausages because usually they're made from the sweepings off the butcher's floor.'

'Minced testicles and eyeballs in some frankfurters, I read. Give me Chinese any day. Hit me with that monosodium.'

Gilchrist's mobile phone rang.

'It's Bob.'

She was silent for a moment, aware of Williamson watching her.

'Hello, s—, hello,' she said with forced enthusiasm.

'I'm sorry to call you there – I know it's awkward – but I wondered if you'd had a chance to look up that car that was burnt on Ditchling Beacon.'

'As a matter of fact—'

'Did the report say anything about a cat?'

'A cat?' she said, her tone clearly reflecting her thought that he was losing it.

'I seem to remember they found a cat in the boot of the car.'

There was silence again.

'Your ex-dancer on Beachy Head?'

No, she was the one losing it. She flushed.

'I'll get back to you later,' she said, breaking off the call. She looked at Williamson. 'We might have a bit of a break. And do you know why? That woman's missing cat.'

'Tiddles to the rescue, then.'

Tingley had called and wanted to meet at lunchtime in English's Oyster Bar. When I arrived he was sitting at the narrow counter, tucking into a plate of oysters in their shells on a bed of ice.

'You're going up in the world,' I said. 'Bit of a change from the Cricketers.'

He didn't look up.

182

'Are you going to eat? The Dover Sole is always good.'

'Sure.' I took the stool beside him and glanced around. Although English's was something of a Brighton institution, with its white painted Georgian fascia and its location just at the edge of the Laines, I'd never been in here. Behind Tingley's head was a framed poster for a play from God knows when signed by an actress called Susannah York. 'Thank you for a third lovely evening' she'd written. Next to it was an old black and white studio portrait of George Robey and below him a more recent actress in a posh dress.

Through the open windows of the pub opposite I could hear a bunch of men singing raucously.

The waitress came over. A tall, pale woman with fine features and an accent. I ordered and when she'd gone into the kitchen, Tingley said:

'Estonian – part of the latest tranche from eastern Europe.'

'The influx causes all sorts of problems when they get into trouble – from prostitution to orphanages. In policing terms—'

'Yes, but you're not a policeman any more.'

I looked down at the stained marble counter.

'Difficult to lose the mindset.'

'But you've never been a proper policeman. When you came in here you didn't scan the room to check out the suspicious characters.'

Now he was looking at me. Was he trying to pick a fight? I glanced at the two glasses beside his plate. One was a wine glass, half-filled with something red; the other was an

183

empty whiskey glass.

'I spotted you, didn't I?'

My voice was light but I was aware of a tightness in it. I looked at photos of Omar Sharif, Albert Finney and Maureen Lipman on the wall behind the bar. He ducked to slurp an oyster from its shell. He looked back at me.

'I've been checking out Milldean. Word is that a guy I pissed off in a pub there the other night is even more pissed off about a raid on a rotten meat warehouse in Newhaven. Name is Cuthbert and, as far as I can see, he's into *everything* rotten. Gang bosses report to him as they park South Vietnamese and Chinese labourers all over the Sussex countryside, and Polish and Lithuanian youngsters in brothels. He's into DVD piracy from China and he's been on the carousel for VAT on mobile phones. All that quite aside from Shylocking on a third of the estate and the fraudulent benefit claims.'

'We know some of that.'

'So why has he never been done? He must leave a trail.'

'Lack of evidence? I never got directly involved in operational matters.'

He put his fork down and shook his head.

'One of two reasons. He's either got the fix in very high up or he's registered as an informer.'

'I don't know which he might be but I can find out.'

'I'll find out,' he said. 'You're too much on the outside.'

'I've got some contacts,' I said, hearing the petulance in my voice.

184

'This involves intel the Israeli way, Bobby, I've told you.' He took a sip from his wine and shucked the last of his oysters.

'Is he linked to the massacre in some way?'

'I'm inclined to think not, but he is part of a bigger picture. This guy has got a competitor. I need to find out more about him. Guy called Hathaway. Into the same sort of shit but a bit more high-end. Maybe better connected. Maybe the man.'

I got back to the bungalow late afternoon and within an hour Gilchrist had turned up. Jeans and T-shirt, her hair tied back. She didn't demur when I handed her the glass of wine. This time I sat beside her on the sofa. She was conscious of me but didn't seem put off by my proximity.

A strong wind had blown up. The window behind us trembled as a strong gust hit it.

'So what have we got, Sarah?'

'The cat from Ditchling Beacon is the Beachy Head cat.'

'Was it chipped?'

'Yes. There were very few remains but we found the chip. So we've got a cat disappearing on Beachy Head just a few hours before a car is torched on Ditchling Beacon.'

'And we've got the body of Finch – a police-man involved in the Milldean operation – thrown into the sea off Beachy Head around that time.'

She leant forward. She was making sure we weren't touching by keeping her knees close to-gether.

'They didn't close the boot when they were

carrying the body to the cliff edge. They wanted to minimize noise. He was alive but probably gagged. And he'd been beaten up.'

'Poor bugger. So whilst the boot was open, the cat jumped in. They came back, having done the deed, closed the lid and drove over to the Beacon.'

'They'd left another car at the Beacon.'

'Leaving a car up there is asking for it to be broken into or vandalized, plus a police patrol is supposed to go by at least once a night.'

'Rendezvous, then.'

'What about the courting couples?'

'Courting couples?' Gilchrist laughed.

'What?'

'That's such an odd phrase,' she said. 'They're not courting, they're shagging.' The window shuddered again. Gilchrist glanced back at it over her shoulder. 'Plus it's either a bit late at night or too early in the morning for that kind of thing to be happening up there.'

'I was thinking of when the rendezvous car arrived. And I've never liked that term.'

She sat back in the sofa and looked sharply at me.

'Shagging?'

I nodded.

'Let me guess. You prefer the term "making love".'

Her voice was sharp and I immediately regretted what I'd said. Even so, I held her look. I was conscious of the emotion welling up in the room. I nodded. And then the question I knew would be next:

'So is that what we did?'

The harshness in her voice was a thin disguise for vulnerability. Another gust of wind. I realized she was hugging her body unconsciously.

'I hope what happened between us was caring, yes.'

She looked at me, her cheeks flushed.

'You shagged the arse off me.' She shrugged. 'It was a one- night stand, ergo, it was a shag.'

I played the sentence back in my head. It should have been bitter or harsh but it wasn't.

'Come on. We were drunk. Did you think it might be more? You knew I was married.'

She reeled back as if I'd hit her in the face. Stood up abruptly. Shit. I could hear the tone of my voice as I'd said those things. I was harsh.

I stood up too. She moved a couple of yards away from me.

'I didn't mean it to sound like that,' I said. 'I'm sorry. My tone of voice was wrong.'

'You chose your tone.'

She moved over to the window, her back to me. She had strong shoulders and a long back.

I felt wretched.

I've never been good with women. I don't mean I'm sexist – at least I hope I'm not – but I haven't spent too much time with them. I've never been a ladies man. I think I'm a good listener, which I hear is a good trait. But then all men think that, and how wrong most of us are.

I was distressed that I'd upset her. I wanted to put my arm around her and hold her close. I watched her long back. She held still.

187

'I'm sorry,' I said softly. 'I spoke without thinking.'

She turned back to me. I looked in her eyes. Yes, definitely too revealing.

I wanted to say so much but I was split because I still cared about Molly and felt we should be back together. I'd already behaved entirely improperly with Gilchrist, messed her about emotionally. It wasn't right to mess her around any more. And yet.

She cleared her throat.

'So the car burnt at the Beacon was the car that had delivered Finch's body to Beachy Head,' she said, walking past me and resuming her seat on the sofa.

I had taken a seat behind my desk.

'Was the car identified?'

She nodded.

'Stolen in Worthing the previous day. Audi A4.'

'But where does that take us?'

'Well, at least we know how Finch got to Beachy Head.'

'But not what he was doing in the two days before then.'

'What about these Haywards Heath blokes – Connolly and White?'

'They were given a hard time by your friend from the Hampshire force, but, as far as I'm aware, they had nothing to say.'

'But maybe it's time they were examined again?'

'Get Jimmy Tingley on it.'

'Then where do we go?'

'We follow the trail backwards.'

I nodded and sat down beside her, conscious of our proximity. She turned to face me. We looked at each other, then she leant towards me.

Tingley was back in the pub in Milldean. This time he was drinking brandy. The barman had made a call and within fifteen minutes Cuthbert was standing beside him.

'I've been finding out about you,' he said.

'That must have been exciting.'

'Well, there's only scraps, but you wouldn't think it to look at you. SAS, intelligence agencies. Bit of a lethal weapon.'

Tingley didn't say anything.

Cuthbert had some heavier men with him than on the previous occasion. He looked round at them.

'But I've got to ask – is this the same person? I mean you look like something I shit out after a bad curry.'

His men sniggered. Tingley smiled.

'Are you going to go on with this macho stuff all night?'

'Well, it's a problem for me. Problematic. You like that? Educated, you see. I mean, I hear this stuff and then I see you and I think someone is having a laugh.'

Tingley didn't go for introspection. To say he was a man of action would be wrong. He was a man of inaction, of calm. However, he didn't soul-search. Never had. He looked at Watts agonizing over the break-up of his marriage, the loss of his job, and he wanted to stay focused on

189

the externals.

Tingley shifted in his seat and looked around him, clocking where the four goons were.

He could take out this room without raising a sweat. He knew which strike to make on each of them. The jab to the throat; the thrust to the diaphragm; the kick to the inside of the knee. He could disable easily enough. Cuthbert would undoubtedly have a weapon. Could he do all that before the gangster drew and used it?

Probably. Tingley stood.

'I thought we might have a useful conversation but in the absence of that I might as well go.'

'I don't think so.'

There it was, in the open.

He took out the bodybuilder first – that rigid V between thumb and first finger whacked into his Adam's apple. As the bodybuilder choked, clutching at his thick throat, his face purple, Tingley was on to the next, stiff fingers thrusting through the beer belly and up deep behind the diaphragm. With a startlingly loud exhalation, the man doubled over.

Two down and nobody had yet reacted. Then Cuthbert started to reach into his pocket and the fourth guy had a knife in his hand. That was quick. He must have had it palmed all the time.

Tingley kicked him in the face and chest and he went crashing backwards, falling heavily. Tingley nutted Cuthbert whilst he was still fishing in his pocket; kneed him between his legs and pulled his jacket down over his arms, trapping his hand in his pocket. As Cuthbert slumped forward, Tingley guided his head down on to his knee. He felt the nose go.

He only had to point a finger at the barman for him to stay where he was. He leant into Cuthbert.

'I thought I could deal with the monkey,' he whispered. 'But clearly I need the organ-grinder. Tell Hathaway I want a word.'

Tingley looked around. Bent down again.

'And don't think about coming back at me. You might be big around here but you will disappear without trace if you try to shit in anything but your tiny, slimy pond.'

He grabbed Cuthbert's hair and raised the bleary, bloodied face.

'Are we clear?'

Cuthbert made a strange gurgling noise. Tingley gave his head a shake then let it drop.

'I'll take that as a yes.'

ELEVEN

Kate didn't have many more pages of the diary to read. She hoped she'd be able to find additional portions of it. There were gaps of a few days between the entries now.

Saturday 30th June
Poor buggers on the night shift were digging up bones in an allotment on Wilson Avenue at two o'clock this morning. Dog bones. Whilst they were doing that, I was tucked up tight with a

young lass who was a bit the worse for wear but seemed to know what she was doing. She reminded me of Frenchy and that actually made me sad. Getting soft in my young age. I wondered about going over to Dieppe for the day when I was next off to see if I could find her, make sure she was all right. It's not the first time that's happened but it's never nice.

Today's local evening paper had asked: 'Trunk Mystery: Solution in Sight?' Its first paragraph claimed: 'Sensational developments in the Trunk Murder were hourly expected late last night following a day of great activity by Scotland Yard officers in London.'

Well, I had to give the locals something too, didn't I? Donaldson had gone up to London in the afternoon and later telephoned us to say he was staying up there overnight.

The paper said: 'His departure has special significance in view of reports that a London man has been visited by police officers in connection with the crime. Another man was also at the Yard for two hours.'

That's as maybe, but Simpson told me Donaldson actually stayed up to take his sister out to dinner for her birthday.

To be honest, I was spoilt for choice for stories to tell the press. No harm in it, was there? The great unwashed liked reading this stuff and we were inundated with it down the nick.

That day, for instance, we'd found a car that had been seen in suspicious circumstances on the coast road at Roedean on Derby Day. Two men had been seen lifting out a trunk. When they saw they'd been noticed, they put the trunk back in the car and drove off. The owner of the car stated it was out of his possession between 31st May and 10th June. Car didn't tell us anything, though, and whatever they'd been up to it didn't seem to be connected.

The knives are long forgotten.

Thursday 5th July
Today it was an empty bungalow on the Downs at Woodingdean. I went with Percy and DS Sorrell. We had a tip from London. We searched the garden and all the rooms. There was brown paper and, in the kitchen, some knives. Won't lead to anything.

I saw the Girl Guide again tonight. She lets me do whatever I want.

Saturday 7th July
Last night Scotland Yard published a list of missing local girls who most tally to the description of the woman we found. There were ten and I'm almost certain I once had a knee- trembler with one of them down that alley that runs from the side of the town hall to West Street. Phyllis Fifer, age 24, from Portslade. She'd gone off to live on a farm in West Sussex.

She was fresh complexioned and freckled. She was a well-built girl who took good care of her appearance. I'm sure it was her. She got upset because I tore her bloomers.

We're busy tracing prenatal cases around the country.

I try not to feel guilt. It's a negative emotion and those emotions just hold you back. Oh yes, I've been on all the right motivational management courses. But I was also aware that with Molly I'd betrayed a trust and behaved like a shit. I was acutely aware of how much distress I'd caused her. That what she was going through was my fault and my responsibility. So, in fact, guilt was dragging me down.

I've never been one to chase women. When I was a teenager, sure, but by the time I was nineteen or twenty I was looking for someone to settle down with. That probably makes me sound boring but I think most normal people are like that. I don't know what possessed me when I spent the night with Gilchrist. I can think of all sorts of excuses: things bad at work, Molly not understanding or caring, me under stress, drink. Lust, of course. And I was drawn to Gilchrist's spirit. Although, if I think about it honestly, it was actually because that spirit reminded me of Molly before her depression.

But no doubt about it, Gilchrist and I did click. I think she was as surprised that she went to bed with me as I was. I think she felt as guilty as I did afterwards. And yet there was this tug.

It was by mutual agreement we had decided not to see any more of each other. I loved Molly and, if I could, I wanted to spend the rest of my life with her. Gilchrist didn't want to be involved with a married man, especially a married man at work.

But now Gilchrist and I were avoiding each other's eyes over an embarrassed breakfast of toast and coffee. Gilchrist looked over at the pile of papers on the sofa. I followed her look.

'The Trunk Murder files. Want to take a look?'

She almost ran over there. I followed. We separated the files. I sat behind my desk, she sat on the sofa and we began to read.

Kate was back on her balcony, memoir in front of her but thinking about her father's visit. And how her hero-worship had changed to something more negative. Family holidays when she was young. They had always been a bit weird as her dad would then write a piece about them. And both her parents were shameless about using that fact to get deals at hotels and restaurants. She used to squirm at the fake bonhomie they received from maitre d' and hotel managers who were hoping for a good write-up.

Her mother was more shameless than her father, more imperious, more strident at check-in desks when asking for upgrades. Kate saw the contempt on the faces of the check-in staff, saw her parents – and by implication herself – tagged as freeloaders and liggers.

One incident still made her face burn with shame at her father's barefaced push and, well, nastiness. It was a press trip to California with half a dozen press families invited to promote a superior camping holiday. On the way out, the rather hunky PR man for the company had got everyone an upgrade to first class. On the four-day trip he'd been pretty good at boosting upgrades and freebies from Santa Monica to Santa Barbara via Las Vegas and the Grand Canyon.

On the way back, the upgrade to first was at the discretion of the airline. Her father had been pretty wrecked from the last-night party. He turned up at check-in bleary-eyed, unshaven, in a baggy T-shirt and scruffy jeans that were too loose at the waist. He looked like a bum.

The tanned man at check-in was gay, of course, with neat hair and a small moustache.

'I believe there's a possibility of an upgrade,' her dad croaked.

The man behind the counter looked at her unkempt father standing before him.

'We like to think of first class as a rather superior party,' he said. 'At which our passengers are the guests.' He touched the corner of his moustache. 'We expect our guests to dress accordingly.'

Kate flushed and looked down as she saw her father stiffen. She knew what was coming.

'Fuck you,' her father said loudly.

The man behind the counter stiffened.

'And that is certainly not the kind of language we tolerate in first class. In fact, we may have to reconsider whether we fly you at all.'

Kate was crimson as she looked quickly from side to side to see where she could stand unnoticed. The man behind the counter pointed dramatically at some chairs off to the left.

'Please,' he said, his voice quavering almost parodically as he tried to do fierce. 'Kindly go and wait over there. If we allow you to travel, you will be informed later.'

Both her mother and father stood in front of him, unmoving. When she had replayed this event in her memory as she got older, she had remembered nuances or suddenly realized things (or perhaps fictionalized things). Like the fact the man behind the counter was gay. Her memory had stored that unassimilated at the time, not totally understanding what was going on but like an animal aware of the atmosphere.

It was typical of her parents that not only did they get the upgrade, but the man also ended up apologizing to them for the 'misunderstanding'.

In the nineties she was watching TV one night and recognized with an embarrassed jolt her parents on the news. It wasn't her parents but it might as well have been. Hand-held camera footage of Neil and Christine Hamilton bearing down on the Man in the White Suit when he was announcing he was standing against Hamilton in a by-election. The same arrogant attitude; the same self-righteousness; the same hard faces. That was her parents at their worst.

By then her father was inside New Labour and her mother was riding on his coat-tails to write high-profile pieces for the qualities.

She didn't mean to be so bitchy about her mum. There was just something about her – always had been. Again, things heard but not understood until much later. Kate sitting on the stripped pine stairs whilst a raucous dinner party went on below.

'Oh, God.' Her mum's voice loud, brittle and bored. 'I suppose that means I'm going to have to give you a blow job tonight.'

So where did that leave Kate? Why didn't it bleed down into her? The genes were there. Was her anti-competitiveness simply a resistance to the obvious, or some perverse version of the same impulse? Could she deny her genes? She guessed she had little to do with it.

She'd avoided going into journalism, though that was the easy option. She looked around and the newspapers were full of kids of famous people. Had they no shame? She accepted that if they couldn't write, they wouldn't be there. But she also accepted that there were hundreds of other journalists who could write just as well, or much better, but didn't have the inside track. She avoided taking advantage of her parents' connections, those newspaper deals made over lunch and dinner with editors and publishers. She reacted against it. Hence her local radio gig. Was she shooting herself in the foot?

She sighed, picked up the diary – and did a double take.

Monday 9th July
The victim's head has been found.

Her mobile phone rang. She checked the number. Answered.

'Kate, it's Bob Watts. Wondered if you wanted to meet to discuss the Trunk Murder with me and a serving police officer.'

'They found the head!' she said.

'I take it that's a yes.'

They agreed to meet in the Hotel du Vin in two hours' time. Kate idly wondered who the serving policeman was but was eager to find out more about the head. She read on.

Actually, it was found back on 10th June before we'd even found the trunk in the left luggage office. The story would be farcical if it weren't so tragic.

A young couple from a lodging house in Baker Street had gone for a walk on the rocks under the cliff at Black Rock on Sunday 10th June. It was about 4 p.m. The tide was out. In a crevice where a pool of water had collected, they saw pieces of newspaper clotted with blood. They were wrapped round a female human head.

I went with Hutch and Pelling to interview them.

The girl – pretty but shy and inarticulate – said she had wanted to pull it from the water but the young man wouldn't let her. They had left it there.

'Why wouldn't you let her?' Pelling asked, puzzled.

The young man, Fred, was pimply, slope-shouldered, with a dusting of dandruff on his shoulders. He shifted in his seat.

'Dunno.'

The girl, Barbara, said: 'Fred thought some person had committed suicide by throwing themselves from the cliff above and that the police –' *she looked round quickly at the officers around her – 'having taken away the remains they required, had swept the other parts into the sea.'*

We all looked at the young man. I'm sure we all thought the same. Halfwit. He seemed to shrink in his seat.

At least they hadn't kept it entirely to them-

199

selves. They'd mentioned it to their landlady and Fred had told his boss. However, we only found out about it when Fred mentioned it to one of his employer's customers. The customer had realized the significance of the information when news of the torso murder appeared in the press.

Hutch decided the girl and the boy should each be separately taken to Black Rock. I stayed with the young man whilst they took the girl to show them the pool.

I didn't attempt any conversation with him. I'm not a snob, but what would we have to talk about? As a matter of fact, I was irritated not only by the fact he had been such an idiot but also by his relationship with the girl – what could such a pretty girl see in him?

They brought her back and left her with me while they took the man out to Black Rock. They were gone a couple of hours. I took full advantage of their absence. The girl proved not to be so shy after all.

Their stories matched exactly, but by now there was no head in the pool.

Jimmy Tingley phoned.

'Just checking in,' he said. 'No real developments my end. You?'

'Nothing here,' I said, glancing across at Gilchrist, feet up on the sofa, frowning as she speed-read the files, occasionally jotting down notes. 'Have you been able to check out the Haywards Heath guys yet?'

'I'm certain they're dirty but I haven't got close yet. Do you want to meet?'

'I'm coming into town for a little get-together to discuss the Brighton Trunk Murder shortly.'

There was a pause on the line.

'First or second?' he finally said.

'You know about them, then – want to join us and then we can have another chat after?'

He agreed and I put the phone down. Gilchrist was looking steadily at me. I smiled and she smiled back, then dropped her gaze back to the files.

Kate arrived first at the Hotel du Vin. A sudden gust of wind just as she stepped off of Ship Street ballooned her skirt out and up, earning a whistle and a few grunts from some builders on the other side of the lane. She went to the loo to comb her hair and sort her make-up, then settled herself on one of the sofas that ran along the wall to the side of the bar. She sipped her wine and gazed up at the rafters far above.

Watts walked in accompanied by a tall woman about ten years older than Kate, with broad shoulders and a long stride. He flashed a big smile as he walked over to Kate whilst the woman deftly checked out the room. She nodded at a man at the bar. Kate glanced across. She hadn't noticed the unassuming man sitting there but now he slipped off the bar stool and walked across to them, carrying a coloured drink in his hand.

Watts made the introductions. Kate tried not to react when she heard Sarah Gilchrist's name – she read the tabloids. She tried not to give her the once-over but, of course, she did. Gilchrist was attractive and had a strength about her. Kate was surprised to see her with Watts. She'd assumed it had been a one-night stand. Were they actually having an affair? She recalled that other wine glass in Watts's bungalow.

'So they found the head?' Watts said.

'And lost it again,' Kate and Gilchrist said, almost together. Kate smiled at Gilchrist. 'It was in the police report.'

'Though the public didn't know until a newspaper report in 1964,' Tingley said. He turned to Kate. 'Hello, I'm Bob's friend, Jimmy Tingley.'

'You know about all this, then?' Kate said, puzzled by his presence. She was worried she was going to lose control of the investigation.

'I've given it some thought from time to time. I like analyzing things.'

'And what has your analysis concluded?' Watts asked.

Tingley took a sip of his drink.

'Rum and pep,' Watts said to Kate, seeing her curious look. 'Otherwise he's more or less normal.'

'First, you've got to figure out how this guy got the trunk into the left luggage in Brighton. The body weighed seventy pounds – that's a lot to lug around. The maximum weight marines are expected to carry in their packs is fifty-five pounds. They're big, fit blokes.'

'He took the train from London,' Gilchrist said.

'Maybe – if that sighting of a middle height man at London Bridge is accurate. But he still had to get it to the station in the first place. Same if he just dropped it off from somewhere in

Brighton. This bloke is going to have difficulty moving this thing around. Such a high-profile case, a taxi driver would remember picking him up and helping him with the trunk.'

'There's nothing in the files I read about taxi drivers coming forward,' Watts said.

'So, perhaps he thought of that risk and he drove to the station. Whether he did the deed in Brighton or elsewhere, he would still have needed to drive.'

'Getting the suitcase to King's Cross would have been easier,' Gilchrist said. 'We need to check how easy that journey would have been from Brighton – and think about why he chose King's Cross. What was its significance?'

'At random?' Tingley said. 'Unfortunately, with just one crime there isn't enough information to do a geographic profile based on the stations.'

'What's a geographic profile?' Kate said.

'A guy called Stuart Kind devised it. He accurately predicted where the Yorkshire Ripper lived by cross-indexing times of attack with locations. He figured out that this man was on a clock – he had to get home. So the later in the day the crime, the nearer to this man's home.'

Kate nodded.

'Ingenious. But I have a question. Why didn't he throw everything into the sea, like he did the head? Assuming that was her head at Black Rock. And what happened to her arms and hands? OK, two questions.'

'Perhaps he worried about the tides and that all the separate parts would end up in the same place,' Gilchrist said. 'Thought he could get away with disposing of the head like that. And that there would be a long gap between the discovery of that and the rest of the body.'

Tingley leant forward.

'Gross as it sounds, a head is relatively easy to move around – heavy though it is. But a torso you've got more of a problem – the weight for one thing. If he'd chucked it in the sea, he'd probably have to do it in the trunk and then there's the problem of floating.'

'And the arms and hands?' Kate said.

Tingley shrugged.

'Don't know. The arms shouldn't have posed a problem of identification unless they had some distinguishing feature like a birthmark – these days it would be a tattoo.'

'And the hands were because of fingerprints.'

'Probably,' Tingley said.

'Though that in itself is interesting,' Gilchrist said. 'It means either that this woman had at some point been fingerprinted, so had a criminal record, or that the killer was ignorant and assumed that just the existence of fingerprints allowed for identification.'

'If she had been fingerprinted, could that be because she was a prostitute?' Kate said. 'Killed by her pimp?'

'Quite possibly,' Gilchrist said.

Kate noticed that Watts had not contributed to the discussion but had been listening intently.

'Let's get back to the head,' he now said. 'If the head they found in the rock pool was the woman's – wrapped in newspaper like the torso

204

in the suitcase – then it's likely he lived around here. He's not going to be travelling far with a head – what would he carry it in, for one thing?'

'A bowling bag?' Tingley said.

'Ugh,' Kate said.

'A man we have in custody walked from near Hove station to the pier with his friend's head under his arm in the middle of the evening a couple of weeks ago, and nobody noticed,' Gilchrist said.

'These days anything is possible,' Watts said, 'but in 1934 I think somebody would have noticed. No, it still suggests he was local. He's not going to make more than one trip from London to Brighton with body parts, is he? He wouldn't want to risk being remembered. And lugging a trunk with a torso and a bag with a head in it at the same time would be risky. Plus, he'd want to dispose of the head at night. He couldn't very well chuck it over the cliff edge in broad daylight.'

'Can we check tide tables?'

'Hang on,' Gilchrist said. 'Are we assuming that he threw the head in there? Why? Why couldn't it have just ended up there – thrown in somewhere else and the tide tugged it there.'

'OK,' Tingley said. 'But we're getting somewhere. So his trip to King's Cross – a special trip or was he going somewhere from there?'

'If he was, he'd have to come back so, again, that's doubling the risk of being remembered,' Gilchrist said. 'Supposing someone had opened the case in the meantime; staff would be on the lookout.'

'So it was a special journey,' Watts said.

'But the same applies to Brighton station,' Tingley said.

'Which same?' Gilchrist leant forward in her seat.

'If we're saying he lived down here, then wasn't there a big risk when he was leaving the trunk at Brighton station that he'd be recognized and/or remembered lugging this trunk the next time he used the station?'

'Hang on – break it down,' Gilchrist said. 'This is important. If he did live in Brighton, as you're suggesting, then he ran two risks turning up at the station with a trunk. One: that he might bump into someone he knew. Who would later remember, when there was all the publicity, that he was lugging a trunk. Two: that as he lived here he might be recognized as a regular user of the station.'

'You mean if he was a commuter?' Kate said. 'Did people commute from Brighton in those days? Plus we think he had a car.'

Tingley shrugged.

'Well, all you're really saying is that he lived down here but not in Brighton. He didn't go up to London much because his business didn't take him there.'

'But that means she was based down here,' Gilchrist said. 'So you'd think they'd be able to figure out who she was.'

'Why was she killed?' Watts said.

Kate replied:

'The police theory from the files we have is that she was probably the mistress of a married

206

man who killed her because she was pregnant.'

'Good,' Tingley said. 'If she was a mistress in London that he visited regularly, then the station might be a problem.'

'Unless he drove,' Kate said.

'But trains were quicker and more frequent then,' Tingley said.

'So it's like not shitting on your own doorstep,' Gilchrist said.

'Exactly.'

'OK,' Watts said. 'Alternative scenario. He was London-based but had a second home here. He didn't come down often but when he did he drove. He brought her down here to kill her. Then maybe never came down again for a couple of years. He was nondescript anyway so no real worries about being recognized.'

Gilchrist nodded slowly.

'But if he's London-based, then he's anonymous and we can't ever locate him. If he's down here, then at least we stand a chance.'

'You mean by the rules of this kind of investigation?' Tingley said.

'What do you mean?' Kate said.

'Well – Jack the Ripper – all the theories revolve around a small number of suspects listed in the police files. So Ripperologists spend all their time trying to prove which one of them did it. But why on earth should the police have hit on the right suspects? So then you get the wild card theorists who suggest it was the Prince of Wales or the Masons or Walter Sickert. But given the fact that with a random killing or crime these days the police haven't got a clue without

DNA or confessions or blind luck, then the chances are the Ripper was somebody totally different.'

Kate frowned.

'And you're saying that applies here?'

'No, no, this is different. There's a surfeit of information – thousands of statements. It's like the Yorkshire Ripper and all those high-profile cases. The police have already got the guys without realizing it – they're in there among the statements. The torso murderer is somewhere in the thousands of statements the police took.'

'But we don't have those statements,' Kate said. 'They were destroyed. We just have a few of them.'

'When were they destroyed?' Watts said.

'In the 1960s on the order of the Chief Constable,' Kate said. 'I assume it was some thirty-year rule.'

Watts looked at her intently for a moment.

'What?' she said.

'Nothing,' Watts said. 'Are there files anywhere else?'

'I'm going to the County Records Office tomorrow. There are files there. There is one other thing too, which isn't in the copies I gave you.'

Watts tilted his head.

'There is a kind of handwritten diary from a policeman involved in the case. Not all of it, just fragments.'

'Which policeman?' Gilchrist said.

'I don't know – I'm hoping the County Records will help me identify him.'

208

Watts still had the odd look on his face. Before Kate could press him, Tingley glanced at his phone – they'd all heard a text alert – and took Watts to one side.

During the discussion about the head and torso, Gilchrist had been thinking about Finch's body washed up at Beachy Head and Gary Parker chopping up his friend. She bought another glass of wine for her and Kate. She warmed to Kate.

'You know who I am, right?' she asked her when they'd both taken a gulp.

'I do. Can I ask – which has caused you most problems – your involvement with the Milldean incident or your fling with your boss?'

Gilchrist stared at her for a long moment then burst out laughing.

'Please, don't sugar-coat it – just ask me straight out.'

Kate flushed.

'Sorry.'

'It's OK. The two together are a pretty powerful combination.'

'Do you regret your fling?'

Gilchrist had asked herself the same question time and again. But now it was her turn to flush.

'If I'm honest, I'm bitter about the consequences but don't regret the fling.'

'But he was married.'

The moral certainty of youth, Gilchrist thought. She didn't know how old Kate was but she assumed she was younger. And she'd felt that same way once, before life kicked in.

Her mother was a feminist, had lived through

the pill and the pressure on women to engage in sex for fun, whether it was fun for them or not. She belonged to that whole generation of women used by men and who ignored their own needs because most women wanted relationships, not one-night stands. Her mother couldn't understand the notion of the mistress. Couldn't understand the idea that women should have solidarity with each other but so many broke ranks to have affairs with married men, ignoring the suffering of the wives.

Gilchrist scanned the room, as she'd been doing since she first entered the hotel.

'What I regret is losing my anonymity,' she said. 'In many ways I hate Brighton – so much "Look at me". But all this exhibitionism, paradoxically, goes side by side with anonymity. When the scandal broke, losing my anonymity was hateful.'

Her phone beeped and she excused herself to read the text. It was from the station. Gary Parker, the man who'd chopped up his friend, wanted to see her.

TWELVE

'I want to do a deal.'

Gilchrist looked at Gary Parker and tried not to show her distaste. This was a man who had chopped up his best friend two weeks earlier and had expressed no remorse, no curiosity, no revulsion – in fact, no emotion at all.

'I don't think a deal is going to work for you. You've killed someone – and in a particularly brutal way.'

'I've got information.'

She sighed, thinking for the moment about the anonymous woman left in the trunk in 1934. She imagined that her killer had acted more soberly, in cold blood, when he cut up her body. She turned back to Parker.

'I'm listening.'

He looked at her coldly.

'No – doesn't work like that. I need to know I'm getting a deal.'

She stood, nodded at Reg Williamson, who was leaning by the door.

'Conversation over, then.'

'Bollocks. Who can authorize a deal?'

'No one. You can talk to me or you can talk to that wall.'

'No deal, no talk.'

She grimaced, sat down again, not wanting to be here.

'Give me a hint,' she said, trying to keep the revulsion out of her voice. She was disgusted by this man.

'I know who did them rapes in Milldean. During the street party.'

There had been three reported rapes during the riots.

'You mean during the riots?'

'Fucking great that was.'

'Who was it?'

'My mate.'

'The one you killed?'

'That's why I done it. He can't be behaving like that with young gels.'

'That was your motive for killing him and chopping him in pieces?'

She couldn't keep the disbelief out of her voice.

His hand dropped into his lap. He stroked himself for a moment. Then he seemed to forget and the hand lay there on his thigh.

'You look like you got great tits. Can I have a squeeze?'

'Watch your language, lad,' Williamson growled.

'Fuck you, fat man.'

Williamson moved off the wall but Sarah raised a hand to stop him.

'Are you saying that's why you did it?' she said.

'We done a lot of kit that day. I was gone, man.'

He lapsed into silence. Gilchrist sat still, looking down at the coffee stains on the table
between them. Parker brought his hand up from
his thigh and started clasping and unclasping it
in his other scrawny hand on the table in front of
him. His nails were chewed down to the quick
and he had 'love' and 'hate' tattooed in blue ink,
one letter at a time, on the knuckles of each hand.

Gilchrist remembered being terrified by a film
she'd seen on the telly as a kid. *The Night of the
Hunter* with Robert Mitchum as an insane
preacher pursuing two little children after he'd
murdered their mother. Much of it seemed to
take place at night or in places with deep, fright-
ening shadows.

Mitchum had been so scary and psychotic. To
demonstrate his preaching on the struggle
between good and evil, he too had 'love' tattooed
on one hand and 'hate' on the other, and he
clasped his big hands together and wrestled
them. She'd been terrified. She shuddered now
at another image of this looming man towering
over a helpless little girl.

Parker broke wind forcefully.

'Jesus,' Williamson said, disgusted.

The smell was appalling, but Gilchrist was at
least relieved to have been dragged away from
the entrance to that particular memory lane.

Parker started up again.

'Some blokes only want to give it up the arse
and they're not fussy whose arse. Women, men,
armadillos.' He showed his ferret teeth and cack-
led. 'OK, maybe not the fucking armadillos.'

He began rocking in his chair.

'These blokes who sew up live birds in the chests of their victims. One guy pulled their lungs out and threw them over their shoulders. There was that guy that skinned his humps.'

'These are all fiction,' she said, exasperated. 'They're not real,'

'Fuck off – that bloke who skinned them was real – and are you trying to fucking tell me people don't do these things in real life?'

'No, you've demonstrated that.'

He had to think about that for a moment.

'Oh, yeah – that. Fucking weird that was. Don't know where that came from. Where's his head? I wanted to keep that.'

'What happened?'

'I chopped him up. I was gonna make burgers but I couldn't get him in the pan.'

She tried to ignore that image.

'I mean – what made you chop him up?'

He tilted his head to one side and looked at her. He frowned. He seemed to have forgotten about the rapes.

'Had this fucking alien growing in him, coming out of his chest. Had to kill the fucker. Plus he wouldn't shut up.'

'The alien?'

'No, you stupid cunt—'

He shook his head in contempt.

'Watch your language with me,' Gilchrist said calmly, as she sensed Williamson straining to come over and smack Parker. 'You said he would not shut up.'

Gilchrist tried not to react to his staring at her breasts.

214

'What wouldn't he shut up about? The rapes?'

'That was always his fucking problem,' he said, dropping one hand back into his lap. 'Always trying to big it up, but nobody was fucking fooled. He was talking bollocks. Pissed me off.'

'So he didn't rape anybody in Milldean?'

'Like he knew what was fucking what. He knew fuck all, the cunt.'

She really loathed this little creep with his vacant grin, his imbecile face, the way he kept ogling her.

'What was he talking about?' she persisted.

'He don't have no fucking clue. Bigs himself up, but it's bollocks. I know more about that fucking lark than he ever did.'

She could see him as a rapist. After what he'd done she could see him as pretty much anything bad.

'What lark?'

Her stomach suddenly growled. She hadn't eaten for what seemed an age. She ran her tongue quickly over her teeth: her mouth tasted stale and of too much coffee. He looked at her, suddenly cunning.

'What they call a bent copper?'

'What do you mean?'

'What do they call a bent copper? It's a fucking joke. You're supposed to say whatsit – you know.'

'Tell me, then,' she said, 'what do they call a bent copper?'

'That's it! Then I say whatsit!'

She tried to be patient. Said nothing as he

215

searched for the punchline.

'Fuck – whatsit – you know – fuckin'...'

He clenched his fist and hit himself on the side of the head a couple of times.

'Fucking done my head in, man. Can't remember nothing no more. What was we talking about?'

'Bent policemen, for some reason. But tell me what your friend was bragging about that got you so angry.'

'Police don't know nothing, do they? Pretend you do but you fucking don't.'

She sighed. Someone let her out of here.

'The Milldean fucking massacre. Fucking mess that was. Bet you don't have a fucking clue about it.'

Her stomach tightened, gurgled again. She leant forward and put her hands lightly on the table in front of her.

'You know something about that?'

'I'm from there, in't I?'

'Were you at the riot?'

He ignored her.

'That bum-boy in the toilet. Another fucking pain in the arse, but then he was all arse.'

'What about him?'

'Spent most of his life on his hands and knees. Chugging or taking it all the way up.'

'What about him?' Gilchrist repeated.

He clenched his fists and shifted in his seat again.

'OK, what's his name?'

'Little Stevie.'

He sniggered.

'What's funny?'

'He had an even bigger dick than me.'

I was having a solitary brunch in a café by the old Town Hall, trying to imagine this square when the police station had been in the basement of the Town Hall. Before the Thistle was built facing out to sea, the Japanese restaurant had been plonked down in the middle of the square and the underground car park had been carved out beneath it. The time of the Trunk Murder.

I was feeling odd. I felt stalled for the moment on trying to sort out the Milldean mess and I was drawn towards this very cold case that Kate had plonked in my lap. I was deliberately not thinking about Molly or Sarah Gilchrist.

Three long pink limousines drew up across the road from me, in front of the side entrance to the old Town Hall. It now housed the registry office and here was the first of the day's gay marriages. It must have been somebody famous – TV vans arrived in the wake of the limousines. I drew back as I recognized a few of the TV people who had harassed me.

In the next ten minutes more people arrived in garish clothes, and policewomen in bright yellow jackets came for crowd control, as a large group of spectators gathered.

Time to move. I paid for my meal and, head down, slipped out of the café and down the street a few yards before turning into the side entrance to a shopping arcade. I walked through it, avoiding eye contact, then up into the Laines. I ducked into The Bath Arms.

217

I ordered a coffee and settled myself in a corner of the old pub away from the late-morning drinkers part-way through their first pints.

I was thinking about the friendship William Simpson and I had inherited from our fathers. And then I was thinking about my father on one particular day.

It was sunny and we were all in the garden. Sally and James, my sister and brother, were bickering, as usual. I was in the hammock, strung between two trees. Mum was reading an Iris Murdoch in a deckchair with a canopy – she didn't do well in the sun. Dad was sitting at a table in the shade writing longhand in one of the cheap exercise books he used. He was in his sixties but didn't look it and certainly didn't act it.

The doorbell rang.

Dad had set up some kind of system so there was a bell attached to the back of house too. It also worked when the telephone rang.

My mother looked alarmed. My father frowned. Unexpected visitors were not welcome.

Mum closed her book.

'Robert,' Dad said, without taking his eyes from his notebook.

I rolled out of the hammock. Smiled at my mother.

I was woozy from the sun so when I opened the front door I was a bit blank.

'You must be Robert,' the woman said.

I was eighteen, with little experience of women. This woman was almost as old as my mother but I still desired her immediately. I

218

suppose she was in her late thirties, early forties. But not only was she beautiful, she also exuded sex. Or maybe that was me, full of testosterone, bestowing on her my own lusts.

She was – the word is apt – glamorous. A beautiful oval face, green eyes, abundant auburn hair. Tall. Big-breasted.

Attractive as she was, there was also an intensity about her that made me nervous. She had full lips, crimsoned with lipstick. When she smiled, there was a twitching of the nerves at the edges of her mouth.

'Is Frank in? Your father.'

Oh, she was trouble. I had a feeling of dread, but also of excitement.

'He's in the garden,' I said. 'With my mother.'

There was movement at the edges of the mouth.

'May I see him for a moment?'

I would have liked to leave her on the doorstep but I knew I couldn't.

'Please,' I said, stepping aside so she could enter our home.

She walked from the hips and I couldn't take my eyes off her. Of course, at that age I couldn't take my eyes off any woman.

I was going to take her into the living room, but I was sure she was a threat and that seemed too intimate as it was full of family photos.

At the same time, I felt for her, didn't want to pain her unnecessarily. Even without knowing, I knew who she was.

I'm not explaining this very well. I sensed this woman was trouble for our family and I wanted to defend my mother from any pain – but I also felt for this woman. Perhaps my feelings for her were callow – simply because she was beautiful.

I took her to Dad's study.

'I'll get him,' I said, ushering her into the room.

Afterwards I wished I'd taken her somewhere else. Maybe if I had, my mother would never have realized who she was.

'And?' my mother said, raising herself in her deckchair and looking back towards the house. My father looked up, frowning. He too glanced at the house.

My father's study looked over the back garden. And now the woman – I realized I'd not asked for her name – appeared at the window of my father's study.

My father rose abruptly.

'I'll see to it,' he said to my mother. But not before she had seen the woman too.

She looked down. Sank back into her deck-chair.

My father strode past me. I didn't look at my mother, though I became uncomfortably aware that I was standing over her. I looked towards the house. As my father entered through the back door, the woman withdrew from the window, fading from view. Now all the window showed was the reflection of our family in the garden. Without my father.

He was in the house for ten minutes. He didn't say anything when he came back out into the garden. He went back to his table and picked up his pen. My mother was looking at the book in her hand.

I swayed in the hammock, thinking about that beautiful woman, watching my mother and father pretend.

'You know the man who was shot in the bathroom at Milldean as Little Stevie,' Gilchrist stated, to get it on the record.

Parker was staring at her breasts again but he was fading. He was probably dealing on a daily basis with withdrawal.

'Fucking little scuzz,' he said, but without heat. 'I gave him one once, just to show him what's what.'

'Why was he there?'

He rubbed his face, blinked a few times.

'About a deal...'

'What's his last name?'

He dipped his head down to his left in an odd gesture, as if trying to see what was behind his left arm.

'The last name, Gary.'

Gilchrist was watching him fade in and out. She was trying to stay calm but she was worried he was going to fade out before he'd given her anything. However, his drifting mind was working in her favour.

'Never had no last name. Just Little Stevie. About a deal...'

'You're saying you know who those people were in the house in Milldean and why they were there.'

He frowned.

'Am I?'

'Are you?'

'Fucking right.'

'How do you know them?'

'What about my fucking deal?'

'I'll talk to somebody. How do you know them?'

'You don't know my dad, do you?'

'Mr Hathaway, good to meet you.' Tingley offered his hand to the tanned, well-dressed man who bore a remarkable resemblance to an older Simon Cowell. Hathaway considered for a moment then gave Tingley's hand a firm shake.

'Hear you've been rearranging my friend's furniture. Mr Cuthbert, I mean. Bit chancy that. You'd better be watching your back from now on.'

'I have other people doing that.'

Hathaway tilted his head.

'Oh, that's right – you're connected to some very secret people, aren't you? Main reason I agreed to see you – courtesy to them.'

'We know some of the same people?'

'Doubt that, but let's say the same kind of people. Our world is a small world.'

'Our world?'

'The shadow world.'

The world beyond the law. Tingley nodded and looked round.

They were in a bar on the boardwalk at the marina. The tables outside overlooked a small harbour, and through the open windows he could see brilliant blue sky and hear the chink and rattle of the hawsers and lines on the yachts moored there. Gulls were screeching.

Bright outside, gloomy inside. The bar was like the inside of somewhere Moroccan, maybe Indian. Rugs strewn around, some bench seating, plump cushions on low divans, hookahs on shelves, turquoise and terracotta tiled walls and floors. Tingley gestured round.

'Business good?'

'Students love it – all this. And the cheap shots.'

Tingley had been checking out Hathaway's business interests online when the text had come through summoning him to this meeting. Although Hathaway's power base was still in Milldean and he was into all the same scuzzy stuff as Cuthbert, he had his fingers in many other pies. He was a major landlord in Brighton and Newhaven and was said to use brutal methods when he wanted people out. He had shares in a recycling plant and there were doubts about exactly what he was recycling. And he ran a security operation providing bouncers for clubs and bars all along the south coast. That operation probably cloaked a protection racket.

Then there were the totally legitimate businesses, like this and other bars, a country house hotel over near Worthing and a small chain of dry cleaners in Burgess Hill, Haywards Heath and Crawley.

He lived in one of the large Spanish-style villas – haciendas really – on Tongdean Drive on the outskirts of the city near the Devil's Dyke.

'So what are you poking around for, Mr Tingley?'

Hathaway's similarity to Cowell was quite striking. He obviously worked out every day. Although Tingley knew he must be in his early sixties, his T-shirt underneath his open suit jacket was tight.

'I'm trying to find out what happened in Milldean on the night of the massacre.'

'Police cock-up, as I hear it.'

Hathaway led Tingley into an alcove and sat down on a low, quilted bench behind an equally low table. He leant back against the wall.

'I find these seats bloody uncomfortable but the kids seem to like them.'

Tingley sat on a similar seat opposite him.

'Do you know who the people in the house were and why they were gathered there?' Tingley said.

'Do you?'

'That's what I'd like to find out.'

'Why come to me?'

Tingley looked him in the eye.

'You're The Man.'

'And what's in it for me?' Hathaway said. 'Anything to trade? No? Thought not.'

'You know I know some important people.'

Hathaway nodded. A pretty young woman walked past the alcove.

'Amy.' She started towards them.

'Hookah?' Hathaway said to Tingley. 'With an "ah" on the end, that is. No? Just me, thanks, sweetheart.'

He watched her walk away, slowly shaking his head.

'Sometimes the way a girl walks is enough to

make you glad you're alive – don't you agree, Mr Tingley? Or, I suppose, the way a man walks, if you're that way inclined, as a surprising number of people are – and not just here in Gomorrah-on-sea.'

'What kind of trade do you have in mind?' Tingley said.

'Your soul?' Hathaway grinned. 'I don't know whether you'd consider that too high or too low a price to pay. Supposing you haven't already signed it away in the course of your secret escapades. Still yours to bargain with, is it?'

Tingley nodded.

'Glad to hear it. Now I'm wondering about these important people you know. I'm wondering – are your important people more important than my important people?'

'Who is his father?' Gilchrist asked Williamson as they walked out into the car park at Lewes Prison, where Parker was on remand. Williamson had his unlit cigarette between his fingers. He shrugged.

'Mother's a single parent living on benefits, three other kids still at home.'

'Milldean?'

He nodded.

'Can we talk to her?' She stopped. 'Does she know what he's done? Has anyone been to see her?'

'He's an adult. No need for his mother to be informed.'

They resumed walking.

'Let's talk to her.'

* * *

Kate was running out of time before her shift started but she was desperate to finish off all the pieces of the diary she had managed to compile. She was sitting on her sofa, looking at her watch every few minutes, calculating then recalculating what was the latest time she could afford to leave.

Monday 16th July
Another trunk murder victim turned up yesterday. In Kemp Street, up near the station. Another woman, of course. No official information was given, but today's newspapers published contradictory stories concerning the contents of the trunk. Hutch wasn't too happy.

'The captain's bloody furious,' Percy said.

I said nothing. The Daily Mail *headline read: 'Trunk Murder Sensation; Second Woman's Body Found.' The line underneath moved away from the facts. 'Discovery of first victim's head and arms last night.'*

The report went on: 'The discovery of the head and arms of the Brighton trunk murder victim, packed into a second large black trunk, with the body of the woman who had been killed apparently by a hammer blow on the back of the head...'

They also declared that a tray of striped cloth stretched across a wooden frame had been found – the missing tray from the first trunk.

Now, maybe I was too extravagant with my story of a trunk stuffed with a dead body and another's body parts – but who came up with the second story? Not me. I'm outraged. Somebody else in the force is leaking false stories to the press.

The press men homed in on the occupants of the house in Kemp Street and a house in Park Crescent where the second murder was actually committed. They tried every method possible to obtain entry to these houses. We had to post officers at both houses to stop them. They offered large sums of money for photographs and information.

The trunk had been in the Kemp Street house for about six weeks and other tenants had complained about the smell. Ironically, neither of the owners – Mr and Mrs Barnard – had a sense of smell so they'd been unaware of anything amiss.

Tuesday 17th July
The new victim has been identified as a prostitute, Violette Kay. A woman in her forties. Her pimp, Mancini, is a bit of a mystery. There's a Soho gangster with that name who has a lot of form but we're not sure if it's the same man. That Mancini was a member of a razor gang. He was a deserter from the forces.

At any rate, this Mancini is much younger than her – she was in her forties, he is in his twenties.

Early this morning – the middle of the night really – Donaldson, Sorrell and Pelling left the Town Hall to arrest him in London. He'd been picked up walking along a road in the middle of the night.

I went with them. We were followed by a
227

number of press men in a fast car. We shook them off in the side streets. When we came back from London, the press car was waiting just outside the borough boundary. It followed us to the Town Hall.

I was sitting in the back seat with Mancini. He was regarded as a ladies' man but he wore a cheap suit. He was only 5'5". I wasn't even going to talk to him but when I did try to make conversation he had this terrible stutter. A stuttering ladies man. Ronald Colman had better watch out.

Later in the morning, Pelling had a meeting with us. He was angry.

'On several occasions throughout the course of this enquiry press men have been successful in securing the substance of the particular enquiry on hand, the result being that sensational stories have been published which invariably have been far from accurate and have had the effect of impeding our work.'

Around now I noticed Percy giving me the evil eye. He couldn't hold it, though. He looked away.

'From the commencement of this enquiry it's been obvious that several of the press men are entirely unscrupulous in their methods of obtaining information. As a result, the remainder – who are far more fair and reasonable – have to do the same to keep their newspapers posted with the sensational stories published by the minority referred to. This means that at times the press has been more troublesome than the actual investigation.

'The stories in the papers about the second

trunk murder are going to cause us serious prob-
lems. It's unlikely that there is any link between
the two killings. There were, needless to say, no
remains of the first victim found in the trunk
containing the second. When we announce the
arrest of her pimp, people will simply assume he
did both crimes and stop bringing us infor-
mation.'

When the meeting had ended Percy came over
to me.

'Hutch wants a word with you.'

Here it was: the beginning of the end.

And there the diary entry ended. Damn, damn.
Kate pushed the rest of the papers into her bag,
grabbed her keys and hurried out of the door. She
got a bus almost immediately, plonked down and
almost tore the papers out of her bag. She groaned. The next diary entry was over two weeks
later.

2nd August 1934
We've finally found out where the brown paper
with the partial word '—ford' on it comes from.
It's the end of 'Bedford', which in turn is the end
of an address a clerk working for the Loraine
Confectionery Company – a sweet and chocolate
shop in Finsbury Road – wrote on paper wrap-
ped around a box of some defective confection-
ery.

She wrote it some time between 1st January
and 22nd May 1934 when she was sending the
confectionery back to an associated company,
Meltis Ltd in Bedford. Both these companies are

229

part of Peek Frean, which has its London depot in Bermondsey.

This is where it gets complicated. Although, apparently, Finsbury Park isn't that far south of Bedford, and anything going between the two goes on a van via Bermondsey, which is off in east London.

When this particular parcel reached Meltis in Bedford with a lot of other parcels, the despatch department would have opened it, passed the contents on and chucked the wrapping paper on the floor.

One of two things could have happened to this wrapping paper. It might have been used to wrap a box of confectionery sold at a discount to staff. It might have been used as packing in either vans or railway containers delivering boxes of confectionery to depots in Glasgow, Manchester, Reading, London – or down here in Brighton.

Now, whether this is going to help, I don't know, but Hutch is acting pretty gung-ho for the first time in an age. By tomorrow he's hoping to have traced every female who has left Meltis since January 1934 and have a list of men working for the company who were off work on 6th and 7th June.

None of this has appeared in the papers yet, for obvious reasons.

Kate had reached her stop and the diary had come to an end, aside from some undated scraps. She let out a little snort of frustration as she got off the bus at the railway station and started to hurry down to the radio studio. Then she paused and looked back at the station. She glanced at her watch, turned and went to find the left luggage office.

THIRTEEN

I was still in the Bath Arms, though by now I was drinking wine, when Sarah Gilchrist called me. She was in professional mode.

'I've been told the man shot in the bathroom was called Little Stevie. He may be a rent boy.'

'I'm in the Laines – can you join me?'

'I'm on duty. The man who told me about Little Stevie is that creep, Gary Parker, who killed his friend in Hove. I think his father is maybe somebody big in Milldean. He's looking for a deal.'

'I hope his father's not Cuthbert,' I said. When Tingley had taken me aside he had told me about his encounter with the gangster. 'Making a deal with him might be tricky.'

'Why?'

'I'll tell you later.'

I phoned Kate Simpson and invited her to join me. I was thinking a lot about the Brighton Trunk Murder.

'I'm supposed to be in the studio but I've been given research time,' she said. 'I'll be right down.'

I thought about William Simpson's father. He

231

had died in the late sixties from cancer after taking early retirement somewhere around 1965 or 1966. My mother had remained close to his widow, Elizabeth, for some years, although they stopped seeing each other eventually. I think my father probably had something to do with that.

The friendship between William and me was encouraged and we did like each other well enough. How friendly we would have been if left to our own devices, I wasn't so sure.

Tingley appeared by my side. I started.

'You should audition for a ghost movie.'

He sat down.

'And you should learn to mask your surprise. I've just had an interesting meeting with Hathaway. He knows what's what. My problem is getting the leverage that will make him tell.'

I thought for a moment.

'He doesn't have a son with a different name, does he?'

The left luggage office no longer existed and there was no one to ask about its previous location. Kate was lingering on the concourse, looking at the iron girders holding up the station's vast, glass roof when Watts called. After the call, she phoned in sick. She took a circuitous route to the Laines to avoid her work. She found Watts and Tingley in the Bath Arms sitting side by side in companionable silence. Both stood when she entered and Tingley bought her drink.

She showed them the pages of the diary she had with her.

'They found that the paper came from Bedford,' she said. 'These days there's a Thameslink service between Brighton and Bedford via King's Cross.'

'I doubt Thameslink existed then,' Watts said.

'But there might have been an equivalent.'

Tingley was reading through the last diary entry.

'He's saying here the paper might still have ended up in a depot in Brighton.'

'Odd coincidence, though, don't you think – that Bedford–King's Cross–Brighton thing?'

'It is,' Tingley said.

'Unfortunately, the diary pretty much ends there. And there's a gap just before when it looks like he's about to get a bollocking.'

'What do you think that was about?' Watts said.

'He was selling stories to the press. Made-up ones mostly. His boss thought they were getting in the way of the investigation.'

Watts nodded. He'd asked but his mind seemed to be elsewhere and he had that odd speculative look on his face again. She frowned at him and he leant forward.

'Kate, remember you said the papers were destroyed in 1964 on the orders of the then chief constable?'

She nodded.

'I assumed it was under a thirty-year rule.'

'Actually,' Watts said, 'I believe that's at the discretion of the Chief Constable.'

'You mean the Chief Constable might have destroyed them deliberately?'

Tingley gave Watts a surprised look.

'Bit far-fetched, isn't it, Bob? If they've been sitting there for all those years, why suddenly worry about what's in them in 1964?'

Watts rolled his glass between his palms.

'Isn't that also the year in which the news about finding the head finally reached the public?'

Kate nodded.

'Renewed interest in the case could be a factor, then.'

Kate was watching Watts's face closely.

'There's something you're not telling us?' Kate said.

Watts shrugged.

'How much do you know about your grand-father on your father's side?'

'I told you – he was dead long before I was born. And he was a career policeman like you.'

'Almost exactly like me.'

Tingley tilted his head.

'He was a career policeman. He joined the force in the early thirties and made chief constable in the late fifties. I'm almost certain that he ended his career as the Chief Constable of this very authority. And under a cloud.'

'When?' Kate said, already guessing the answer.

'Around 1964.'

Gilchrist and Williamson looked at each other, both with handkerchiefs over their mouths. The boyfriend was locked in the bathroom. They could hear him through the door moaning and mumbling to himself.

'I'm starting to feel like Dirty fucking Harry,' Williamson said, drawing a ragged breath. 'All the dirty jobs...'

'No offence, Reg, but if you were Clint East-wood, I wouldn't mind so much.'

To hell with the sick-fuck boyfriend, he could wait. The paramedics were gathered around the unconscious woman sprawled on the bed. Her open mouth was a gory red well. Blood was gushing out of it, down her cheeks, soaking into the pillows and once-purple duvet. She was covered from head to foot in it. She was unconscious.

Gilchrist held down bile as she looked at the pair of pliers that lay beside the woman. There was a bowl on the bedside table. It was bloody. There was a pile of the woman's teeth in it. Other teeth were scattered over the bed.

'Actually, Clint, I still hate this job,' she muttered.

'You and me both,' Williamson said. 'You and me both.'

I watched Kate's expression change as she took in the implications of what I'd told her.

'You mean my grandfather was the one who ordered the destruction of the Trunk Murder files.'

'If I've got my dates right, quite possibly – but the dates might be wrong.'

Kate thought for a moment.

'How weird a coincidence is it that I'm doing this research now? But why would he do that?'

'There's more, I'm afraid.'

'Go on.'

'I'm not sure but I think he may have started his police career here...'

'Back in the early thirties?'

I nodded. Kate sat back.

'Wow. Just bloody wow.'

She took a long swallow of her drink. Tingley and I exchanged glances.

'Small world,' he said.

'Smaller than you think,' I said. 'My dad was a policeman too.'

Kate put her drink down.

'He's a writer, isn't he?' she said.

'But he was a policeman back in the thirties.'

Kate frowned. The thirties was ancient history to her.

'I thought you said he was alive.'

'He is. He's ninety-five. He's the George Bernard Shaw of the crime genre. He was running marathons until he was eighty-five.' I shook my head. 'And he's a bastard.'

'As a father, you mean?' Kate said. 'Tell me about it.'

'No, more than that.'

Tingley had been watching me closely. He'd picked up on a tone in my voice.

'Where did he serve?'

I gave a small smile and jabbed a finger towards the floor.

'Here. That's how he met your grandfather, Kate.'

There was silence around the table.

'Kate, you're wondering if either your grandfather or my father wrote that diary.'

236

'I'm wondering more than that,' she said.

'If she's wondering the same as me,' Tingley said, 'she's wondering which one of them was the Brighton Trunk Murderer.'

Kate was in a fog and not just because of the alcohol she'd consumed on an empty stomach. She didn't like the man who wrote the diary and she thought he was keeping secrets that the missing bits of it might reveal. From what Bob Watts had said, perhaps his father had written the memoir. Or her grandfather. Then again, perhaps neither of them had.

As for the idea of either of them being the murderer, well, of course, if this were fiction, one of them would be. But this wasn't fiction. This was real life.

Tingley was talking. She didn't listen at first but then she tuned in.

'I'm thinking he got the idea to put her in the trunk from precedent: 1927 at Charing Cross Station. The mainline cloakroom. A trunk was delivered by taxi, but the porter didn't remember the man who was with it. It wasn't airtight so the cloakroom attendants started to smell it quite soon. Inside – under brown paper – was a woman divided into five parts by amputation at shoulder and hip joint.'

'Did the police get the murderer?' Kate said.

'They did, by tracing the taxi and finding where he picked up the person with the trunk. Spilsbury was the man who did the autopsy. He concluded the woman had been knocked out, then asphyxiated. He also said that because of the skilled way she'd been cut up the murderer was a slaughterman. In that he was entirely wrong.'

'So the great Spilsbury wasn't infallible,' Watts said.

'Far from it – and something for us to bear in mind.'

Watts looked at Kate.

'What do you see when you think of the Trunk Murderer?' he said.

'I see either your father or my grandfather.'

Watts smiled.

'Not really,' she said. 'My imagination has been colonized by the movies. I think in film images. A man standing beneath a yellow gas-light, the light falling at an angle and spreading a long shadow on the cobbled street. It's an image that I've got from Hitchcock's *The Lodger* morphing into *The Exorcist*.'

'And this is your killer?'

'Yes – and in black and white, despite the yellow light – if that makes sense.'

'Sort of.'

'Then there's a man in a homburg and topcoat, his shoes polished, walking with deliberate steps down a rain-glistening alley.' She smiled. 'Except in reality it was summer so it was probably daylight and he would have been sweltering.'

'Strange, isn't it,' Tingley said, 'how we picture him through a series of mirrors, representation of murderers from that period in photos and TV and books and our own imaginations. I see him smoking a pipe and in a heavy three-piece suit – even in the summer.'

'I don't see him at all,' Watts said, rather sadly, Kate thought. 'But I wonder if he intended to kill her? If he did, then chopping her up would be cold-blooded, thought out. If he didn't, it would perhaps be more difficult, much more upsetting.'

'And how did he live with that for the rest of his life?' Kate said.

'Maybe he was her pimp so he was pretty insensitive anyway,' Tingley said. 'Maybe he killed others, in other ways.'

'Maybe I'll find out tomorrow when I go to the records office in Lewes.' Kate pointed at the handwritten pages in front of Tingley. 'I'm absolutely certain I'll find out who our anonymous scribe is.'

Kate was about to leave when Watts's phone rang. It was Gilchrist.

'I don't think I can do that now,' Watts said. 'It's Gilchrist,' he said to Kate and Tingley. He looked at Kate. 'Do you want to meet her when her shift finishes to give her a debrief?'

Kate liked Gilchrist. Kate was tipsy. She thought for just a moment.

'Sure.'

An hour later, she was meandering rather than walking into Ha Ha to meet Sarah Gilchrist. She tried to sober up with strong coffee. She had done a reasonable job by the time Gilchrist arrived looking drawn and tense. Kate watched the way she seemed to shoulder her way into the bar. She nodded at Kate but didn't come over until she'd got a drink. She stood at the bar, shoulders high and tense, until the barman handed her a glass of wine, then she came over to Kate and sat down stiffly on the sofa beside her.

'Glad you've got a drink,' Gilchrist said. 'I hate women who go in bars and don't buy a drink until their friends arrive. Or just order tapwater. They want to be in nice places but they don't want to pay to be there. They seem to have a problem understanding how capitalism works.'

Kate watched her for a moment. Gilchrist responded to the scrutiny.

'Rough day,' she said quietly.

Kate nodded and listened while Gilchrist outlined the discovery of the man in the bathroom and his girlfriend unconscious on the blood-soaked bed.

'They were both under the influence of GHB. A fun drug, supposedly, unless you take too much. Taken to excess, it causes hallucinations. They were seeing floating furniture, clowns, witches.' She took a swig of her drink. 'And somewhere in this he decided it would be a good idea to pull her teeth out with a pair of pliers. We found eighteen.'

Gilchrist shook her head.

'Drugs are killing this town.'

After ten minutes or so they moved to the back of the restaurant. It was quieter there, although they could still hear noise from the front of the restaurant.

'I'm sorry that I haven't engaged fully with the Trunk Murder,' Sarah said, swirling her red wine in her oversized glass. 'I've been preoccupied.'

'Clearly – plus your career has been jeopardized – how could you not be preoccupied?'

Gilchrist shrugged.

'If I've got this right,' she said, 'the Trunk Murder victim had been pregnant for four months. Do you think she knew? Was she scrupulous about when her periods were happening?'

Kate put down her drink.

'I think so. And being pregnant and unmarried would be a big deal. In those days, if you weren't married, you needed to get married if you were pregnant.'

'Yes, you're right – she knew.' Gilchrist flexed her shoulders. 'A woman knows, though doesn't always want to admit she knows, right? So she chooses her time to tell the man. If she's a mistress, she waits to use it as a lever for him to leave his wife?'

'I've been wondering if she got pregnant deliberately or knew the rules?'

'Rules?' Gilchrist said.

'You know – that mistresses are just that – no claims on the man.'

Gilchrist smiled.

'I don't think it has ever worked quite like that. I believe it's rare that a mistress just wants to be a mistress – she wants to move up in the pecking order.'

'Was that how...'

Gilchrist, still smiling, gave Kate a look. Kate flushed.

'How it was for me with Bob? No – that was strictly a one-night thing.' Gilchrist took a bigger swig from her wine. 'I wouldn't do that to another woman – except I did.'

241

'So what does that make our unidentified woman in the trunk?'

Gilchrist reached over and squeezed Kate's arm. 'I think you're doing a great job for her. It's about respect, isn't it?'

Kate felt that she was trying to breathe life into the sad remains of the victim's body.

'I wonder what she was like?' she said. 'Was she clinging? Demanding? A bitch? Gullible? Giving? Unselfish? In love? Was there someone else who cared for her and, if so, why did that person not come forward?'

'Even if she were any of those negative things, nothing can justify what he did.'

'Of course – and as soon as you start using words you're building a construct of this woman which may or may not be true.'

Gilchrist waved at the waitress and tilted her glass to get another round for them.

'A fiction,' Kate continued. 'One of many possible stories.'

The waitress brought their fresh drinks and their food. They'd both chosen the fishcakes with salad leaves.

'I think the police were right,' Gilchrist said. 'She was the lover of a married man who made a fuss when she got pregnant.'

'Obviously the abortion option would have been tried,' Kate said. 'She said no. It would have been a backstreet abortion in those days. Four or five months pregnant – she'd be starting to show, or soon would be. She needed a commitment from him.'

'But if she had a job – would she not have been

missed at work?' Gilchrist said. 'By her friends? What happened to the place where she lived? Presumably he kept her. Maybe he owned it. But what about the neighbours? What did he do with all her stuff? Her clothes?'

Kate thought for a moment.

'They compiled a list of eight hundred missing women and managed to trace seven hundred and thirty of them – quite extraordinary really. Do you think the victim was one of the seventy unaccounted for?'

'I'm sure of it. They had her but they just had too much material.'

'Shame we don't,' Kate said, thinking about her grandfather's destruction of the Brighton files.

FOURTEEN

Gilchrist dozed on top of her duvet. She felt like shit. Not because she was hungover after the early part of her evening but because she was knackered after the rest of her night. There had been an alarm that a five-year-old girl had gone missing. A thirteen-year-old in Hollingbury reported he'd seen a long-haired white man drag the girl into a car – a blue or turquoise Ford Escort. The force had a new system when a child went missing. It flooded the area with police and interrupted local radio and television pro-grammes with pleas for help. Gilchrist had been called in. Although she'd had a couple of drinks, she was OK to work. She'd spent a fruitless night rousting registered paedophiles in the area.

This morning it turned out the kiddie had spent the night with her best friend four doors away. Gilchrist wondered if it was a wind-up, wonder-ed what other crime had been carried out when the police were fully occupied with that.

She yawned. She was hoping for word back on a possible deal for Gary Parker today. Her seniors would want to keep her out of the loop but they had to tolerate her because Parker would only deal in her presence – presumably so that he could ogle her. Gilchrist wanted to interview his mother but she was out of town, nobody quite knew where.

Vice were investigating Little Stevie. Oddly, he didn't ever seem to have been arrested – highly unusual if his occupation was as Parker sug-gested.

The problem was that nobody senior to her gave a toss. Since Watts had resigned, there were no senior officers who cared about investigating Milldean.

The phone rang and she reached forward to answer. She listened for a few moments and put the phone back down. Now she was awake.

From Kemp Town, Kate drove along the coast to Rottingdean, the sea sparkling to her right, then cut up across the slow curve of the Downs. When she reached Lewes she parked in the

Cliffe car park by the river and the brewery, and trudged up the steep hill, past the War Memorial to the High Street. She was horribly hungover.

The records office was in the Maltings, a couple of hundred yards from the castle, which was off to her left beneath an arched defence gate and past the Barbican – little more than the keep remained.

She turned into the cobbled castle close and was perspiring by the time she passed a bowling green on her right. A sign told her that until the sixteenth century it had been the jousting field.

She was early for the records office so walked across to a viewing point. A plaque there told of the Battle of Lewes at which Simon de Montfort had defeated a larger royal force in 1264 and paved the way for Parliament. A little map showed the disposition of the troops on the Downs whose folds and soft slopes were spread out in front of her.

She took a long drink from her bottle of water and two more painkillers. At 8.45 a.m. precisely she walked into the records office and took the stairs. The room upstairs had creaking floors and high ceilings. The walls that did not have bookshelves were bare. All the floor space was occupied by rows of long tables.

The Trunk Murder files were waiting for her at reception but she was only allowed to take them one at a time. The first was a buff-coloured foolscap file on which somebody had written, in now-faded blue ink, 'Trunk Murders File – Mancini'.

The first items in the file were two black and

white photographs of creased and ripped pieces of brown paper. Someone had painstakingly put the pieces together to make what, according to the note on the bottom of the photo, purported to be a brown paper bag. She guessed this was the oil-soaked paper the victim had been wrapped in.

There was a letter and two brief notes from Spilsbury, the Home Office pathologist, with his initial conclusions about the remains he had examined. He referred to the victim as 'the latest cut-up case', which Kate found cold.

Next she came to the photo albums proper. The albums – little more than folders really – were all tied together by a loosely knotted piece of string. Kate untied the knot and separated the first folder from the others.

This was the part of her visit she was most squeamish about, for within these folders were photographs of the woman's remains.

There were about a dozen people in the library by now and most of them seemed to be making use of the books just behind Kate. Taking a deep breath, she opened the folder.

It took a moment to make sense of the first photograph. When she did, she flushed and quickly closed the folder. She waited for the elderly man immediately behind her to move away before she opened the folder again and forced herself to look.

The woman's torso had been laid on a table and this first shot was a close-up from between where her legs should have been. It showed the ragged, raw stumps of her thighs and, between them, startlingly clear, her vagina and anus. The black flesh of the stumps looked horribly like the ends of cuts of meat.

She felt shame on the woman's behalf. Ludicrous as it was, given that the woman's limbs and head had been hacked off, she felt the humiliation of her being exposed in this way even after death.

She turned to the other photographs. The torso had been photographed from every angle. The second and third photographs showed the torso from the sides, the arms cut off below the shoulder like some obscene Venus de Milo. The fourth was taken from where her head should have been. She had strong, shapely shoulders but her neck was abruptly terminated in another cut of meat.

Kate swallowed, looked across at the two librarians behind the reception desk, wondered what they were thinking about her wanting to see these files. She felt grubby.

She had the bottle of water in her bag but there was no drinking or eating allowed in here. Or use of pens, for that matter. She glanced at the pencil she'd brought.

The second album contained eight photographs of 'limbs discovered at King's Cross Railway Station'. In the first photograph the woman's legs were laid out on a table in front of a dark brick wall. It seemed like a basement or a workshop. It seemed very cold. It was, presumably, the mortuary.

Kate felt tears welling up at the same time as she thought how comical they looked, these legs lying alone on a table. She could have believed they were false, had it not been for the way that the thighs and the rest of the legs were separated a couple of inches to demonstrate how they had been hacked in half at the knee.

She'd been horrified at the thought of Spilsbury handling the feet as if they were shoes, but from the photograph she could see that the feet had not been detached after all.

Spilsbury's autopsy report had stated the feet were well looked after, but the tops of the toes seemed to be covered with corns or blisters. The right big toe was bent at an angle and the right little toe crossed over its neighbour as if she had in fact been wearing too-tight shoes. But were all these things a consequence of her body parts being crammed into a suitcase?

The third album contained a dozen photographs linked to the other Trunk Murder, that of the prostitute Violette Kaye. Most of them were photographs of the room in which she had been killed and the one in which she had been discovered.

The last two, however, were of Violette Kaye squashed into the trunk, her legs bent, her head pushed down towards her chest, her face swollen, teeth bared. She looked hideous, but it wasn't her fault. Mancini had made her like this, had taken her dignity away.

There were no more files, no police report saying exactly which policemen had answered the call from the left luggage office at Brighton railway station. She left the archive empty-handed and queasy.

* * *

Gilchrist found Brighton phantasmagoric, dreamlike, crude. So many wannabe artists. So much bilge talked. Then, to see the young people spill out of the railway station on a day like this. Men in T-shirts, girls in micro-minis. Raucous voices: shrill, shrieking girls; guttural, hoarse boys. Girls tottering on unfeasible heels; men swaggering, shoulders back, crotches thrust out.

It was horrible to watch because she knew all that testosterone, all that female we-want-babies, all that din, was an unholy cocktail that would end in sex, sure, but mostly in violence, rape and misery.

'Modern life, eh?' she said to Williamson, scowling.

'Your version of it.'

'Meaning?'

'I don't quite see things like that.'

He was looking almost benign as he watched the teenagers flood by.

'Meaning?'

'These are just kids out to have fun. They aren't the children of the anti-Christ.'

'Yes, they are. I can give you statistics.'

'We can all do statistics. Doesn't mean anything. When did you turn into a *Daily Mail* reader?'

'The *Daily Mail* is much misunderstood,' Gilchrist said.

'By whom?'

'Its readers, mainly.'

Williamson barked a laugh.

'Why are we here, Sarah?'

'I told you – I had a phone call.'

249

'But you didn't tell me what it said.'

'A man said to come here and wait by the flower stall to learn something to my advantage.'

'Something to your advantage? Jesus, Sarah. We're here because of a crank call?'

'It's to do with the Milldean thing.'

'Did he say I could come along?'

'He didn't say you couldn't.'

Kate had lunch in Lewes at Bill's, down beside the river. It was as crowded as ever. As she ate, she was thinking about the murderer. Would he put what he had done out of his mind? Would he savour it? Had he told anybody? Had he boasted like Violette Kay's killer, Mancini, apparently did? What price did he pay? Did he feel guilt? Remorse? If the victim was his mistress, did he and his wife stay together? Could his wife smell death on him?

She imagined him dismembering the woman. Wearing a hat. A tiepin. Maybe those elasticated metal things to hold the sleeves of the shirt up. His shirt would have had a detachable collar. Would he have taken the collar off whilst he was using his saw on her? Would he have put on a pinny, maybe with a floral design, frilly round the edges?

She'd printed an essay off the Internet that George Orwell had written in the thirties about the perfect English murder – and murderer. Kate looked at it now. Orwell's view was that the murderer should be 'a little man of the professional class' – a dentist or a solicitor, say – living an intensely respectable life somewhere in the suburbs. It would be best if he lived in a semi-detached house so the neighbours could hear suspicious sounds through the wall.

Orwell thought he should be either chairman of the local Conservatives or a leading Nonconformist strongly against alcohol. His crime would be a guilty passion for his secretary or the wife of a colleague or rival. Having decided on murder, he'd plan it in detail but slip up in one tiny, unforeseeable way. He would see murder as less disgraceful than being caught out for his adultery.

Was this the Trunk Murderer? If so, what slip had he made?

'He's not coming,' Williamson was saying when Gilchrist's mobile phone rang. The number was blocked.

'Hello,' she said.

She heard a matter-of-fact voice.

'Hope you've got home insurance.'

The line went dead. Williamson looked at her.

'Oh fuck,' she said.

Kate saw Tingley enter the café and order a coffee at the counter. He walked towards her and sat down beside her.

'How's it going?'

'Just reading George Orwell's theory about the English murderer.'

'Anything in the archive? Have you found out who your diarist is?'

She shook her head.

'Just some gruesome pictures. What are you

251

doing here?'

'Passing through. Saw your car in the car park and guessed where you'd be.'

'That predictable, eh?'

He shook his head.

'There aren't many options in Lewes.'

A harried waitress brought over Tingley's coffee, slopping some of it on to the table as she put it down.

'I've been reading up on Sir Bernard Spilsbury. Do you know why he was the only forensic pathologist ever to have been knighted whilst still working?'

Kate shrugged.

'Because his knighthood unduly impressed juries. They automatically believed him. He was a Sir, for goodness sake. But, of course, he wasn't always right. He was a scrupulous man but he was also egotistical and dogmatic. He was quite capable of jumping to conclusions beyond the limits of the facts. He fancied himself a kind of Sherlock Holmes. He wasn't.'

'So what do you think he got wrong in this case?'

Tingley soaked up the spilt coffee with a napkin.

'I think we agree that the police did a damned good job of tracing most of the missing women in Britain aged around twenty-five. And, if our dead girl wasn't brought in from abroad – though it's quite possible she was – the likelihood is that she is among the seventy or so missing women not traced.'

Kate nodded agreement.

'Assuming,' Tingley said, matter-of-factly, 'Spilsbury was right about her age.'

Kate's eyes widened and she started riffing through the pages of her notes.

'What was his evidence for that conclusion?'

'I don't know. He drew the conclusion after examining the torso. But here's the funny thing. Much of the evidence for establishing a woman's age is in the skull – the fusing of bones and so on. Since the skull wasn't there – how *did* he reach that conclusion?'

Kate thought for a minute.

'I read that, in the Mancini murder case, a friend of Violette Kay's reported her missing, but because she was outside the age range Spilsbury had proposed the police didn't take her disappearance seriously.'

Tingley nodded.

'They focused entirely on women within the narrow age range Spilsbury proposed. But do you remember the police surgeon who first examined her?'

'He thought she was older.'

'That's right – he put her age at about forty.'

Kate sat forward.

'But if the police surgeon was actually correct, then the whole of the police investigation was flawed.'

She tapped the table.

'And there's nothing we can do about that now. We've reached a dead end.'

'Not necessarily,' Tingley said.

Kate frowned.

'We could find the body – find where the

victim is buried.'

'How?'

'It would be a pauper's grave, right? Brighton would have buried her. They'll have records.'

'But even if we dig her up, how would that help us to identify her?'

'DNA,' Tingley said quietly. 'You can extract it from bones.'

'I thought you could only identify people from their DNA if you have their DNA on a database. And there wasn't a database in her day.'

'There are other ways.'

'Actually, you're right. I read this book saying that everybody is related to five women way back when. We can all be traced back. So we'd be able to figure out quite a lot about her.'

Tingley nodded.

'Ancestral DNA. DNA breaks down into one hundred and seventy-seven different parts, some of which indicate ancestry. Let's say we come up with Native American, European and sub-Saharan strands. We won't, but just suppose. You only get that combination in the Caribbean. Then we get voluntary tests from a couple of hundred males and females from the same area. Then we compare their DNA and family history with our victim to identify which island, or even town, they come from.'

'They can do that?'

'Sure – remember that little boy they found chopped up in a sack in the Thames? They traced him right back to his village in Africa. There have been some really interesting studies of the ancestral DNA of phaseolus vulgaris.'

'Phaseolus vulgaris?'

'Yes – the common bean. It has two major geographic gene pools.' Tingley caught the look on Kate's face. 'But maybe that can wait.'

'I think so. How do we find out where she was buried?'

Tingley thought for a moment.

'Well, the local council will have records of who is buried where. But hang on – didn't Spilsbury take the body back up to London to examine it?'

Kate was silent for a moment.

'No, no – he took internal organs but the body stayed in Brighton, I'm sure.'

'Did they cremate in those days?'

Kate squeezed his arm.

'God, I hope not.'

The fire brigade was already there. Two engines outside, two firemen on top of ladders hosing the flat through the blown-out front windows. There was a terrible smell that caught at the back of her throat.

'We think we got it before the rest of the house took fire,' the fire chief told Gilchrist. 'But I'm afraid your flat is pretty much gutted.'

Gilchrist was both seething and frightened.

'Can I go in?'

'Tomorrow, sure.'

'It was arson,' she said.

'You surprise me, officer. I think you'd be best getting away from here for now. Come back tomorrow.'

'Is there anything left?'

'We don't know yet. I'm sorry.'

Williamson was looking awkward, standing on the pavement, trying to keep an eye on Gilchrist without making it obvious, trying to hide his concern.

Gilchrist went over to him.

'Looks like I don't have anything except what I'm wearing. Weird feeling.'

'Is this to do with the Milldean thing?' Williamson said.

'Oh, I think so.'

'You're being warned off?'

'I think that's the gist of it.'

'Is it working?'

Gilchrist looked up at the steam and black smoke billowing out of her window. She could feel the shakes starting but she knew that was adrenaline more than anything. At least, she hoped that was what it was.

'I'll get back to you on that.'

Tingley said he had to see a man about a son – whatever that meant – so Kate drove back into Brighton, parked in the Church Road car park and walked along to Brighton Museum. On the ground floor she passed Dali's Mae West sofa – bright red lips on four legs – and the Rennie Mackintosh furniture that looked great but that she'd never want to sit in. She took the stairs to the local history unit.

Behind the counter a bald-headed man and a woman in linen were talking. They turned in unison.

'I wondered if you kept records here of where

people are buried,' Kate said.

'Good question,' the man said. He looked at the woman. 'Do we?' She shrugged.

'Not sure but they'll certainly have records at Woodvale Crematorium.'

Kate took a phone number and on the way back to her car got through to a woman called Sally at Woodvale. She explained what she wanted.

'She may have been cremated,' Sally said. 'They were doing cremations by then.'

Kate didn't want to hear that.

'The council would have buried her. They would have gone for the cheapest option, wouldn't they? Which is cheaper – cremation or burial.'

'Oh, a pauper's grave, for sure.'

'Can we try, then?'

'When was she buried?'

'I'm not entirely sure,' Kate said. 'She died in June 1934 and the police did an autopsy. I'm not sure how long they'd need to keep the body – well, her remains. Three months?'

'Let's try six,' Sally said. 'You have no name for this woman?'

'That's the problem.'

'OK – I'll see what I can do.'

I was feeling sorry for myself when Gilchrist phoned. I never thought I'd be the kind of person to pine but I was pining for my former life. The man who'd yomped 200 miles in six days during the first Gulf War, now acting like a wuss. I was really getting into the unfairness of it. Me, the poster boy for routinely arming the police. I took a lot of shit for that, then six months later every other chief constable in the country was clamouring for it. By then, for me, it was too late.

'Someone has burnt my flat down.' Gilchrist, breathing heavily.

'Are you safe?' I said, immediately on my feet.

'I'm fine. I wasn't intended to be in it – they got me out on a wild goose chase. They were warning me off, I think.'

'Do you know who they are?'

'Just a voice on a phone. Do you have any more ideas?'

'I'm waiting on Tingley. You've lost everything – that must be dreadful.'

'Actually, I haven't. Most of my stuff is in store after my last move. I lost some nice CDs and, I assume, all my clothes. I think I can survive without the *Mamma Mia* DVD.'

'Do you want to stay here?'

There was silence on the line.

'Tempting but probably not a good idea.'

'Do you want to come over at least?'

'What I want is to go and find those Hayward Heath bastards and confront them.'

'So much for being warned off. I'll come with you.'

Death hadn't touched Kate yet. Her grandparents on both sides had died when she was too young to remember them. At university she knew a couple of students well enough to say hello to who died from overdoses. But nobody close to her had ever died. She had never suffered that

258

anguish. And never visited a crematorium before.

Woodvale was a big cemetery but it wasn't exactly Arlington or those cemeteries for the war dead she'd seen in Normandy – line after line of white crosses. Normandy and Brittany had been regular holiday destinations when she was little, and her father had made them visit three or four of the World War Two battle sites and attached cemeteries for articles he had to write.

She went the wrong way at first. She drove up Bear Road, a steep, narrow road out of the clutter and noise of a bad road junction. It was a windy day, puffy white clouds scudding across the sky. She drove into the Woodvale cemetery. With its abundance of trees and colourful bedding, it might have been a country park.

She drove down a narrow, pockmarked road with gravestones among the trees – some ostentatious, others much less so. She followed the sign to the lodge, a Victorian flint and brick house on the right-hand side of the road. Below, she could see the road go down to connect with the hustle of the Lewes Road and the big shopping complex there.

It struck Kate as strange to have such an oasis of calm so near the bustle of rush-hour Brighton. But then that *was* Brighton – this hodgepodge of disparate things colliding – sometimes clashing – but somehow *working*. Not necessarily working together, of course, but definitely working.

She looked for cypresses as she drove through the cemetery. Those precise, evocative exclamation marks with their acutely delineated shadows

259

so associated with death. But there were none. She went into the lodge, conscious of the heavy scent of rhododendra.

There was a narrow counter with a long, open office behind it. A pretty woman with a mass of grey hair and a tattooed ankle came over.

'Is Sally here?' Kate said.

'I'm Sally.'

'We spoke on the phone – about the Trunk Murder victim?'

The woman nodded and walked over to a cluttered desk. She picked up a sheaf of papers.

'I found the grave,' she said. 'At least I found where it roughly is.'

Kate tilted her head.

'We have grid references for a block of plots. I know roughly where she was buried but I don't know which the exact grave is. And it's in an area where other burials may have taken place across where she was buried.'

'What does that mean if we're thinking about exhumation?'

'It means we're not sure which is her body.'

Kate nodded.

'I think in the circumstances she might be quite recognizable.'

The woman shrugged. She handed over the papers.

'The woman is buried in the cemetery across the road,' she said. 'But these days her plot is one of a number given over to wildlife.'

Kate thanked the woman and went back to her car. She wound her window down. It had been raining and there was an earthy smell in the air.

She drove slowly, avoiding the potholes in the road, past stone crosses on plinths, stained and lichened mausolea, headstones tilted at odd angles poking out of tangled undergrowth.

The entrance to the other cemetery was directly opposite. She drove in, turned right and drove up towards Woodland Grove.

The cemetery was deserted. She drove between a wall on her right and graves on her left. She took a left and parked beside a white van. An estate car was on the other side of the van.

The cemetery sloped away below her. Beyond it she could see, on the next hill, the racecourse. There was a giddy curve of houses, the railway station where all this began on another hill, and the sea beyond. Always the sea.

She checked the map and walked up the slope between newish gravestones. People who had died in the past five years. Now there were a few people in the graveyard. A couple laying flowers and a man on his own looking down on a small grave, lost in thought.

Quite a few young people buried here. Car accidents? Drugs? There were toy animals on a number of the graves. That of a three-year-old child was piled with teddy bears and other soft toys.

At the rim of these recent graves was longer grass, a grove of trees. She walked over. There was a sign: 'This area has been designated as a nature reserve.'

The ground around and beneath the long grass was uneven – as well it might be, given that it was covering a score of graves. These were the

261

paupers' graves. People buried by the parish at the cost of the parish in unmarked graves. And the woman – the remains of the woman – found in the trunk at Brighton railway station was one of them.

Kate had no idea where in the twenty square feet her grave was.

She looked into the long grass. Looked up at the blue sky. A sudden wind shivered the trees. And when she looked back at the plot of ground, a man was standing at the other end of it.

Surprised, she took a step back.

He was tall, skinny, in a long black raincoat. He was in his thirties, maybe early forties. He stood, feet together, hands clasped in front of him, head bowed, as if in silent contemplation of the plot.

Then he lifted his head, just a little, and raised his eyes to look at her. He gave her a mischievous, malevolent look from that strange angle, made more sinister when he smiled. He called out to her, his voice deep, an edge to it.

'What Katie did next, eh, darling?'

Then he turned and ambled away.

FIFTEEN

'Well, something is kicking off,' I said the moment Gilchrist had got into my car. 'What happened to your flat is the worst, but I've just had calls from Kate and Tingley. Kate had a scare put into her – some guy hassled her up at the cemetery.'

'The cemetery? What was she doing there?'

'She's found the grave of the Trunk Murder victim.'

'Oh, that. Clever girl. And Tingley?'

'He's found out who Gary Parker's father is.'

Gilchrist snapped her head round.

'How the hell has he done that? *We* don't know yet.'

'He has his methods. Anyway, somebody is getting really rattled or pissed off – or both.'

'Gary Parker's father?'

'No, that doesn't make sense. The timing is wrong for him to come down heavy on us if his son is wanting a deal.'

'I want to talk to that gap-toothed bastard, Connolly, in Haywards Heath.'

'Tingley is on to him too. We're going to pay him a visit. But we've got to collect Tingley from Gatwick first.'

'Tingley's been away?'

263

'Not unless Lewes counts. A meeting. As usual, he was enigmatic.'

Tingley was waiting for them at the South Terminal. He slid into the back seat. Gilchrist told him about her flat but was really just waiting to ask one question.

'Who is Gary Parker's father?' she said.

'Not who you'd expect,' Tingley said.

Kate was trying hard not to freak out. The man at the cemetery had chilled her to the bone. What could he possibly want from her? Surely nothing to do with the Trunk Murder – this wasn't one of those silly thrillers where secret societies protected a secret for centuries. Was it?

Wrapped in a rug, she was on her balcony. Tonight, the music in the square was just Amy Winehouse and something unrecognizable involving a heavy bass beat. She had a notepad on her lap and a pencil in her hand. She was trying to focus on the Trunk Murder but all she could think about was that thin man standing at the other end of the burial plot.

When he walked away she thought of following to ask what he meant, but there was no one around and she wondered if he might attack her. Then she thought he might have done something to her car. When she got back to it she got in gingerly and locked it immediately, before starting the engine and testing the brakes.

She'd entered her flat nervously too, but there was no sign of any kind of break-in. She'd phoned Watts and told him what had happened. He'd told her to stay in the flat until he got over there later in the day. Told her to keep her mobile beside her.

It rang now, playing the irritatingly perky tune she couldn't figure out how to change. Her parents' number flashed up on the screen.

'Hello, Kate,' her father said in an oddly hearty voice. 'How are things?'

'Things are fine, Dad, thanks.'

'Everything going OK, is it? You're feeling OK?'

Her father never asked anything about her except when he was checking up on her for his own peculiar reasons.

'I'm fine, Dad. Why do you ask?'

There was silence on the line for a moment. Then:

'Nothing unusual happened?'

It was Kate's turn to be silent as she pondered his asking her this question after her encounter in the cemetery.

'Not really, no.'

'Not really – what do you mean, not really?'

'I mean no. How's Mum?'

'Mum's fine,' he said impatiently. 'She's wondering when you might be coming up to London again for a visit.' He cleared his throat. 'In fact, we were both wondering if you might like to come and stay for a few days. We don't see nearly enough of you.'

Stranger and stranger.

'I've got work, Dad.'

'Don't you have leave due?'

'I haven't been there long enough to get leave yet.' And if I had, she thought but didn't say, I

265

wouldn't want to spend it at home.

'Maybe next weekend, then.'

'Maybe – it depends on my shifts.'

Another silence. Finally:

'OK, then. Well, you take care, Kate. And phone me if you need me.'

'Will do, Dad.'

'Love you.'

'Bye, Dad.'

She dropped the phone in her lap and listened to Amy Winehouse's by now poignant views on rehab ricocheting round the square. She thought for a moment about other singers she'd liked, who'd arrived but hadn't stayed long. Whatever happened to Macy Gray?

But really she was thinking about her dad calling. It *had* to be more than coincidence. The man in the cemetery was something to do with the grey areas of her father's life. The many grey areas. In threatening her, the man was sending a message to her father. And her father had clearly received it.

There had been concern in her father's voice as their conversation had gone on. It was a long time since she had heard that. It would have touched her had she allowed it to. There was fear too. She had never known her father to be in a situation he didn't fully control. Maybe this was it – the first time.

Kate pulled the throw up over her shoulders and waited to hear from Watts.

'James Tingley – you tease,' I said. 'Who would have thought it?'

'I'm not teasing. I'm trying to get it clear in my head. I'd thought it would be Cuthbert – same Cro-Magnon mentality. I'd hoped it was Hathaway so we could do a deal that would explain your situation. But it's neither.'

'We get that,' Sarah said. 'So who is Gary Parker's father?'

'Another close friend of Mr Watts here. This whole affair is bedevilled with them.'

'And that close friend is...?' I said, trying to listen to the satnav instructions at the same time. I was driving down dark, winding lanes to the north of Hampstead Heath.

'A certain Mr Winston Hart.'

'You're joking!' I said, almost missing a turning.

'Who's Winston Hart?' Sarah said.

Tingley looked wolfish.

'The Chair of the Police Authority that forced Bob's resignation,' he said.

Kate had gone back inside her flat from the balcony, double-locked the French windows and pulled out the Trunk Murder files again. She was conscious that she was spending far too much time on this but, frankly, she didn't have much else in her life. Her last relationship had gone south, her job was boring as hell ... and so it went.

She looked again at the remaining two undated scraps of the diary.

My background is Northern. You don't look at the mantelpiece when you're poking the fire. I

*didn't bother too much about faces – I was more
interested in bodies. So that was unusual for me.
Noticing the face so much, I mean. Nobody
would have thought she was forty. She looked ten
years younger. In fact, she looked like Carole
Lombard, that movie star. Spitting image.*

Who was he talking about? Just another of his
many women? Kate was thinking about what
Tingley had said about Spilsbury getting the age
wrong. Oh, there was something here, for sure.
But what exactly?

The next entry was more factual.

*Come September and we'd looked at about 3,000
statements from the public. We had about 1,000
letters from Germany. But now I was out of work
so far as the Trunk Murder investigation was
concerned. The Scotland Yard boys, Donaldson
and Sorrell, went back up to London. Unofficially they had another twelve months to
solve the case. The operations room in the Royal
Pavilion was wound up.*

*I told the local press that Scotland Yard would
be investigating 'a secret list of fifty men,
selected because of their association with
certain sorts of women'. Of course, that wasn't
entirely true – in fact, I'd plucked the number out
of the air.*

*I was in trouble, though. The powers that be
were giving me a hard time about my extra-
curricular activities. There was talk of disciplinary action. Possibly resignation. Perhaps
criminal proceedings. Ha bloody ha.*

Kate assumed it was the diarist's habit of leaking stories to the press that was the problem. But she wondered about his way with women. Wondered whether sometimes his seduction method was too forceful.

She needed to explore whatever files were available in the National Archives in Kew. That was the repository for all the old Scotland Yard files, and she hoped there would be material in there that existed nowhere else. Failing that, there might be something that would help her to identify whoever was writing this diary.

'You're only paranoid if people haven't really got it in for you,' I said triumphantly – but my mind was whirring. First, I couldn't figure the man Sarah had described as the son of the effete Winston Hart with his stupid moustache and his middle-class pretensions. Second, did that actually mean I was right and he was somehow part of a plot against me?

'I'm tempted to abandon Connolly and head for Hart,' I said.

'No,' Sarah said. 'We have to talk to Connolly – he's in this up to his neck.'

'I've seen Hart,' Tingley said. 'And we're here. Drive past the house, Bob.'

We'd reached an imposing Elizabethan farm-house, alone on the road, with a wide drive to one side of it. I noticed that lights were on in various parts of the house. I drove about a hundred yards past it and pulled into a passing point.

'You've seen Hart? And?'

'Not now, Bob.'

I sighed.

'So what do we do?'

'We go up and knock on the door,' Gilchrist said.

'What if he won't see us?' I said.

Tingley just grinned.

Somebody rapped on Kate's door. She had a fisheye lens set in it. She looked through it but nobody was there. The chain was on but she didn't open the door. Her heart thumping, she stayed with her eye glued to the fisheye. Still nobody there. She retreated to her sofa but couldn't take her eyes off her door. All she could think, however, was that to knock on her door you had to get through the locked outer door to the whole house.

She phoned Watts.

'This is not a good time,' I said when I heard Kate's voice. Tingley was straddling Connolly, Gilchrist was over by the window looking out, rubbing her chin. Connolly was struggling to get his breath. Tingley punched him again, very precisely. Connolly's breath bubbled in his throat.

'Enough now, Jimmy. You've made your point.'

'Have I?' he said, slapping Connolly across the face. 'Do you feel I have, Billy boy?'

'Fuck you,' Connolly spluttered.

'Tough guy,' Tingley said, drawing his fist back.

'Enough.' Gilchrist this time, striding across

from the window to grab Tingley's arm.

Tingley kept his arm raised but didn't try to get out of Gilchrist's grip. Instead he reached down with his other hand and smoothed Connolly's hair. After this oddly gentle gesture, he drew himself off Connolly and, in the same fluid movement, stood upright. In the process, with a quick twist and shake, he freed his arm from Gilchrist's grip.

Gilchrist grasped at thin air and looked momentarily bemused as she watched Tingley go to sit on a narrow sofa. Connolly lay on the floor beside Gilchrist, his chest heaving. He gave her a malignant look.

He pulled himself to a sitting position, all his weight on his right arm. His left arm hung useless by his side. His face was engorged with blood, his eyes bulging. He looked over at Tingley, who ignored him, fixing his own eyes on the stacks of DVDs beside the rogue policeman's giant plasma screen.

Connolly had readily let us in but then had taken offence at something Gilchrist had said and lunged at her. Tingley had intervened, and before I had even begun to react, Connolly was on the floor.

'Someone has been trying to get into my flat,' Kate was saying in my ear.

'Call the police. No, wait.' I called to Gilchrist. 'Is Reg on shift now?'

'How would I know?' She saw my look, thought for a minute. 'I think so.'

I handed her my phone.

'Give Kate his mobile number. And tell her

271

we'll be over as soon as we're finished here.'

I'd doubted the value of fronting Connolly. We weren't going to strong-arm him into telling us anything. Tingley felt the same. He'd been monitoring Connolly and his colleague, White. But Gilchrist had been keen to confront him. And confront him she had.

'You murdering scum,' she'd said the minute we'd got into the house. Not the most tactful opening gambit and the reason everything had kicked off.

'What the fuck do you all want?' Connolly rasped, his voice hoarse. The open-handed blow to the throat does that to the voice box. The bubbling breath was the consequence of that and the punch in the diaphragm. The temporarily useless left arm was a nerve thing: Tingley's precise attacks on the elbow and that bundle of nerve endings just below the shoulder joint. Connolly would be feeling major pins and needles soon. Then a lot of pain.

'We want to know what happened at Milldean the night that everybody got shot. What was behind it?'

'You're Watts, aren't you?' Connolly said as he pushed himself up on one arm to his feet. He went over to a big armchair and dropped into it. 'Mr High and Mighty.'

'Why did you steal that phone from the kitchen?' Gilchrist said.

Connolly bared his gappy teeth.

'What is this – amateur hour? If I have something to disclose, don't you think you should approach it with a bit more subtlety? Asking me

272

straight out ain't going to get you anywhere.'

I agreed with him. Even so, I said:

'We're on a clock. No time for subtlety.' I waved my arm around the large room. 'Nice place. Must have cost a bob or two. You must be good at handling your copper's salary.'

'That's subtle. It's Bob, isn't it? Are you thinking you were one of the bobs who paid for it?'

Tingley snorted. I looked over at him but he still seemed to be focusing on the DVD collection, tilting his head to read spines. Connolly looked over at him.

'Anything you fancy, feel free to borrow it.' Connolly's voice was getting stronger. 'You're handy, by the way. I'll remember that for next time.'

'Won't do you any good,' Tingley murmured.

'What was that?' Connolly said, leaning forward, belligerent again.

'I said I can't see your ultra-violent gay rom-coms – I'm guessing you keep them in the bedroom.'

'Let's go,' Gilchrist said, heading for the door.

'We've only just got here,' I said.

'This was a mistake. My fault. Asshole isn't going to tell us anything. He doesn't realize he's next.'

'Oh, here they are,' Tingley said. *Reservoir Ducks. Lock, Stock and Mockney Cockney. Gay Gangs of New York.* The whole gay gangsters-r-us collection. You must have *The Very Dirty Dozen* and *The Quite Wild Bunch* in your bedside cupboard.'

273

'What do you mean I'm next?' Connolly said.

'He's not stupid,' I said. 'He knows what's what.'

'Somebody is knocking off the shooters,' Gilchrist said. 'And assuming it's not you – because you're too much of a blunt instrument – then you're on the list. My flat was firebombed.'

'That's just pest control,' Connolly said, but it was clear his heart wasn't in it. He rubbed his dead arm, gave Tingley another look. Then he turned to me.

'You should know more than me what's going on, Chief Constable. Ex-Chief Constable, I mean.'

'Why would I?'

Connolly looked at me and shook his head.

'Don't treat me like an idiot.'

'That's a tough call,' Tingley said.

'You're next,' Gilchrist repeated, standing over Connolly. 'Being a policeman won't protect you.'

'Yeah?' he said. 'I'll take my chances. Besides, I'm retiring on health grounds. Going into the security business.'

'Anyone else retiring?' I said.

Connolly shrugged.

'Whoever is still alive,' he said.

Kate's bell rang again. This time it was the outer door.

'Hello?'

'DS Reg Williamson from the Brighton nick,' a tinny voice said. She recognized the name from Sarah Gilchrist. She buzzed him in.

274

He was a lardy man, pasty-faced, but with something sympathetic in his eyes. He smelt of sweat and tobacco in about equal proportions.

'Somebody has been trying to get into your flat,' he said.

Kate told him what had happened.

'Well, there's no sign of forced entry on the front door of the house, but then another flat could have buzzed someone in. There is nobody in the common parts of the house now. I'll check the other flats to see if they have a guest who rang your bell by mistake.'

Kate double-locked the door behind him. Her phone rang while he was out. Watts.

'We're on our way,' he said.

Gilchrist was kicking herself for persuading the others to go to Connolly's place. It hadn't done any good. Hadn't even made her feel better – which, if she were honest, had been the point of it. She realized she needed to wait for what Gary Parker was going to say, wait for more on Little Stevie, maybe talk to Philippa Franks. She sensed from what Connolly had said that the investigation was going to be shelved.

She watched the road ahead and cursed herself until Tingley started talking about his conversation with Hart.

'Hart was a student here. Drunken encounter with a married woman on a hen night – this was back in the day when you did a pub crawl in your own town, not in Prague or Budapest or the south of France. Thinks no more about it. Does his degree, goes off, eventually settles back

275

down here, gets in the papers a bit once he's involved in local politics.

'This woman gets in touch with him out of the blue about their son. She's a divorcee now; life hasn't been kind to her.'

'She blackmails him?' Watts said.

'I think you mean she asks for the financial support to which she's entitled,' Gilchrist said.

'Hart goes down the DNA route,' Tingley said, ignoring them both. 'Quietly, because he's married with family.'

'Then he coughs up?' Watts says.

'To be fair, it doesn't sound like this woman is trying to screw him – financially, I mean – but Gary as a teenager is a handful so she has a lot on her plate. When Gary is a bit older, she asks Hart to pay for the rent on a flat for him. Hart agrees.'

'Is that when Gary figures out who his father is?' Gilchrist said.

'Not immediately,' Tingley said. 'But, yes, the flat is in the name of one of Hart's companies, and at some unspecified point Gary figures it out.'

'He blackmails Winston Hart?' Watts says.

'Apparently not.'

Gilchrist pondered for a moment.

'So, actually, this doesn't take us anywhere. Gary Parker isn't suggesting that Winston Hart had anything to do with the Milldean thing, is he?'

'You tell us,' Watts said, glancing towards her. 'You're the one who's spoken to Gary Parker.'

'I'm now wondering if his mention of his

276

father and his claiming knowledge of the massacre are actually linked, as I had assumed,' she said glumly.

'So long as he can tell us about the massacre, we don't necessarily need the bigger picture straight away,' Tingley said.

'I do if Hart was involved in setting me up.'

'Jesus, Bob, will you forget that conspiracy stuff.'

Watts shot a look at Tingley. Tingley shot it back.

'I pushed Hart about what might have been going on behind the massacre. He told me that he had a call from your friend Simpson the night before the meeting at which you resigned. But it was just to tell him about the package Hart could offer if you agreed to resign and that Simpson would phone during the meeting.'

'Did he know William before then?' Watts asked.

'That didn't come up.'

Gilchrist was thinking about the man who had threatened Kate. It couldn't be to do with the Trunk Murders. It had to be linked to something in the present – but was it necessarily the Milldean massacre?

'He was just pushing you to resign, wasn't he?' Gilchrist said. 'You don't suspect him of anything else, surely?'

Watts didn't answer. Instead, he put his foot on the accelerator.

Heading back to Brighton, I was sticking pretty much to the outside lane, going too fast as usual.

277

Gilchrist was sitting beside me, Tingley behind her. I'd slow to get past a cluster of cars then watch in my rear-view mirror as their headlights faded. Occasionally, I know, I tailgated when drivers were slow to move into the middle lane.

Men, once they had grudgingly given way, immediately accelerated in the middle lane to make it difficult for me to overtake. Once I'd overtaken, they'd slow to the speed they actually wanted to be doing.

I was thinking about William Simpson. I'd assumed he was the messenger from a government that wanted me to resign, but perhaps he was the one pushing for me to go for his own reasons. I was also trying to figure out how this threat to his daughter, Kate, fitted into the story.

'Is this police driving?' Tingley said.

'It's the driving of a man used to having a chauffeur,' Gilchrist said.

'There's a kind of method in it,' I said.

'Which is?' Tingley said.

'We're being followed.'

There was this one car. I'd been aware of it for some time. I assumed it was a male driver I'd passed who'd booted up to show he had a penis too. Except he was keeping back maybe half a mile and he was keeping the same pace as me.

Didn't waiver.

I'd lose sight of him on long looping bends, but once we hit a straight there he'd be, maintaining a constant pace, keeping the same distance behind.

I drove faster. This car did too. I drove slower. It came nearer then stayed in place.

We hit a few hundred yards of overhead lights.

'The dark Rover?' Tingley said. I nodded. 'You're thinking he's armed?'

'Maybe,' I said. 'Are you?'

In the rear-view mirror I saw him shake his head.

'I'm a police officer, for God's sake,' Gilchrist said. 'We don't need to run away.'

'I suspect whoever this is doesn't respect the law,' Tingley said.

'It may be my paranoia,' I said.

The logical part of me was thinking: why the hell should they be following us? What benefit can they gain? They must know we're going back to Brighton. But I was also conscious of Kate being threatened, of Gilchrist's flat being firebombed.

Tingley was watching out of the back window.

'No, he's following and he wants us to know he's following.'

'Can you get his registration?' I said.

'It's masked.'

'Naturally.'

'It always happens in badly scripted films,' Gilchrist said. 'There's never a good reason for following someone except to inject a bit of false excitement into the story.'

'I think in this case it's intended to intimidate,' Tingley said.

'But who is it?' Gilchrist said.

'That's the interesting question,' I said. 'Shall I try to draw them in?'

'How?' Tingley said.

'I haven't the faintest idea.'

The road narrowed to two lanes just after the signs for Burgess Hill. A car had pulled out in front of the car that was tagging us. I went into a couple of sharp bends faster than I should have. I accelerated up the hill on the other side of the last bend.

There was a turn-off at the top of the hill where the road again went into a couple of – more gentle – curves. If I could take the turn off before he came out of the last of the bends, our pursuer would, I hoped, think I was still on the A23 into Brighton. He would carry on and I could come back on to the road behind him.

I came off OK, went across a short bridge and took the slip-road back on to the Brighton road. I stopped on the slip-road about twenty yards short of the A23 and switched off my lights.

'Clever boy,' Tingley murmured.

The Rover went barrelling by a few moments later. I waited until it had gone round the next bend then pulled back on to the A23.

'Headlights on or off?' Tingley said.

'On, I think – we're going to hit overhead lights soon anyway so we can't really hide. I'm just hoping he won't notice us.'

It took a couple of miles to get within sight of the Rover. It had slowed, presumably because its occupants thought we'd come off the road and given them the slip. We came into the lighted area near Pyecombe service station and I dropped back. It would go dark again for the last couple of miles before hitting the outskirts of Brighton.

'The rear registration is masked too,' Ting-

280

ley noted.

We were about a quarter of a mile behind the Rover so lost it through the next couple of bends. When we came on to the long, straight stretch just outside Brighton, I drew nearer.

'You're going to have to close up for the roundabout,' Tingley said. 'He has three options there.'

'I know it,' I said. This was the tricky bit – not losing them without them noticing us.

I drew to within two hundred yards of them. I'd been hoping for more traffic so there could be cars in between us. With luck he would only be aware of our headlights when the overhead lights resumed at the roundabout.

The Rover slid left into the lanes that went on to the road to Hove and Worthing. I stayed in a Brighton lane for the time being. I saw lights on full beam close in behind me, then a big four-by-four overtook me on the inside lane, heading for Hove and Worthing.

I eased in behind the four-by-four. It hid me from the Rover but it also, I realized too late, hid the Rover from me. Just when I was fully committed to taking the Worthing road, I saw that the Rover had moved back on to the Brighton road and was heading for the roundabout.

'Shit,' I said. 'Watch where he's going.'

Tingley and Gilchrist were both straining to see as my lane took me round a tight sweep of bend.

'Couldn't see,' Tingley said.

'Nor me,' Gilchrist added.

At the small roundabout ahead I swept back on

to the loop that would take me down to the main roundabout. I would have two choices there.

'What do you think?'

'Head straight into Brighton,' Gilchrist said and Tingley grunted agreement. I took the left into Brighton but couldn't see the Rover on the long road ahead of us.

'Let's get to Kemp Town,' Tingley said.

Kate was alone when Watts, Tingley and Gilchrist arrived at her flat. Reg Williamson had left about half an hour earlier. Kate had liked him. She had been comforted by his shabby presence.

'Detective Sergeant Williamson told me about your flat,' Kate said to Gilchrist as she handed out coffees. 'I've a spare room here if you'd like to stay.'

'That might not be a bad idea, in the circumstances,' Watts said.

'If you're sure?' Gilchrist said.

'It would be great,' Kate said. 'Theoretically, it's my parents' room but they never stay here. I'll dig out the spare keys and show you the magic that makes the lock work later.'

'OK, well, I'm going to go,' Watts said. 'Give you a lift, Jimmy?'

'What's the plan for tomorrow?' Kate said. 'I'm going to go up to the National Archive to look at police files for the Trunk Murder.'

She sensed that nobody else was particularly interested in the cold case just at the moment. To be honest, she wasn't either but she felt she needed to persevere. And she was thinking that when in London she might call in on her father.

'I'm getting back to Hathaway, see if he has anything for us,' Tingley said.

'I'm on shift but I'm going to see if I have anything of my flat left,' Gilchrist said. 'And I'm going to talk to Philippa Franks.'

Only when Watts and Jimmy had left did Kate realize that Watts hadn't said anything about his own plans.

SIXTEEN

Gilchrist was still waiting for word of a potential deal with Gary Parker. He had been interviewed again twice in her absence but had refused to say anything more until he got his deal. Somebody was stalling – maybe somebody was putting pressure on Acting Chief Constable Sheena Hewitt.

Gilchrist wondered if Winston Hart at the Police Authority was also putting pressure on Hewitt to make the deal for his son. But maybe he was just worrying about the scandal when the press found out about his connection to a sick killer.

She sat at her desk looking out of the window at the rain sheeting down. It was only 6.30 a.m. and she was waiting until a more civilized time to phone Philippa Franks to arrange to meet. She wouldn't be put off this time.

She'd come into work via her flat. She'd stood on the pavement and looked at the boarded-up windows. She'd been renting so had no emotional attachment to the place but she was pissed off about her belongings. There wasn't much there of personal significance. She was pissed off because she hated shopping and was going to have to hit the high street today to get some clothes.

Kate had offered to lend her anything she needed, but Gilchrist couldn't see herself getting into Kate's clothes.

Now, sipping at her too-hot coffee, she thought about the man who had been shot in the kitchen. She could believe that there was nothing sinister about his death, that a sniper had simply reacted too quickly, perhaps because he thought the object in the man's hand was a gun. But who was he?

Could he have been the man who had actually been watching the house? Gilchrist had assumed that person had been a policeman, but perhaps the watcher was Edward's snitch. But why was he inside the house? So he could be clear where everybody was? Was he in direct touch with Macklin, the gold commander, just before the raid, or was he in contact with Foster, the silver commander actually in charge of the operation? Were either men in on it or were they being fed false information?

So many questions. Still too few answers.

She'd been patient enough. She phoned Philippa Franks just before seven a.m.

* * *

Kate took an early train up to Victoria then the District Line to Kew. It seemed to take forever. She dozed on the first and yawned on the second. At Kew she walked down a quiet street of Victorian terraced houses to the National Archives. The building was on a kind of shopping estate so first she nipped into M&S on the site to buy a healthy lunch. She also bought some underwear for herself and guessed at Sarah's size to get some knickers for her. Bras were a little more complicated.

In the archives she called up her files then went outside to sit on one of the benches by the lake. She ate her sandwich watching the ducks dipping for food. She looked up at the blue sky and the plump white clouds. It was so peaceful, so ordered.

She sighed and looked at her notes. There were only two files she hadn't already seen. They referred to a Director of Public Prosecution's proposed action against a policeman for leaking information to the press about the Brighton Trunk Murder. This, Kate felt sure, was her anonymous narrator.

She was wrong. When she went back in and got settled with the files she saw that the first DPP file was about a man called Bowden, a policeman for twenty-seven years, head of Hove CID for thirteen years.

He'd established a relationship with a freelance journalist called Lindon Laing. Kate knew that name from the memoir. Under duress, Laing told the Brighton Chief Constable 'Hutch' Hutchinson that Bowden had already leaked a story to him some years earlier about somebody called Major Bailey, so Laing thought he'd ask him about the Trunk Murder. When Laing was asked if anyone else close to the investigation had been feeding him stories, he said no.

Kate paused for a moment. So when the anonymous memoirist had been summoned to Hutchinson's office after the Chief Constable's lecture about leaks, it might not have been about his relationship with Laing. What, then?

She read on. Laing said he had asked Bowden about the Trunk Murder on the afternoon of 30th October 1934 – the day the CID man was retiring from the police force. Unfortunately for Bowden, he was still on his final shift when that night's *Evening News* came out. Laing's story was splashed on the front page with the headline, 'I know the man'. Laing had quoted Bowden saying he knew who the killer was.

Bowden insisted he hadn't told Laing anything he shouldn't have done, that he had in fact told him he didn't think they'd ever find the culprit.

Kate looked at another document, an opinion from a barrister, dated 12th November, about whether Bowden could be prosecuted for public mischief. According to this, Bowden had been 'trying to curry favour with the newspaper because they had agreed to buy his memoirs after his retirement'.

Another document suggested that the man Bowden had referred to was a suspect called William Augustus Offord of 152 Fortess Road, Kentish Town. He came under suspicion very early because his handwriting was similar to that

286

on the paper 'and he had known immoral associations with a number of young women'.

This was clearly hokum. Not the existence of Offord – she was sure he was real enough. But she knew from her other reading that the words on the paper had not been written by the killer.

The second file was much thinner, containing only a few sheets of flimsy paper. The first sheet was a memo dated April 1935. A policeman in Reigate sent it to Pelling, Brighton's head of CID, with a letter from an unemployed nurse attached. She was asking the police to locate the present whereabouts of a friend of hers. This friend had worked as a cook and housekeeper for a doctor in Hove who had also employed the nurse.

The nurse claimed that her friend had disappeared and was pretty much suggesting that the doctor might have done away with her. Kate guessed that the nurse had a grudge against the doctor – she assumed she was unemployed because he had fired her. But his name drew her attention. Dr Edward Seys Massiah of 8 Brunswick Square, Hove.

Dr Massiah. Kate didn't realize she was tapping her pencil on the desk until a man nearby cleared his throat. She put the pencil down. Dr Massiah. She was remembering the start of the memoir. The writer saying that he had taken his girlfriend, Frenchy, to a doctor in Hove. Kate realized she'd been holding her breath and slowly exhaled. The writer had referred to the doctor as Dr M.

* * *

287

'Hello, Lizzy.'

Lizzy Simpson, William's wife and Kate's mother, looked at me in a calculating way. I'd always found her chilly. When I had status I always felt she simply tolerated me. I believed she was actually a sociopath, unable to empathize with other humans, so that in order to fit in she forever had to conjure up the simulacra of emotions she didn't know how to feel.

I could see she was trying to figure out how she was supposed to be with me. She'd known me a long time. We were, by nature of my friendship with her husband, supposedly close. But I was no longer high status, no longer potentially useful. Rather the reverse.

I wondered if her husband had briefed her against me. I smiled as the word 'briefed' popping into my head in relation to a husband talking to a wife. In their case, I'm sure that was exactly how they conducted business.

She mistook my smile and pasted one on her own face for just an instant. Her sourness had affected her undoubted beauty. Her mouth turned down at the edges, her skin was taut against her high cheekbones. Her pursuit of thinness had made her gaunt. The cords of her neck were hawsers, her legs were sticks.

I was two steps down from her so our eyes were at the same level.

'Bob. How nice. Is William expecting you?'

'I doubt it.'

She turned, throwing over her shoulder:

'I'll tell him you're here.'

'I assume I don't need to wait on the doorstep.'

She didn't reply.

I went into the wide hallway. I hadn't been in this house for several years but nothing seemed to have changed. Period prints in heavy frames on the walls, stripped pine floor and staircase, waxed not varnished, of course. Opulent flowers on a table – lilies and some exotic succulents.

I went into the sitting room to my left. Marble fireplace with a log fire laid but not lit. Two deep sofas with scatter cushions in expensive fabrics laid across them. Two floor-to- ceiling windows looking over the square.

Some of their art was on the walls. Lizzy liked BritArt. They had a small, early Damian Hirst just inside the door. There was a collage made of elephant dung and discarded snake skins by an artist whose name I had forgotten.

I walked to the window. How could someone who was essentially a public relations guy afford to live in one of these multimillion-pound Holland Park villas? Had he done a Mandelson and borrowed money from one of the party's generous friends? Well, that was a question but not one of the ones I intended to ask.

'He'll be down in a moment.'

Lizzy's voice was as tight as her face. She sat on the sofa at the far side of the room, bony knees together.

'I hear you've been seeing a lot of our daughter.'

I sank into the sofa opposite. She pointed at the lapel of my jacket.

'You'll never get that pollen off.' I looked at the brown dust from the lilies I didn't realize I'd brushed against.

'We've been working together on something.'

'Her men aren't normally as old as you.' Her smile was mocking. 'Though her women sometimes are.'

I let that go, though I realized I hadn't given Kate's sexuality a single thought – why would I?

'How's work, Lizzy? Got some interesting projects?'

'I'm doing a couple of tellies, a few profiles. But I've been commissioned to write a novel.'

'Sex and sleaze in Westminster?'

'Naturally. *Très* discreet, though.'

'I didn't think those books were supposed to be discreet.'

'Well, you know – relatively speaking.'

'Bob – what a surprise.'

Simpson was standing in the doorway. He didn't come forward to greet me, I didn't stand.

Lizzy uncoiled from the sofa.

'Lovely to see you, Bob.'

Simpson closed the door behind his wife and replaced her on the sofa.

'I can't do anything for you, you know,' he said. 'You made your own bed.'

'Other people tucked me in.'

Simpson's mouth twitched in slight acknowledgement of a smile. I hadn't really noticed until now how sinister he looked. That Prince of Darkness tag that used to be applied to spin doctors certainly applied to the way he looked now. His hair had gone grey but his eyebrows and goatee beard were black. His mouth was an ungenerous slash.

I thought about how pretty and warm his daughter was. How come?

'You've been seeing a lot of my daughter,' he said, reading my thoughts.

'So I gather. You know she's been threatened because of you.'

'What?'

'You know. Don't pretend you don't. What are you into? Is it linked to the Milldean mess?'

Simpson looked at me, then out of the window. He pouted a little.

'It's none of your business, Bob. Let me just say that it was a misunderstanding.'

'*Was?* Does that mean you've got it sorted.'

Simpson always had a poker face. Like most politicos, you could never tell what he was really thinking. But I thought I saw something in his eyes.

'She's still in danger, isn't she?'

'Absolutely not,' he said.

'But it's not sorted.'

'Just a little local difficulty, Bob, that's all.'

'Tell me about Little Stevie.'

'Who's Little Stevie?' he said, looking genuinely puzzled.

'One of the victims. The one who was shot sitting on the loo.'

'Can't help you there. Why would you think I'd know?'

'He was a rent boy of some sort.'

'I repeat my question.'

'Was it blackmail? Are you still being blackmailed – did your account just get passed on to somebody else when Little Stevie was killed?'

'Blackmailed about what?' Simpson uncrossed his legs and leant forward. 'Do you mean about my sexuality? You know I swing both ways – is that what you're referring to?'

Although we'd never talked about it, I did know. There was an occasion years ago when Simpson and I had gone one lunchtime to hear some free jazz in the ICA.

It had been too free, even for me, but it was summer and hot and the wine had flowed freely. When the wine ran out, we'd left together and as we were walking across St James's Park in the heat of the afternoon he said: 'This is the kind of day to have a cool shower then spend the rest of the afternoon in bed with somebody.'

I laughed and nodded my head.

'Shall we?' he said.

I laughed again and gestured to the people sitting on the grass.

'Who did you have in mind?'

He looked at me for a moment.

'I was thinking you and me.'

It hung there as we threaded our way between the sunbathers. I remember distinctly wondering what the fuck I could say to that. I liked the guy but I wasn't interested in sex with him. As best I recall, I pretended that we were just joking.

'Another time, gorgeous,' I probably said.

'You're on,' he definitely said.

It was never referred to again.

Simpson laughed now without warmth.

'I still remember your face as you attempted to fend me off without hurting my feelings. Price-less.'

'I think you knew Little Stevie,' I said

He gestured with his hands.

'Prove it.' He leant forward again. 'Bob, let me give you some advice. Forget this obsession about the massacre. Get what remains of your life back together. Do your little radio spot about the Trunk Murders—'

'You're offering me career advice?'

I was pushing down the anger. I hated his imperturbability, hated the fact he'd been part of the train wreck of my recent life. My wife may have been right – I was looking for someone to blame because I wasn't willing to take the responsibility myself. Maybe so, but I felt justified in focusing on my former friend. My anger seethed because I couldn't see how to get him.

'Your daughter is a good girl.'

'Yes. Sometimes the apple falls far from the tree. She's tediously good. Does she ever have fun?'

'Lizzy suggested she was bisexual too.'

'There's a lot of it about. Family tradition. My father swung both ways. He liked the theatricals. A lot of married actors liked to go backstage, so to speak. He had flings with Olivier and Michael Redgrave, to hear him tell it. Maybe with your father too – who knows?'

'Does Lizzy know? That you're bisexual? Would it upset the apple cart at home if it came out?'

He snorted.

'You obviously haven't met her friend Erica.' He sighed. 'Bob, I have no idea why you've come today. I'm truly sorry your career has gone down the pan. I can understand your lashing out. But lashing out at me will achieve nothing but more grief.'

'So far as that goes, I know you're somehow involved. Maybe you were actually the one pushing for me to be fired. What I don't understand is that I thought we were friends. Why screw me over?'

'Ah, yes – friendship. Forged in youth, tempered in battle and all that. But don't you think we were pushed together by circumstances? Our fathers. Do you even know how our fathers met?'

I shook my head.

'In Brighton in the thirties. They were in the police force together.'

'I know that,' I said.

'Ask your father about it.'

I didn't respond. He sighed.

'You and me – we never really had much in common, except the odd girlfriend. Politics and police – they don't mix well, you know.'

He got up in one fluid motion from the sofa.

'Bob. I saw you as a courtesy. There's nothing here for you. If you try to embroil me in this, I say only one thing. Hunker down.'

I walked over to him. We were of a height but I was broader. I stood closer to him than he liked. I wanted to hit him, wanted to pummel him back into his soft sofa. He saw it in my eyes and stepped back. He didn't take his eyes off me, though.

'You're out of your depth, Bob. Let it go. Accept your fate.'

I moved past him, opened the door and went out into the hall. As I swung open the front door, I called back:

'Never.'

Which was a reasonable parting line, except that I hadn't a clue what I could do to change things.

Tingley pressed the doorbell and heard it ring somewhere in the back of the house. He looked across at the Union Jack fluttering on top of the tall flagpole stuck in the middle of the impeccable front lawn. He shook his head. Tongdean Drive.

A small, neat man opened the door and stepped aside to allow Tingley to enter. Neither man said anything. Another, bigger man was waiting in the wide hallway to lead Tingley through to the back of the house.

Hathaway was sitting in a faux-Victorian conservatory which looked out over a long stretch of garden, mostly given over to another neat lawn. Tingley presumed that the building at the bottom of the garden housed a swimming pool.

The gangster, in cashmere pullover and neatly pressed blue slacks, didn't rise but gestured to a seat opposite him. Tingley sat, aware that the man who'd led him here was standing just behind him.

There was a sports programme playing on a massive TV screen. Hathaway pressed the remote and turned to Tingley.

'So have you figured out what's in it for me, Mr Tingley?'

Tingley shrugged.

'My eternal gratitude.'

Hathaway leant forward and smiled a brilliant smile.

'Now that's worth something if, as I'm assuming, your gratitude is a liquid currency?'

Tingley shook his head.

'It doesn't change into anything more concrete, if that's what you mean.'

'Shame – that's exactly what I mean.' Hathaway eased back into his seat. 'Then I don't see exactly how I can help you.'

'You've checked my references.'

'But you don't want a job.' Hathaway grinned again. 'Do you?'

'You know what I mean.'

'I know that – as best I can gather – you have been a very bad boy on your government's behalf. Very bad. Tsk, tsk. I know that your friends and my friends in the shadow world are about equal. I don't know that I can tell you anything you don't already know.'

Tingley looked up and behind at the man standing guard over him.

'Do you think I could have a glass of water?'

The man looked at Hathaway.

'Yeah, I'll have a beer and a bowl of chips – tell the cook.' He looked at Tingley. 'Beer better?'

Tingley shook his head.

'Next time,' he said.

Hathaway gestured at the man's retreating back.

'He wasn't a threat to you, you know. Or

296

protection for me. Knowing what I know about you, if you came here to take me out, there'd be little he or I could do about it.' Hathaway patted his chest. 'I don't carry a weapon. I'm no longer into chop suey or any of that Bruce Lee shit.'

'Nor I,' Tingley said quietly.

'What is your martial art of choice? Just out of interest. That Brazilian thing? I hear the Hindi system is pretty effective.'

Tingley shook his head.

'It's an Israeli thing – a street-fighting thing.'

Hathaway smiled with his perfect teeth again.

'The Jews have a *mano a mano* self-defence system?' He laughed coarsely. 'I assume it's a post-World War Two thing. Back then it was grovelling and pleading, wasn't it?'

Tingley simply looked at him. Hathaway continued to chuckle then said:

'Tingley, I play consequences. You're a bright guy, you've figured that out. That's why I know I can send my boy out of the room and I'm going to be safe from you, despite what you did to Cuthbert – who is straining at the leash to do terrible things to you, might I note.'

'Consequences?'

Hathaway pointed a finger at Tingley. 'You harm me and you lose – in ways too horrendous to describe on such a sunny day – every single person related to you or close to you. Every person remotely connected to you. Every person who remotely knows you. Every person you passed in the street today.'

'The Colombian way,' Tingley said.

Hathaway shrugged.

'Them and others. Colombian drug-dealers, Russian mafia, Albanian headbangers, ex-IRA psychopaths, Serb war criminals turned villains – a bloody United Nations of sick crooks have transformed the nature of violence in the UK. We home-grown boys have got to big up to keep up.' He shrugged again. 'Nature of the beast. Capitalism, that is. The unacceptable face of.'

Hathaway's man returned with a tray and handed Tingley a glass of water. As Tingley took a long drink, the man put a pint glass of beer, a bowl of chips and salt and pepper on the table. Tingley drained his glass and handed it back.

'Thanks.'

Hathaway pushed the bowl of chips towards him. Tingley shook his head. Hathaway put the salt and pepper in the ashtray and pushed them to the other side of the table.

'You have a problem with condiments?' Tingley said.

'Only the word.' A smile at the corners of Hathaway's mouth didn't make it any further. 'I'm a recovering saltaholic. Don't ever bring crisps into my presence.'

Tingley waited as Hathaway tucked in.

'OK, I'm going to give you something,' Hathaway said through a mouthful of chips. 'Just so you'll go away. You poking about is potentially bad for business. There's a delicate balance and I don't want you upsetting it.' He reached for his glass of beer. 'Never got this modern thing about drinking from the bottle. Disgusting habit. Got it from the Aussies, who are, by and large, a disgusting people. I happen to have it on good authority they shag kangaroos.'

'Wouldn't the tail get in the way? Even supposing they could catch up with one?'

Hathaway's eyes glinted.

'Maybe it's koala bears. My point remains the same.'

'Only the country is different,' Tingley said. 'Could you get to the point? I'm not getting any younger.'

Hathaway's smile was at half-wattage.

'There's a close relationship – you might call it a synergy, if you were so inclined – between some local politicians, some national politicians, local criminal entrepreneurs such as myself, elements of Her Majesty's constabulary and those government employees who live in the shadow world.'

'I gathered that much.'

'That terrible business at Milldean was a settling of certain scores and the removal of a threat. Threats plural, to be precise.'

'Threats to whom?'

'That would be telling – because that's where that delicate balance comes in.'

Tingley made a stop sign with his hand.

'Are you going to be specific or are we going to go round in circles again?'

'I can't be specific –' Tingley started to get out of his chair – 'but I know a man who can.'

Tingley sat back, aware the man behind him had moved nearer.

'Multiple threats,' Tingley said. 'That doesn't scan at all.'

Hathaway shrugged.

'You have a better theory?

'I've got a question. If what you say is true, who is bumping off all the police?'

Hathaway wagged a finger.

'That would be telling.'

'And who threatened William Simpson's daughter, Kate?'

'William Simpson. Now there's a name to conjure with.'

'Well, show me the bloody rabbit in the hat, then.'

Hathaway took another handful of chips.

'I don't believe you one little bit,' Tingley said.

Hathaway chewed. He had strong jaws and ate quickly.

'Look,' he said. 'I think you need to talk to a government department I know you're familiar with. They'll have the skinny.' Hathaway wiped his mouth with his napkin. 'I have a number you should call.'

Anna opened the door to my father's house. She was slim and petite with badly bleached blonde hair and a pale face. There were dark rings under her eyes but she smiled cheerfully when she saw me and led me upstairs into the sitting room. He was by his broad bay window, feet up on a stool, half-hidden by the wings of his big chair.

My father didn't get up as I walked over but he watched me, his head tilted, and gave a little smile. He indicated the wingback chair opposite his.

'Is Anna getting you coffee?'

I nodded.

'You're becoming a regular visitor.'

I sat and got straight to it.

'We're investigating the Brighton Trunk Murder,' I said.

'Gives you something to do, I suppose,' my father said. He dabbed his mouth with a white handkerchief. I looked at the liver spots on the big hand, the thick purple veins, the fingers bent to the side by arthritis.

'Who was she, Dad?'

'A tart. Violette somebody. Man who did it got off, God knows how. Mancini also known as Notyre. Went round the music halls after he got off doing a show where he sawed a woman in half. Very bad taste. Used to brag to people how he'd done it and got off. Publicly admitted it later – thirty years after – in the press.'

'Not that murder,' I said. 'The first one. The one the police never solved.'

'That lass. Found her legs in London, rest of her in Brighton. With them two murders Brighton got a new nickname: the queen of slaughtering places.'

'That's right. You were a policeman then, weren't you? Alongside William Simpson's dad.'

My father had scarcely talked about that phase of his life. I didn't know until I was well into my twenties that he'd even been a policeman.

He turned his head to me awkwardly. It seemed like it was on a stalk, his body still facing forward. Looking both robust – the shoulders and the paunch – and puny – the bony wrists and the scrawny neck.

'A bogie, aye. That's a part of my past I prefer

not to recall. Didn't want that life but in those days you did what jobs you could get. The police force is just like any organization. They use you then they cast you off.' He looked at me. 'You know that now.'

'Why did you leave?'

'No advancement if you weren't from the officer class. Lot of tedium, boredom.'

'I thought you were forced to resign.'

He looked straight ahead. He made an odd clicking noise in the back of his throat.

'It were thought best.' He nodded, forming extra chins with loose folds of skin around his jowls. 'Good thing I did. Best thing I did. It got me started writing, introduced me to a new way of life.'

'You did well.'

'I did well by you and your mother. Made your life possible.'

'Why did you resign?'

'Tuppeny 'apenny stuff. Nowt worth bothering about.'

'You were under suspicion for the Trunk Murder?'

'Don't be daft. Why would you think that?'

'Mum said you had an eye for the ladies.'

'Seems you inherited it.'

My dad had a fierce stare and when I was younger it had freaked me out. Even these days I usually couldn't hold it. However, my dad looked down first, at his clasped hands, mottled with age.

'You know the secret of getting women?' he finally said.

302

'Good looks, money and power?'

'I didn't have any of those things. No, what you look for is someone good looking who's obviously insecure. She'll probably have a certain way of walking, she'll touch herself on the hips or sometimes on her breasts. She's both sensual and insecure. Sow that wind and you'll reap a whirlwind right enough.'

'Dad, I'm not sure this is a proper conversation between father and son.'

'But you think accusing your dad of murder is proper?'

'I was just trying to find out. Secrets and lies, Dad – they get in the way of proper relationships.'

'I can imagine murder would too. Don't pontificate at me, Bobby. The genre I write in is predicated on secrets and lies. Usually family ones. But then at the end the secrets are revealed, the lies exposed.'

Anna came in with my coffee. My father watched her leave the room then turned back to me.

'Graham Greene was a suspect, you know.'

'Graham Greene was suspected of the Trunk Murder?'

'One of dozens, but yes. One of his fancy women shopped him.' He saw my quizzical look. 'He used to bring them down to Brighton at the weekend. Stayed at the Grand. That's when the razor gangs were around on the prom and up at the racecourse.'

'*Brighton Rock*?'

'Yes, though that didn't come out for a few

years – just before the war. I knew a maid who worked at the Grand. Told me the disgusting state he and his girlfriend of the moment left the sheets in.' He looked at me again. 'Apparently the famous writer was a back-door johnny. Can be a messy business.'

I felt squeamish hearing my dad talk about such things. I pushed away the thought of his sex life with my mother.

'How did that make him a suspect?'

'He was having nightmares about taking taxi rides with a woman's body in a trunk. A cast-off lover telephoned us.'

'Did you interview him?'

'No – too delicate a task for a junior. I was on guard in the interview room, though.'

I nodded.

'That's the first time you met him. Did you talk about the case when you met him later?'

'I told him at the Foyle's lunch I'd been a policeman in Brighton in the thirties and he brought it up.'

'What did he say?'

'Said he'd been questioned then asked me the same thing you keep asking me – did we know who did it?'

'And did you reply to him or were you as enigmatic as you are with me?'

My father pursed his lips but said nothing. I leant over and put my hand over his. It was impulsive but I also felt embarrassed. There had been little physical affection, or indeed contact, between the two of us over the years. My father looked down at my hand – big, long-fingered –

304

covering his own hand. A smile twitched at the corners of his mouth.

'Tell me, Dad, please.'

My father reached over with his other hand and patted mine on top of his.

'I don't think you really believe I've murdered anyone. So what did your mum tell you?'

'I told you,' I said, impatiently, defensively. 'She didn't. She hasn't poisoned me against you, Dad.' I ducked my head. 'You did that.'

I sighed.

'Tell me about your friendship with William Simpson's father.'

My father shrugged.

'We met in Brighton, on the force. He was more ambitious than me. Keen to get on – a high-flyer for those days. Like yourself. We got on well enough.'

'Did you both investigate the Trunk Murders?'

'That were over half a century ago, lad. How do you expect me to remember?'

'You remembered Graham Greene.'

'We were pals, I remember that. Pally enough that he told me once he played for both teams. Brighton opened my eyes to a lot of things, I can tell you that.' He scratched his chin. 'Why are you asking about him? You should be sorting out the mess that got you the sack, not bothering about some decades-old case nobody gives a toss about.'

I left some ten minutes later. I couldn't figure out how to take the conversation any further. I remember saying to him once:

'There's stuff we never talk about.'

He'd shut that approach right down.

'Too much talking these days,' he'd said quickly. His face cracked into a kind of grimacing smile. 'Too much *sharing*.'

I stepped out of his house on to the busy road and waited for a break in the traffic to cross to the river bank. I took a walk along the towpath. There were youngsters sculling on the river. Their coaches shouted instructions from little motorboats alongside them, the engines echoing across the water. I sat on a bench for ten minutes watching a long, grey heron, motionless on the thin stalks of its legs, in the shallows near the bank.

Dad had always been tough. At the age of seventy he'd still been stronger than me. Still arm-wrestled. All that macho stuff.

'You joined the army to please your dad,' Molly used to say. Bitterly.

True. I didn't want to become him, but when I was growing up I wanted his respect. It was hard won. If ever I got it.

I got the train at Barnes Bridge and changed at Clapham Junction for the Brighton train. As I walked across the echoing, roofed footbridge at Clapham, I pondered the route the killer might have taken if he'd come from London. And wondered, just for a moment, whether my father might know who the killer was.

SEVENTEEN

Philippa Franks had a flat in a rusting, paint-peeled sixties block on the seafront at the far end of Hove. Gilchrist drove down there late afternoon after her shift ended. She rang Philippa's bell then waited in her car. The rain had finally let up but the sky was grey and brooding.

'Thanks for seeing me,' Gilchrist said when Philippa slid into the passenger seat.

'Yeah, well...'

They didn't speak as Gilchrist drove to Shoreham and parked behind the Arts Centre. They walked in silence back down the High Street to a rambling old pub that backed on to the wide river estuary. It was late afternoon and the pub was quiet. They took their drinks into the little paved garden. The tide was out so they sat looking out over mud flats.

They chinked glasses and Gilchrist got started.

'I really need to know what happened upstairs in Milldean.'

'I don't know what happened, as I've already told you. And why have you got to know? You've got your job back.'

'Oh yeah, and promotion is just around the corner.'

'At least you're still in the police.'

307

She wasn't looking at Gilchrist.

'You're retiring on health grounds?'

'It's been offered. It's probably for the best. The shifts were making it difficult with the kids. My mum's great but you don't want to take advantage.'

'You have children?' Gilchrist said. 'I didn't know that.'

'I don't broadcast it. You know what organizations are like.'

'How old?'

'Emily's eleven, Jackson is nine.'

'Jackson – that's an unusual name.'

'My ex-partner's idea – I don't even want to get into why. You want kids?'

'Not yet,' Gilchrist said, perhaps a little too quickly. Franks glanced at her. Gilchrist continued: 'Was your partner the man I saw you arguing with in the veggie in Hove?'

Franks looked startled.

'You mean the organic place?'

Gilchrist nodded.

'No, that was someone else. Another relationship going south.'

'He looked nice.'

'He wasn't,' Franks said. She looked at Gilchrist almost warily. 'You were there? You heard us?'

Gilchrist flushed and shook her head.

'I was thinking of coming in, put my head in the door, saw you having this intense discussion and thought I'd better go elsewhere. It was just for a minute.'

Franks shook her head.

'Jesus. There's no privacy in Brighton.'

'Small place,' Sarah said.

'Small minds,' Franks said. She saw Gilchrist's look.

'Not you,' she added quickly. 'I hate this town. So smug, so full of itself but so parochial.'

She looked back over the glistening mud.

'Philippa – why won't you talk about what happened?'

'Why do you bloody think?'

'You shot someone?'

'I didn't shoot anybody.' She was fierce. 'So what do you mean: why do I bloody think?'

Franks swirled her wine in her glass. Gilchrist waited. Finally Franks looked at her, her mouth twisted in a curious expression of disgust.

'Because I'm a coward.' The words came out as an expulsion of breath. 'Look what's happened to Finch and Foster. I'm just a straightforward gal. I've got my kids to think about.'

'Can't you tell me who fired first?'

'If I did know who fired first, I wouldn't say. I've a feeling it wouldn't be healthy. But anyway, you know how those decisions go. A split second to decide, a lifetime to repent. Everybody was hyped. Someone started firing, everyone else joined in thinking they were in danger. It's hard not to go forward in those situations.'

Gilchrist thought for a moment.

'You know they torched my flat. Have you been threatened too?'

Franks nodded.

'Who?'

'Voice on the phone.' She sighed. 'Once you've got kids everything changes. They are your absolute priority. It shackles you.'

'There's no guarantee you or your children are safe even if you do keep quiet. It looks like whoever they are have decided to take no chances. All the deaths surrounding this case indicate that. The only way for you to be really safe is to go public.'

Philippa stared at her drink.

'At least tell me who went up the stairs first,' Gilchrist said.

Philippa swirled her drink round in her glass. Flat-voiced, she said:

'The big Haywards Heath guy went up first, the one with the teeth missing – Connolly. Then Finch, then White, then Harry Potter. I'm a mere woman so, of course, I brought up the rear.

'Connolly, White and Finch were supposed to go straight to the front of the house whilst Harry and me took care of the back bedroom and the bathroom. But White stumbled at the top of the stairs and his gun went off. He was blocking our way. Next thing I hear Finch – I think it's Finch – shout "This is an armed police raid", then almost immediately there's a volley of shots. I don't know how many – three or four, perhaps.

'By now White is back on his feet and heading to the front of the house. It's pandemonium. Everybody is hyped.' She drew a ragged breath. 'So then I heard a single shot along the corridor. All the shots were really loud in that confined space. My ears were ringing. I looked and Finch was standing in the bathroom doorway, lowering

310

his gun.'

She shook her head.

'And that was it. Your team came up the stairs and I was in the corridor, deaf and feeling sick.'

'So Finch shot Little Stevie in the bathroom.'

'Little Stevie?'

'That's the name of the victim. Some kind of rent boy.'

Franks looked at Gilchrist for a moment.

'A rent boy. Really?'

'Unusually, he doesn't have a record.'

'That is unusual.' Franks finished the rest of her drink. 'My round? I could do with another.'

'I'm driving. A tomato juice will do.'

Gilchrist watched Franks walk, stiff-shouldered, to the bar. Was she telling the truth?

Tingley's meeting at Gatwick was almost surreal. He met the contact from one of the intelligence services in a seedy cafe area near to Domestic Arrivals. The man had flown in from Edinburgh. He was tall, stoop-shouldered, in an elegant suit but with dandruff on his shoulders. His face was pinched, his eyes hooded.

They sat at a tiny round table under bright fluorescent lights that made the man's skin look sallow and tired.

'Why did Bob Watts get dumped on?' Tingley said.

The man shrugged.

'Because he'd fucked up.'

'There's more to it than that.'

The man looked at his polished right brogue for a moment, jiggling his foot.

311

'I'm not entirely clear why my agency sent me to meet with you.'

'Because your agency and me go back a long way.'

'But what I'm about to tell you is highly sensitive.'

'So am I, especially when I'm mucked around. Just tell me, please.'

'Telling is almost invariably a bad idea.'

'You don't have a choice, as I'm sure you've been informed. I'm calling in a large number of favours.'

The man stretched his right hand out and examined his nails for a moment. Satisfied with them, he looked at Tingley with an insincere smile.

'Yes, I gather you've been quite a help to us over the years. Operations few people know about...'

Tingley said nothing. The man nodded.

'The targets in the house were the man and woman.'

'The ones in bed together?'

The man nodded.

'What about the guy sitting on the toilet?'

'Collateral. But not innocent.'

'What about the man killed in the kitchen?'

The foot jiggled again.

'An informer. Dispensable.'

Tingley wanted to hit him. He'd met people like this before. Every nation had them, every period of history. People who kill remotely, who don't have to see the cost of their decisions in human misery.

Tingley lived with the bad things he'd done. He believed that one day he'd answer for them. But at least his bad deeds were always in war, overt or covert, and face to face. It didn't mean he had a right to kill those he'd killed but it made some kind of sense.

He watched the man's foot. The shoelace was unevenly tied, with a long stretch hanging over the side of the shoe.

'Mind you don't trip on that,' he said, gesturing at the shoe. The man didn't look down.

'What had they done?' Tingley said.

The man told him.

When I got back from London I drove over the Downs into Ditchling and bumped into Ronnie, the neighbourhood cop. Traffic was at its usual standstill because of cars parked on the High Street, so he led me into an alley near the church to tell me the body in the burnt-out car had been identified.

'It was Edwards, sir. I believe his snitch had started the whole Milldean thing.'

'Wonder who was using his credit cards in the south of France?' I said.

'Probably sold on.'

I nodded. I wasn't sure that Edwards's death took us any further than his disappearance had, but I needed to think through a few things. I thanked Ronnie and wandered into The Bull. I was pleased to see the big log fire was burning.

The music was turned off, thank goodness. The new landlord had introduced non-stop music into the quiet space. Bob Marley, Lionel Ritchie – I'd

313

been there with all of that. I play music all the time in the car but in a pub I like silence.

On the odd occasions I bought crime fiction, it made me laugh to read of this or that policeman's musical interests. This one's a jazz fan, that one is into prog rock, another's an opera buff and there's one north London cop who likes country and western.

My musical tastes are more eclectic. Dissonance is my preference but one of the perks of my old job was getting invited to Glyndebourne for the opera and the Brighton Festival for world music.

It amused me too that the barmaids in this pub were so ill-suited to their job. They exuded arrogance and boredom because they were usually the good-looking daughters of local wealthy people. Tonight, it was a final-year student at Sussex with good legs and a sour mouth. She didn't notice any of the customers because she kept her head down. Since there was a pile of people at the bar, it was irritating that she served only who was next in her narrow line of vision, however long others had been waiting.

When I eventually got my drink I sat down beside the log fire. It had started raining and my mind drifted as I gazed into the embers. Three policemen dead. Foster, Finch and Edwards. Presumably the ones who could talk about who was behind what had happened.

But what about Connolly and White, his Haywards Heath sidekick? I felt sure they took the lead in what had happened in the house in Milldean. Were they under threat or were they the ones doing the threatening? What was William Simpson's involvement? Blackmail because of Little Stevie or something more? Was he the man pressing to get the investigation closed down? More to the point – was he the man arranging to have people knocked off?

I was contemplating the odd coincidence that our fathers were both around during the Trunk Murder investigations. I was still curious about how much my dad really knew. I was pretty sure he'd written the diary, even though I didn't recognize the handwriting as his. I'd also been trying to get hold of Tingley but he was as elusive as ever.

Judging by the intriguing individuals drifting into the pub – mostly men, largely macho, often dodgy – I guessed there had been racing at Plumpton, a few miles down the road.

I couldn't stop chewing over my encounter with Simpson. I knew I'd missed something. There was a look on his face when I focused on Little Stevie. Inscrutable, to be sure, but a hint of relief. It was there for just a moment then was veiled again. He was expecting something else. Something worse. I'd known this guy a long time. I was pretty certain I was right, I just didn't know how to get him. It was bloody irritating. What had I missed? What else was there?

A guy came and stood in front of me, blocking my view of the fire. He was standing feet planted, legs apart, shoulders squared. Not big but thickset. Looking down at me.

'I know you, you cunt,' he said.

Which isn't the most neutral of conversational

openings. I looked up at him. Didn't recognize him. I shrugged.

'Remind me?'

At this point I was aggravated but calm. However, from the pugnacious way he was leaning over me, I thought it appropriate to uncross my legs and drop my hands on to my knees. The problem with the army training I've had is that it's easier to think about the way to kill someone than it is ways merely to disable. And one of the first things you're taught is that if you get the first punch in, you're probably going to win the fight.

So, one part of me was resisting the – strong – urge to rise and smash the side of my hand into the base of his nose, driving the bone up into his brain. That's the death option. Or I could just reach out, grab his balls and give them a good twist.

I smiled at my thought processes, since I was worrying that the second was a bit crude for a family pub, but I was having no such worries about the first option, which was, ultimately, cruder.

'You don't know me,' he said. 'But you're the guy who backs murderers.'

I was drinking a glass of Zinfandel and I had been enjoying the taste of it and the memories it evoked – I had spent a year on a police exchange in California. I took a healthy mouthful.

'That's under investigation,' I said calmly, although already I was irritated by the gel in his hair, the suede jacket and the way he was pushing his cock in my face.

316

This guy was muscular but paunchy. I could drive my fingers up beneath his diaphragm and he'd be crippled for the rest of the day and unable to draw a proper breath for a week. I could kick his feet from under him and as he fell ... Frankly, I could do anything.

'You're blocking my view of the fire,' I said.

'You policemen think you own the world.'

One or two people could hear and turned their heads but mostly the boisterousness of the pub hid what he was saying.

'Ex-policeman,' I said, my fists clenching. 'Do you want to get to the point?'

I think he must have glimpsed something in my eyes, or seen my body tense. He took a step back but he held his ground. I felt my anger bubble. But I was also conscious of the situation. I hadn't reamed anyone out in a pub since I was in the military, and even then it was before I made rank.

Fuck it. He wasn't who I wanted to lash out at, but he'd do. I started to rise.

'Mine's a cranberry juice – sorry I'm late.'

We both looked. Molly was standing beside me. She sat down in the chair opposite. The paunchy guy and I looked at each other. The steam went out of both of us, though neither was going to admit it.

'OK, then,' I said to him, turning to Molly. He shuffled past me back to the bar.

I sat down opposite her.

'How are you doing?'

She laughed at the incongruity. She'd always had a lovely laugh.

'I mean, thank you for turning up when you did,' I said. 'And how are you doing?'

'How do you think I'm doing?'

'A glass of wine?'

She shook her head.

'I told you – cranberry juice.'

She saw something in my face.

'Surprised?' There was an edge to her voice but not the hostility I'd been used to lately.

'A little,' I admitted.

'It's been a week.'

I reached for her hand but she pulled it back into her lap.

'Must be tough,' I said.

'It's nice to start feeling things again.'

'Really? I thought the point of drink—'

'Was to stop feeling? Well, yes, but that's not a good way to live your life. And there's not enough alcohol in the world to shut out some feelings.'

'I'm so sorry about what happened. If we could talk—'

Molly pushed the palm of her hand at me.

'It's too late for talk.'

I looked at the fire.

'So why did you come in here?'

She shrugged and looked down at the table.

'Sentiment? I saw your car in the car park.'

I nodded and smiled. She looked at me.

'Of course, I was also prepared to find you in here with *her*.'

There was little intensity in her voice, but even so I reared back.

'I wouldn't do that,' I said.

318

'What – you have no problem shagging her but you draw the line at going to the local with her?'

Her voice had risen. One or two people looked over again.

'I didn't mean that.'

She looked at her hands.

I'd always put my work before my marriage and my kids. Molly was a woman I'd pursued and wooed (after a fashion) and swore to spend the rest of my life with, even before we got married. But I hadn't kept that promise.

I wanted to. When I thought about it – and given that I was a man, I tried not to think about it very often – I was desperate that we were not still together. Oh, I missed Molly. She was difficult, but when we chimed we could talk for hours, laugh for hours over the littlest things.

'Molly.' I leant across the table but she stood up.

'Take care, Robert.'

'You too,' I murmured as she walked out of the pub.

Kate had decided against seeing her father in London. Not cowardice, she told herself, just timing. She was curled up on the sofa in her flat sipping a mug of green tea. Her head was spinning from what she'd stumbled on in the National Archive. She was excited about the discovery of a suspect, Dr Massiah, and the possibility he was the Dr M referred to in the memoir. She was frustrated that she could find no other documents about him.

And she was knocked sideways to have found

at the back of the second file a memo about the discovery of the torso at the left luggage office that mentioned in passing the names of the police officers present.

Knocked sideways because there were two names she recognized.

Her doorbell rang. It made her jump – she still wasn't over the scare she'd had – but then she heard someone climbing the stairs and the insertion of a key in the lock. A moment later, Sarah Gilchrist came through the door.

'Hi,' Kate said, sitting up.

'Didn't want to startle you with the key in the door, so thought I'd scare you with the bell,' Gilchrist said.

They both smiled.

'There's some green tea,' Kate said, indicating the teapot on the table.

Kate watched as Gilchrist went into the kitchen and returned with a mug. It had hit her with some force today that she had a major crush on Gilchrist.

'Did you get any clothes today?' Kate said.

'Didn't have time,' Gilchrist said, pouring her cup of tea.

'I bought you some underwear in M&S,' Kate said. Gilchrist looked at her. Kate felt suddenly embarrassed.

'There was a store right next to the Archives and I was buying myself some and thought that just in case you didn't have time. I guessed your size and they're probably not very flattering—'

Kate realized she was blushing.

'Thanks,' Gilchrist said, sounding distracted.

'That was thoughtful of you. How was your day in Kew?'

'Great,' Kate said. 'I've got a new suspect and my grandfather may be the mystery memoirist – or possibly Bob's father.'

Gilchrist laughed.

'You're going to have to run all that by me again.'

'I found a police report about the original discovery of the body and it listed the policemen who were in attendance. Our autobiographer described how he was there. One of the names is that of my grandfather. And another is called Donald Watts.'

'Crikey. And who is the new suspect?'

Kate told her about Dr Massiah and the Dr M in the memoir.

'But I don't know what happened in the investigation,' she ended. 'There were no more documents about him.'

Gilchrist was paying more attention now. She sat in the armchair opposite the sofa, balancing the mug on her knee.

'You're thinking that the Frenchy referred to in the memoir may be the victim?'

Kate nodded.

'That's great.'

'Maybe,' Kate said, standing up. 'But then there's this.'

She went over to the table and brought back the fragment of memoir about the older woman who looked like Carole Lombard. Gilchrist read it.

'I was wondering why the head was cut off,' Kate said. 'Was it because she would be instantly recognizable?'

'That he cut the head off meant the killer was worried *someone* would recognize her. And looking like a movie star would make it more likely.'

'I'd assumed Frenchy was young, but there's no reason why she shouldn't be this older woman. Especially if Tingley is right and Spilsbury got it wrong.'

Gilchrist studied the fragment again.

'I don't know – the tone of voice in this—'

Kate's phone rang. It was the radio station manager wanting to change her next shift. When Kate turned back to the room, she saw that Gilchrist had put the sheets of the memoir down and was staring at Kate. Kate flushed again.

'What?' she said, panicked for a moment that Sarah could read her mind. 'What?'

I'd parked in the public car park below the community hall in Ditchling. As I reached the bottom of the incline, I was aware of a figure to my left detaching from the shadows of the building. At almost the same moment I heard hurried footsteps behind me. I turned to see the man from the pub, face contorted, as he wielded a baseball bat above his head.

Wielding a weapon with accuracy whilst running isn't easy. This man was running downhill with a couple of pints inside him. His momentum was leading him. As he reached me, I bent low and he went over my shoulder. I gave him extra propulsion as I straightened. He hit the ground with a terrible wet crunch. I heard that horrible, hollow sound as his head cracked against the tarmac. I turned to face the man who'd come out of the shadows. He was about five yards away, his bat ready to whack a ball – or my head.

'Be proud to be British,' I said. 'At least use a bloody cricket bat.'

The second man didn't respond either to my bravado or to the plight of his colleague. He just moved in a half-crouch two yards closer.

I was out of practice at this stuff. Which is why I wondered too late how many others were in the car park. A third man came up behind me and whacked me hard across the small of my back. I arched and grunted, and fell backwards. Knowing as I fell that, once I was on the floor, it was all over.

Kate was feeling strange and embarrassed about the evening. She really liked Gilchrist. OK, fancied her. But she was worried that Gilchrist had guessed and was put off by the thought. Gilchrist had gone to bed early, leaving Kate to ponder this and her notes on the Trunk Murder.

She wondered about her grandfather. He'd died long before she was born and her father had never really talked about him. Nor had she been curious until now. She wasn't upset about this family link to the Trunk Murder, although she disliked intensely whoever the memoirist was.

She might not be so pleased if her grandfather turned out to be the murderer but, then again, doesn't everybody hope for a villain when they research their family histories?

That brought her to her father. Part of her estrangement from him was because once he was in government she'd had to give up wondering about his involvement in *anything*. She was sure he'd been behind getting Watts fired. Now, of course, in light of the threat to her in the cemetery, she was wondering if he'd done far worse.

Gilchrist knew she'd blanked Kate for a moment and in the process freaked her a bit. She was sorry for that. It was simply that, though she was touched by Kate's thoughtfulness and intrigued by what she had discovered about the Trunk Murder, her mind was elsewhere. She was almost entirely focused on the present. Specifically, what Philippa Franks had told her. It sort of made sense but Gilchrist was cautious. She was remembering how upset Franks had been on the night of the tragedy. Was that normal post-trauma emotion or was there something else?

Gilchrist excused herself from Kate and retreated to the spare room. She put the underwear in the chest of drawers. One of the top drawers was taken up with framed photographs placed face down. Family photos, she guessed, to be brought out when her parents were using this room.

Gilchrist was lying in bed but she couldn't sleep. The room was hot, the duvet heavy. But it wasn't really that. It was all this stuff going around in her head. And something else. In work today, in the canteen, she'd seen Jack Jones, the CSI officer who'd been involved in analyzing the Milldean crime scene. The man she'd once had a fling with. The man she'd confided in about her one-night stand with Bob Watts. The man who'd sold her to the press.

She should have confronted him but she didn't. At the time she thought she was being mature, rising above it. Now she was wondering if she'd just been cowardly.

And that brought her on to Bob Watts. And what, for want of a better term, she'd been thinking of as their second-night stand. Neither of them had referred to it again. Both had retreated to a kind of default position. There was no intimacy between them when they were together. The passion when the lights went out had shrivelled in the glare of the day.

She finally dozed off thinking about Bob Watts. The room felt hotter.

I didn't go down. The man who was close enough to whack me across my back was close enough for me to engage with. And because it was a hit right across my back, it didn't do me serious injury, even though it did hurt like hell. If he'd rammed the bat into one of my kidneys, or across the back of my head, he would have been more effective. As it was, the main blow was to my spine. It jarred me, but he'd need a lot more force to snap it.

I twisted as I was falling, and grabbed first the bat, then his forearm. Pulling down on his arm, I swung my legs off the ground and drove one knee into his side, the other into his neck.

I fell on him, my body a dead weight, and that was it. Except that the one man who seemed to have a bit of savvy was now standing over me, pondering where his bat could do most damage.

It was clear that this was nothing to do with the altercation in the pub. These guys had been sent to deliver a message. A message I wasn't wild about receiving.

I scrabbled around and grabbed the bat of the man I was lying on. I brought it up just as the other bat came down. The thwock of contact was hard and loud, and I felt the impact shudder down my arm.

The man above me was now off-balance so I snaked around, swivelled at the hip and my outstretched legs swept his legs from under him. He fell backwards, abandoning his bat to break his fall with his arms, keeping his head off the tarmac.

I looked around to see if there were more roughnecks waiting to tip in. Seemed not. I launched myself on to him, pinning him to the ground.

I hissed in his ear:

'You gonna tell me the message you were supposed to deliver?'

He struggled but I was pinioning his arms.

'Back off,' he gasped.

'Fuck you,' I said.

He shook his head, breathing badly.

'That was the message. I was to say you had to back off.'

'Who's the message from?'

'Me,' a voice said, as someone knocked me unconscious.

EIGHTEEN

'Some people are crap at delivering messages,' Tingley said, standing by my hospital bed.

'That's not how I see it,' I mumbled, wincing as I tried to sit up.

'Well, as I understand it, you don't know who sent the message and you don't know what the message was since they knocked you unconscious.'

'The medium is the message,' I whispered. I couldn't get my breath.

'What?'

'Nothing.' I coughed. 'Presumably they would have left the message had they not been disturbed.'

I'd regained consciousness in the car park to find a gaggle of people crowding around me. Racegoers who'd disturbed my attacker. The two thugs still standing had hauled the two on the floor into a white van and sped the wrong way out of the car park.

After I vomited on their shoes, the racegoers had given me space. Someone had called Ronnie, the community policeman, and he had got me into hospital in Haywards Heath. I'd been kept in overnight in case I had concussion from the whack on my head. This morning the doctor had decided I was probably OK.

'I could have told them that last night,' Tingley said. 'You and your hard head.'

'Somebody got the number plates, but the van will be stolen or the plates will be cloned,' I said. 'And I didn't get a look at the man who said the message was from him.'

'Did anyone else?'

'Apparently not – baseball cap pulled low – you know.'

'At least for once it was the appropriate head-gear,' Tingley said.

After a moment I smiled and gingerly touched the lump on the back of my head.

'I've got stuff to tell you,' Tingley said. 'But not here.'

'I'll be discharged later this morning.'

I winced again.

'Let's meet at The Cricketers.' Tingley said. 'But soft drinks for you.'

'Will I like what you have to say?'

Tingley waggled his hand.

'Etsy ketsy,' he said.

'Which is Greek to me,' I said.

'I'll see you at one.'

Gilchrist and Reg Williamson were on their way to Lewes Prison to take a new statement from Gary Parker.

'On the direct orders of Sheena Hewitt, eh?' Williamson said as they drove out of Brighton. 'The deal must have been done. Wonder what the scumbag is being offered.'

'I don't know, Reg. There isn't much room for

manoeuvre.' Gilchrist was excited, as she hoped Parker might have some real news for her.

'You're kidding, Sarah. They'll go the temporary insanity route, he'll be put in some country club loonie bin, get tested in a couple of years and come out in three.'

'Well, he *was* under the influence of a lot of drugs,' Gilchrist said.

'The guy's a scumbag born and bred.'

'Reg, can I ask – do you think those awareness courses you've taken have been working?'

Ten minutes later, Gilchrist was tending to agree with him.

Parker was looking even unhealthier than the last time she'd seen him. His face was puffy and sallow, almost green, and his eyes were sunk into their sockets. His mouth was even filthier too.

'You know what I discovered?' he said. 'I discovered that poncey people like cock and twat as much as the rest of us.' He sniffed. 'Actually, they love it more.'

Parker's solicitor was sitting beside him. He was a harassed man in an ill-fitting pinstripe suit. He stared at the table as Parker was talking.

'Is that your news?' Gilchrist said. 'Next you'll be telling me there are gays in Brighton.'

Parker sniggered.

'Well, it's arse bandits I'm talking about. Easy money to be made down at Black Rock. Fucking perverts turning up, cock in one hand, roll of twenties in the other.'

'You're saying you've been a rent boy?' Gilchrist said.

'Stick it up your tight arse. I've kicked their

fucking heads in, pissed on them, then taken their money is what I've done. Easy bloody money.'

Gilchrist's mind wandered for a moment. Black Rock was where the head of the Trunk Murder victim had been found, then lost again. Then and now there were posh apartments above. Now there was also a lot of nocturnal activity in the bushes below. It was a well-known cottaging place, but Gilchrist hadn't heard much about gay-bashing there. She guessed it was the closet gays who were being attacked. They weren't going to report it.

'What has gay-bashing got to do with Little Stevie and the Milldean thing?'

Parker started jiggling his leg but said nothing.

'I thought we were supposed to be moving forward in this meeting.' Gilchrist addressed herself to the lawyer. He adjusted his glasses on his nose and looked from her to Parker. Parker didn't know which nervous tic to focus on. He was actually quivering. Gilchrist knew he was being given methadone and other medication to help his withdrawal from the cocktail of drugs and booze he'd been living on for years.

Parker chewed at his finger.

'Bloke I was at school with. Bunked off school with, really. We was mates. Turns out he takes it up the bum. Likes chugging it too.'

'Little Stevie.'

Parker looked at Gilchrist.

'You've got a mouth on you – bet you've chugged a few in your time. Will you chug me?'

'Mr Parker,' the lawyer said quietly.

330

'That must have messed you up,' Williamson snarled. 'Your mate being gay. Did you bash him?'

'I give him one up the arse is what I did. Fucking poof.'

Williamson leant forward.

'You lost me there,' he said. 'You punish a homosexual by sodomizing him?'

'So you're gay, too?' Gilchrist said.

Parker stubbed a finger on the table.

'Course not, you ignorant bint.'

'Mr Parker—' the lawyer said, his voice gloomy.

'You do someone, even a bloke, that's the power. You let yourself be done, that's something else.'

Gilchrist forced a laugh, though she never felt less like laughing.

'Oh, it's that prison thing – you're only gay if you're on the receiving end.'

'Don't know about that—'

'Dream on, Parker,' Williamson said. 'You're a jobbie jammer – and, as for sucking men off, is that why your teeth are such a bloody mess?'

'All right, that's enough—' the lawyer said.

Parker swivelled his eyes between Gilchrist and Williamson.

'I ain't gay, you dyke bitch, and you, you fat bastard.'

'If you're not now, you will be by the time they've finished with you in prison.' Williamson said. 'You'll be able to get the Flying Scotsman up you by the time some of those boys have finished with you. Sorry – Flying Scotsman is before your time. It's a train, boyo – and not a diesel.'

The lawyer was on his feet.

'I think that's the end of this discussion.' He looked down at Parker. 'Mr Parker.'

Parker was still looking from Gilchrist to Williamson, his horrible teeth bared in a grin. He pointed at Gilchrist.

''S OK, Mr Whatsit. As long as she frigs me. Or she could do the milkmaid's shuffle.'

The lawyer looked exasperated and sank back in his seat. Williamson was clenching his fists. Gilchrist touched his arm.

'What about this friend of yours?' she said. 'Little Stevie.'

Parker seemed to have forgotten his request.

'He was a rent boy. Made a lot of money in Brighton.'

'We have no record of him. Besides, I would have thought, given the number of consenting adults, this would be a place where you wouldn't make money.'

'He wasn't on the streets. Conferences. Especially the political ones. All these happily married men wanting to stuff him. He made good money.'

'You kept in touch, then?'

'Saw him around.'

'And?'

'And fucking what?' He was scrunched up in his seat now. Gilchrist looked at the ceiling, talked to it.

'And how did he end up dead in Milldean?'

Parker glanced at his lawyer. The lawyer

332

nodded.

'He met this bloke. Did him. Bloke left his wallet behind.'

'So he nicked it.' Williamson said. 'And we're talking blackmail?'

Parker didn't look at him but said:

'We're talking the massacre in Milldean. You fuckers kill him and all his friends. That's why I'm nervous – you're all in it.'

Gilchrist stared a hole in the table.

'Did Little Stevie tell you whose wallet he had nicked?' she said.

This was the crunch question. This was the deal.

Parker flicked a glance at his lawyer. His lawyer looked straight ahead.

'Do I have a name to give you?' Parker leered. 'Well, yeah.'

Tingley was waiting for me in The Cricketers, sitting at the bar with a rum and pep in his hand. He bought me a tonic water and led me over to a dark corner. I was walking stiffly – my back was in bad shape.

'Etsy ketsy – haven't heard that for a while,' I said.

We'd been in the Balkans together for a bit and a Greek officer had tried to teach us some colloquialisms. 'Etsy ketsy' was phonetic Greek for 'so so' – provided you used the hand wiggle and maybe a little shrug.

'Just popped into my head,' Tingley said, then got down to it. 'OK, according to the man from the shadow world, the couple in bed were the targets. Little Stevie was collateral.'

I thought for a moment.

'I don't buy that. If we're placing Simpson somehow at the centre of this, then the target is the rent boy.'

'But that might not be all of it,' Tingley said. 'I don't know how much I believe of what I was told, but it was plausible.'

'Those men are always plausible. That's their stock-in-trade.'

'I know that,' Tingley said, his tone of voice making me feel foolish.

'I know you know,' I said. 'So what was his scenario?'

'The couple in bed were Bosnian Serbs and, therefore, potential business rivals for the Brighton crime families. But they lucked into Little Stevie.'

'And?'

'They bought him.'

'I thought he was just for rent.'

Tingley gave me a look.

'They were trying to blackmail the government.'

'Didn't know you could blackmail a whole government,' I said.

'Yes, you did.' Tingley was getting impatient. 'Terrorists do it all the time.'

'These weren't terrorists, though. So it was Simpson they were trying to blackmail?'

'They were hoping to implicate him in something, yes, but I don't think it was just the rent boy thing.'

I frowned.

'He isn't high enough up the food chain for the government to be worried, is he?' I said. 'Friends though they are, the PM would have cut him loose without hesitation. Unless it had implications for others higher up. Did your man know?'

Tingley shook his head.

'He said it was beyond his pay grade. Suggested we ask Simpson.'

'That's going to work.' I touched the lump on the back of my head. 'Did your contact say if anyone else locally was involved?'

'He said – and I quote – "There may have been other local ramifications, yes." But, again, I don't have the detail.'

Tingley moved his glass around the table.

'Maybe Simpson is in deep with one of the local crime families. He grew up here, didn't he?'

'As did I,' I said. 'We didn't move in their circles.'

'University days. Drugs?'

I thought for a moment.

'Maybe. But what about me? Maybe we're missing something. Did I have to be removed because I was a threat to somebody on the force? Was I threatening some comfortable deal between police officers and local crime people?'

Tingley steepled his hands.

'There might be some of that,' he said. 'But how did they know you would react in that way? It was your reaction that got you booted out. They couldn't predict that.'

'Maybe I was collateral damage too. Big foot, bigger mouth.'

Tingley smiled.

'Then you became an embarrassment. So, actually, nobody was out to get you – this wasn't planned to bring you down.'

I wasn't going to admit that. I wasn't able to. I looked beyond him to the row of spirits behind the bar.

'Why was this man happy to tell you now?' I said.

'Timing. New way of doing things. Some familiar faces won't be hanging around the corridors of power any more...'

I frowned.

'You mean Simpson's on his way out? Hmm. Maybe.' Kate popped into my head. 'How are we going to tell Kate exactly what's going on with her father?'

Tingley shrugged.

'Not my area of expertise.' He looked across the room. 'I want you to have a chat with some-one I know.'

'That's always interesting. Who?'

Tingley gestured towards a table in the opposite corner of the pub.

'A grass.'

I'd noticed the short, middle-aged man with the comb-over when I'd come in. He was with a strikingly pretty woman, taller than him. She was wearing full make-up and might have had plastic surgery to define that jawline. But there was a puffiness about her face. I'd wondered if she was an alcoholic and he the man who kept her drinking under some kind of control. There was an empty bottle of white wine and two empty glasses on the table alongside two further glasses. His was almost full, hers almost empty. They were doing a crossword in the paper and she was looking bored, but maybe that was because she wanted another drink.

'What's he got to say for himself?'

'Let's find out,' Tingley said, leading me across the room.

Sheena Hewitt looked older. The Acting Chief Constable's face was gaunt and there were dark shadows under her eyes that her inexpertly applied make-up couldn't conceal.

'What's so urgent, Sarah?' she said, tapping her pen on her desk. She sounded weary, too.

Gilchrist was seated in an uncomfortably low chair to one side of the desk, conscious of her knees sticking up in front of her.

'I had a further interview with Gary Parker this morning. He told us that the male prostitute known as Little Stevie was attempting to blackmail William Simpson, the government adviser.'

'He has proof of this?'

'Not direct proof, no, ma'am.'

'Then it's hearsay evidence. There's nothing to be done with it.'

'But, ma'am, it's a lead.'

Hewitt sat back in her seat and dropped the pen on her desk.

'Sarah, the Milldean affair is old news. The Hampshire investigation has concluded no individuals should be prosecuted. Nobody is publicly pressing for any further enquiry and I don't intend to stir things up again. Enough damage has been done to the reputation of this force already. My job is to contain it and move on. All the officers involved have left the force, retiring on the grounds of ill-health. You are the lucky one. You are working again.'

Gilchrist was indignant.

'But, ma'am, that means nobody is being held to account for what happened.'

'Our lax procedures are largely responsible and we are making strenuous efforts to put new ones in place.'

'That's just a whitewash,' Gilchrist said heatedly. She saw Hewitt's face. 'Sorry, ma'am.'

Hewitt leant forward and stabbed her finger at Gilchrist.

'DS Gilchrist, the Milldean affair is not your case, nor has it ever been. You are meddling in things to the detriment of this force and your other duties. You will desist forthwith or you will face disciplinary procedures. Am I clear?'

Gilchrist's face was burning with a mixture of anger and frustration.

'Am I clear?'

'Yes, ma'am.'

'Then you're dismissed,' Hewitt said, picking up her pen and pulling a sheaf of papers towards her.

The woman picked up her glass and went to sit at the bar when Tingley and I approached. The grass's name was Stewart Nealson. I was expecting him to be shifty but he was articulate and open.

'Bob here is interested in knowing a bit more

about what the families are up to.'

'What they're up to?' Nealson touched his nose. 'The usual dodges and scams. But they're under a lot of pressure from outsiders. Specially on the smuggling racket through Newhaven and Shoreham.'

'What do you hear about Milldean?' I said.

Nealson looked over at the woman at the bar.

'A real mess from every side you look at it. And best kept away from.'

'The Bosnian Serb connection?' Tingley said.

'Not a people you want to piss off.'

'Tell us about it,' I murmured. Tingley and I had not enjoyed our Bosnian tour.

'And Hathaway and Cuthbert?'

'Not involved, as far as I'm aware. Though Cuthbert's on the warpath for you, Jimmy. You need to watch out.'

A thought occurred to me.

'I don't suppose you've heard anything about Cuthbert in relation to Ditchling last night, have you?'

Nealson smoothed down his comb-over.

'Well, he would have been in the neighbourhood. He always goes to Plumpton races – prefers it over the jumps to flat-racing. Plus he has a bit of business going on, of course.'

I exchanged a glance with Tingley.

I thanked Nealson and we left about five minutes later.

'How's he connected to the gangs?' I said as we walked through the Laines. 'Seems too straight.'

'Accountant,' Tingley replied. 'Strictly legit

and only handles their legit businesses, but he hears things.'

'Taking a bit of a risk, isn't he?'

'His missus has expensive habits. Most of what he makes goes up her nose or down her gullet.'

I was contemplating her ruined beauty when my mobile rang.

'Gilchrist,' I mouthed to Tingley.

'Had another meeting with Gary Parker,' she said.

'And?'

'He gave us William Simpson's name. I told Hewitt. She's not interested.'

'I've a feeling we can do something,' I said. 'I feel certain we're closing in.'

'That's not my feeling,' she said. 'My feeling is that we don't have a clue what's going on.'

'We have clues aplenty. It's fitting them together that's the problem. Let's meet later at Kate's place.'

Gilchrist ended the call. She was lying on the bed in Kate's spare room. She was restless. She jackknifed off the bed and went over to the chest of drawers to change. She opened the top drawer and saw the framed photos lying face down. Absently, she turned them over.

I eventually found a parking space near Kate's flat – Brighton is not car-friendly – and walked the few hundred yards to her door, working out what I needed to say to her. When she buzzed me in, Gilchrist was sitting on the sofa. Gilchrist gave me an intense look.

'Kate,' I said. 'You don't need to worry about this stuff that's going on now. It's nothing to do with that scare you had.'

'Are you excluding me?' Kate said.

'Just didn't want to bore you,' I said. 'You're in if you want to be.'

'Let me find some booze,' she said, disappearing into the kitchen.

'Something I want to show you in my bedroom,' Gilchrist hissed at me.

'You haven't found the head in there, have you?'

She looked totally thrown.

'The Trunk Murder victim?' I said. 'Forget it – bad joke.'

Gilchrist looked exasperated.

'You know, frankly, I don't really care about that.'

'About what?' Kate said, walking back in with a bottle of wine.

The doorbell sounded.

'That'll be Tingley,' I said.

Kate headed for the door. Gilchrist laughed for no reason and stood to usher me towards her bedroom. The moment we were in there she handed me a framed picture.

'Is that Kate with her parents?'

It was a much younger Kate, and William didn't have his goatee, but it was unmistakably the family. I nodded.

'Then we need to talk,' she said, striding back into the living room.

Kate was ushering Tingley in.

'Was your meeting with the Godfather useful?'

341

Kate said to Tingley.

'Hathaway? Not really. But he put me on to someone else who was much more interesting. And today Bob and I got a little tickle from an acquaintance of mine.'

Gilchrist looked from one to the other of us.

'Oh, what – there's some stuff only the boys should know?'

Tingley looked down.

'Some of this information specifically affects Bob,' he said. 'I'm not trying to exclude anyone. If Bob wants to share it with you and Kate, fine.'

'It's fine with me,' I said. 'But Kate, it also specifically affects you because of your father.'

Kate shifted in her seat.

'Tell me,' she said.

'Your father is behind some bad things,' Tingley said, his voice unusually gentle.

'Tell me something I don't know,' Kate said, barking a laugh that couldn't quite conceal her ... conceal her what? Dread? Alarm? Fear? There was something, but I didn't know her well enough to know what she was feeling.

'He could end up in prison for a very long time,' I said quietly.

Kate looked at her glass of wine, picked it up and took the smallest of sips.

'It was only a matter of time,' she said tone-lessly. She put her glass back down on the table, very precisely. I glanced at Gilchrist. She looked like she was about to burst.

'Did you get anywhere else with Philippa?' I said to her.

She took a breath. Exhaled.

342

'I thought I had. Now I'm not so sure.'

I frowned, but she gave a slight shake of her head.

'Finch killed Little Stevie,' she said. 'That's the first thing she said.'

'And the rest?' I said.

She shrugged.

'According to Tingley's source,' I said, 'Little Stevie wasn't the main target. It was the couple in bed.'

'Who were?'

'That we still don't know specifically. Bosnian Serb gangster and his moll, apparently.'

'Moll?' Kate said. Then, after a pause: 'How is my dad involved with Bosnian gangsters?'

'We think his link is with Little Stevie,' I said.

Kate reached for her glass but stopped, her hand still outstretched.

'OK,' she said. 'OK.'

Gilchrist was looking at Kate.

'I'm sorry,' she said.

Kate grimaced.

'As I said: long time coming.'

Gilchrist stood and nodded at me.

'I think you and I should have another crack at Philippa Franks,' she said.

'If you think I can help. When?'

'Now?'

They took Watts's car. The moment they were in it, he turned to her:

'What's going on?'

'I recognize Kate's father,' she said. 'William Simpson. I couldn't think where at first.'

'You've probably seen him on the telly,' Watts said. 'He does a lot of broadcasting.'

'No, from somewhere else. Somewhere here.' She took a big breath. 'I saw him having an argument with Philippa Franks in a cafe in Hove a few weeks ago.'

Watts was silent for a moment. Tingley murmured:

'Bingo.'

'Hence our need to get back to her,' Watts said. He looked at Tingley in the rear-view mirror. 'Do you want to come with us?'

'You don't need me. Let's talk later.'

Watts dropped Tingley on the seafront opposite The Ship and drove on in silence.

'I assumed it was a lover's tiff,' Gilchrist said.

'It may have been. Even so, it's heady stuff.'

Watts parked near the entrance to the block of flats and Gilchrist rang Franks's doorbell.

'It's me again. Sarah.'

There was silence, then Franks buzzed them in. They took the lift. Watts seemed embarrassed by their proximity in the lift, but maybe Gilchrist was imagining that.

Franks's door was ajar. They knocked then walked in. She was standing on her balcony looking out to sea. The noise of the traffic going by on the main drag below ricocheted into the confined space. She saw Gilchrist's expression.

'I'd always wanted a place overlooking the sea. Imagined myself sitting out on the balcony of an evening with a glass of wine, listening to my favourite music, watching the sun go down. But the traffic along the sea front – who knew that sound rises? The fact is I can't hear the music because of the blare of the traffic and the sea frets usually obscure the sun.' She lifted her glass. 'At least there's still the wine.' She nodded at Watts. 'Cheers, sir.'

'Call me Bob,' he said.

'It won't get you anywhere,' she said.

'How do you know William Simpson?' Watts said.

Franks was startled. It was clear she was about to deny it, equally clear that she realized there was no point.

'H–how did you...?'

'The man I saw you with – that was him, wasn't it?' Gilchrist said.

Franks sighed.

'It's not easy meeting men when you work our hours and you have two kids.'

She sounded tipsy.

'Is there anything you want to tell us about you and William Simpson with regard to the Milldean operation?' Watts said.

Franks looked puzzled.

'Nothing at all. Why?'

Gilchrist reached out to squeeze Franks's arm.

'We think that Simpson is somehow involved with what went wrong there and since you were involved with him...'

Franks's eyes flashed.

'You think he asked me to shoot somebody?'

'What happened in that house?' Watts said.

'I've already told Sarah,' Franks said. 'Jesus. Let's go inside.'

There were two big sofas in the sitting room.

345

Franks took one, Gilchrist and Watts took the other.

'It's looking like the couple in the bed were a hit,' Watts said.

After staring at him for a moment Franks said: 'And?'

'I wondered if you knew anything about it.'

She bridled and over-enunciated as she said: 'I was nowhere near the front bedroom. And why would I be doing hits? It's absurd – I'm a single mum, for Christ's sake, not a contract killer.'

'I'm sorry. I'm not saying you did anything. I just wondered what you knew.'

'I've told Sarah what I know. And I also told her that my life and the lives of my children had been threatened.'

Watts looked at Gilchrist, who nodded then turned to Franks.

'And your relationship with William Simpson has nothing to do with this?' Gilchrist said. 'Was that argument in the restaurant really about your affair?'

Franks gave her a hard look.

'Fuck off, Sarah. How dare you? You presumed on our friendship earlier to get me to talk to you. But this, coming to my home like this – my *home* – and asking me this shit – this oversteps the mark.'

She got up from her sofa, swayed for just a second.

'In fact, I want you both to leave. Conversation over.'

Gilchrist stood but noted Watts stayed where

346

he was.

'Philippa – we're just trying to figure this out. It's a bad coincidence that you've been having a thing with a man who seems to have some involvement with what happened in Milldean.'

'You think those threats I got came from William Simpson? He's a shit but he's not that much of a shit.'

'But your relationship—'

'It hardly was a relationship. A few meals and hurried sex whenever he was down here.'

'What about Little Stevie?' Watts said.

Franks turned and peered down at Watts.

'Little Stevie?'

'The rent boy I mentioned earlier,' Gilchrist said.

Franks looked from Watts to Gilchrist.

'What about him? How would he connect to William Simpson?'

Gilchrist and Watts both looked away. Franks swayed a little.

'Oh Christ. Well, isn't that just the icing on the bloody cake?'

NINETEEN

Kate unbolted the door and took the chain off to let Gilchrist in.

'Anything you can tell me?' she said lightly as Gilchrist came through the door.

Gilchrist towered over her.

'God you make me feel so big,' she said, laughing. Then she turned solemn. 'How close are you to your father?'

'Isn't that obvious?' Kate said.

Gilchrist chewed her lip for a moment.

'So how are you feeling about all this?'

'I don't understand it, to tell you the truth.'

'Bob wants to nail him.'

Kate turned away.

'That's fine with me,' she said. But Gilchrist didn't believe her.

I went to see my father before I went to Simpson. Although I wasn't as het up as Kate about the Trunk Murder, it almost seemed like family business. It wasn't about the victim – in face of all the millions of other atrocities in the world, I couldn't really get too worked up about that – but it was family.

Anna let me in.

'Back again,' my father said.

348

'There's a diary among the archive papers. Well, half of one.'

'And you're trying to figure out who wrote it?'

'I'm pretty sure you wrote it.'

He didn't say anything.

'We think it might point in the direction of the murderer.'

'You think? You mean you don't know?'

'The part of the diary we have doesn't say anything incriminating in so many words—'

'Not much use without the rest of it, eh?'

His smile was vulpine.

'Why are you taunting me?' I said.

'I'm not, Bobby. It just amuses me to see my son, the ex-Chief Constable, doing some proper police-work for the first time in his high-flying career.'

He tilted his head.

'But how do you propose to get the rest of this diary? Behind a cabinet? Misfiled somewhere? Didn't you tell me that when you were having the station redecorated you found a sealed-up room in the cellar with a load of files in it? Are you hoping to do the same trick twice?'

Finding the sealed-up room was true. Material in there included all the evidence boxes connected to the unsolved murder of a schoolboy in the sixties.

'I don't think we can do that twice, no. Did you write the diary?'

He grimaced. I think he was trying for a smile.

'I remember writing something. We had a lot of spare time stuck in this tiny room in the Royal Pavilion.'

'I thought the investigation was inundated with stuff. You couldn't keep up.'

'Aye, well, most of it was rubbish.'

'Even so,' I said.

'Even so – there's always an even so.'

He looked at me for a long moment.

'Do you want to know who did it? Who the Trunk Murderer was?'

I laughed – this was unexpected.

'Well, yes.'

He grimaced again.

'I haven't a bloody clue.'

I shook my head.

'Dad.' I bit the bullet. 'All these women in your diary.'

'You know I've bin a ladies' man all my life.'

'Whether they wanted to or not?'

'I didn't get many turn me down, I'll tell you that. And the ones who pretended they didn't want to – well, there were no blood on the sheets when I were done, so what does that tell you about them?'

'What about Frenchy?'

'Frenchy – my God. Couldn't pronounce her real name then, can't remember it now. She got on that ferry on the end of the West Pier and floated out of my life.'

'Where did you meet?'

'On the prom in Brighton. February 1934. She was over for the day from France. We went to see *The Gay Divorcee*. Fred Astaire coming to Brighton to get a quickie divorce. Always preferred Gene Kelly myself, but, to be honest, I didn't see much of the film.'

'Was it unprotected sex?'

'Aye, and she fell pregnant. We didn't know it. She'd come over once a month and we'd get to it. She was fiery. Then in May she comes over and says she's pregnant.'

'So you sent her to Dr M, the abortionist.'

'You found that part of the diary, then. Massiah. He was something. She wanted to keep it, wanted me to marry her. Daft wench. I refused, so finally she came back over fourth of June and I paid for her to have an abortion. Coppers' rates – still wasn't cheap, but he was a society abortionist so I reckoned she was in good hands. I phoned after and they said it had gone fine.'

'So she wasn't the Trunk Murder victim.'

My dad gave me a surprised look.

'Dad, you saw the body. Was it her or not?'

He looked out of the window towards the iron bridge.

'There were hardly any distinguishing features, were there? I mean, what was left of her was just a naked woman. I never gave her body a good look anyway.'

'But you suspected it might be her? How?'

'Spilsbury's report mentioned what he called a pimple under one of her breasts. Frenchy had made a joke of having three nipples for me to suck on. That's a mole, I said. Suck on it all the same, she said. I'd never met anyone quite like her.'

Again, I tried to mask my discomfort at my father talking about sex.

'Do you think Massiah botched the abortion and Frenchy was the victim?'

351

'I think it's a possibility.'

'So why didn't you at least mention the possibility it might have been Frenchy? It could have changed the focus of the investigation.'

'Sod 'em. By the time I was wondering whether it was her, they were giving me grief about my little arrangement with the press.'

'But didn't you want to see justice served for someone you'd known and been fond of?'

'Fond of? She were nice enough, but it were just sex. I've had more meaningful relationships with my fist, believe me.'

'What happened to Massiah?'

'It went nowhere. They were going to put him under observation but Billy Simpson's dad – ambitious bugger – jumped the gun and went and accused him. Massiah just sat at his desk and wrote a list of names of well-connected people in Sussex and high society he'd had dealings with. Implicitly threatening that he'd name names if he was put on trial. They dropped it.'

'Then as now,' I muttered.

Damn – maybe this old case was getting to me more than I realized. The enormity of the thought that my father had known this woman, had had sex with her, had perhaps made her pregnant – and had kept quiet about it.

'Why did you get fired?' I said.

'Who says I was fired?' he said. He brought his hands together. Separated them again. He grunted.

'I was leaking stories to the press. That's all. Inventing them, really. The press were ferocious back then, as now. The press corps wanted

352

stories every day. Needed stories every day. I supplied them.' He sniffed. 'The stories weren't exactly accurate but they gave the press their headlines.'

'What kind of thing?'

'I'd just take bits of routine work and make more of them. Claim we were following something up, looking for someone. Sometimes we were, sometimes we weren't, but none of it really amounted to much.'

'Meaning?'

'I did a lot with a man called Lindon Laing – always thought it was a queer's name but I don't recall that he was. He was a stringer for the *Daily Mail* and the *Evening News*. He paid me good money for a story – at the end of 1934, I think – that I based on something and nothing. I told them we had a clue to the victim's identity based on the fact her name began with the letter M.'

'Was that a real lead?'

He was impatient at the interruption.

'I don't remember now. I doubt it. It was probably some link to Massiah. Other times I'd say that Captain Hutchinson is anxious to interview someone. That he'd asked all the other police forces in the country for help. Something and nothing. What you have to remember is we were inundated with accusations. Ex-wives trying to set their husbands up. Neighbours trying to set neighbours up. Then there were people who'd gone on holiday and not sent postcards so were presumed murdered. None of this stuff came to anything.'

'You didn't know that.'

He ignored me.

'Tell me about the women, Dad.'

'I've told you. I like women. Always have. And they've been kind to me. Always have. Frenchy, now – don't know what she saw in me but she must have seen something.'

'What did you threaten them with?' I said. 'The ones you didn't bother to get to know too well?'

He rubbed one hand over the other.

'Women are pliable, Bobby. You know that. And they want the same as us, they just don't know how to admit it. I helped them do what they wanted to do.'

I looked down.

'What did you say? That if they said anything you'd have them up on vice charges? Ruin their reputations?'

'It was enough to be a policeman. But a couple did complain. Word did get round.'

'You went to trial?'

'Nobody would go that far. So they had no grounds for firing me or reprimanding me.'

'And the Carole Lombard lookalike?'

He looked blank for a moment. Blank and old.

'I'd forgotten about her. She was quite something. Must have been twice my age. Bonny lass. She was down with some older, rich bloke having a dirty at the Grand. I don't think he was much cop in bed.'

'But you were with the French girl—'

'I met her on the pier and within five minutes we were underneath it.'

'The French girl?'

'No, the other one. She said: "I've always had a thing about uniforms." I don't remember what I said. Next thing, we're under the pier, she's stuffing her knickers in my mouth and we're having a knee-trembler. Wouldn't even let me get the johnny on. Fine by me – I've always hated them bloody things. It were parky too, I can tell you. Then it were "Thank you and good-bye".'

I chewed my lip, thinking about what Tingley had said about the pathologist Spilsbury being fallible.

When I said goodbye to my father I wasn't sure I would be seeing him again. As I waited for the overground train to central London, I wondered about him as a rapist. I also wondered about Frenchy as victim. But mostly I was wondering about the older woman he'd been with, the Carole Lombard lookalike. I didn't think he was a murderer, but was it possible that she was the Trunk Murder victim?

A taxi took me to Millbank and the City Inn just behind the embankment. Tingley was sitting in the spacious foyer beneath a complicated map that was also art.

'He's here,' he said. 'He has a couple of mind-ers with him.'

I was trying to figure out the map.

'PR type minders or heavies?' I said absently.

'Heavies.'

I nodded and led the way up a spiral staircase to the bar above. It was a vast space with sofas and chairs running to a wall of long windows.

Simpson was sitting by the windows, alone on a sofa, a tall glass in front of him. A bulky man was sitting a few yards away with a coffee, and a second, slighter man was on a stool at the bar.

Both watched as Tingley and I walked over to Simpson.

'Forgive me for not standing,' Simpson said as we stood on the other side of the coffee table. He looked at Tingley. 'Don't believe I know your friend.'

'Tingley,' Jimmy said, sitting in the armchair opposite Simpson. I sat in the chair beside him.

'You're on the brink of harassing me,' Simpson said to me. 'And that could get very nasty for you.'

'What we know is pretty nasty for you,' I said.

Tingley shifted his chair to put it at an angle to Simpson's sofa. It also meant the man at the bar and the man behind Simpson were both in his view. Not that I could imagine for a moment anything kicking off in here.

'Tingley – ah, yes. Our security services put quite a lot of work your way. You should bear that in mind.'

Tingley smiled, crossed one leg over the other.

'And that means I know a lot of stuff of a very sensitive nature. You should bear that in mind.'

'Why did you call this meeting?' Simpson said, reaching for his glass.

'To get the truth,' I said.

'The truth?' He laughed. 'That only exists in bad fiction, doesn't it?'

'Why didn't you come to me for help?' I said.

'At what particular stage of your plodding

career and my meteoric rise?'

'At the stage when you were deciding to have a blackmailer killed.'

He stretched his arms out along the back of the sofa but said nothing. We looked at each other. It turned into a staring contest.

'What is it that you think you've got on me?' he finally said.

'Didn't know you were into rough,' I said.

'Oh, Robert. Surely you know – a little bit of everything does you good.'

'But it didn't work out with Little Stevie.'

'Little Stevie? Sounds like a little scut. They all try it on.'

'OK, then. But are you going to explain what happened?'

He slapped the arm of the sofa. A little puff of dust bounced into the air and slowly dispersed.

'My dear chap – you've come to get a confession! How wonderful.' He crossed his legs revealing bright red socks. 'But this is not a crime novel and I have absolutely nothing to confess to.'

'So why have him killed?'

He pouted.

'Is that what this is about? The death of a rent boy.'

'What else did you think it was about?' Tingley said. He wasn't looking at Simpson, he was looking at the man at the bar, who had his mobile phone to his ear. I saw a curious look cross Simpson's face. I flashed a look at Tingley.

'William,' I said. 'We know you're up to your neck with the gangster families who rule

Brighton. We know you were being blackmailed by a rent boy who stole your wallet. We know your daughter was threatened because you're in hock to the crime families. And we know Bosnian Serb gangsters had possession of your blackmailer. Your high-flying government career is well and truly over.'

Simpson looked from me to Tingley and shook his head.

'Robert, there was a time when I thought you were politically most astute. Of late, I've become aware that you're a plodder. You have no feel for nuance. These scurrilous allegations – what can you possibly do with them? If so much as a hint leaks into *Private Eye* or a national newspaper, so much shit will rain down on you that you will drown before you can even reach for a hat.'

He gave a nod to the man sitting at the bar.

'If, however, you decide to do things above board and take me through the courts, I will, of course, have more respect for you.'

He stood.

'But I will also destroy you and your family.'

That teatime I went to see Molly. She opened the door and when she saw it was me turned away and walked back into the sitting room, leaving me to follow if I chose. I closed the door and followed her into the sitting room.

She was wearing a baggy trouser suit and looked pretty good. Except that she had logs burning on the fire on a sunny summer day. She sat down in her chair but said nothing to me. I sat down in the chair opposite.

'Thanks again for intervening the other day.'

She shrugged.

'Do you want a cup of tea?'

Her voice was harsh.

'How's it going with the drink?'

'Grand, just grand.'

'Look,' I said. 'I feel like a cog has come loose and I can't find a way to put it back on.'

She pushed her tongue behind her teeth, thrust out her lower lip.

'How do you think *I* feel?'

I sensed a softening in her.

'I know. I'm sorry.' I shook my head. 'Really sorry.'

She didn't respond. I pushed my luck.

'I want to be here to take care of you.'

Her tone didn't change so it took me a moment to register what she said next.

'Yeah, well, you can fuck off. You've fucked up this family. Family is meant to mean something. You make a commitment. You *made* a commitment. To our kids. To me. Our wedding day. Such a wonderful day. Remember when everybody clapped?'

I saw her grind her teeth, knew the calm was over.

'You *shit*,' she said. Then: 'How does it feel to have ruined my life?'

'Truly terrible,' I said.

She had a lovely mouth. I watched as she worked it.

'Good,' she said, a dying fall.

* * *

359

Tingley met me in a bar on the Brighton board-walk. When we'd left Simpson in London we'd talked a little but then gone our separate ways. Now, he looked at me.

'So are you telling me this guy is going to get away with it?' Tingley said.

'For the moment it would appear so.'

There was an elderly couple leaning into each other, making their slow progress across the beach. The brim of the woman's hat was blown up by the wind and she was holding it on with her left hand. His head was down, his chin tucked into his muffler. They had linked arms and she laughed, open-mouthed.

'Terrific,' Tingley said, swirling his drink in his glass.

'We haven't got the evidence – and we missed something.'

'We did.'

'How can you drink that shit?' I said.

He said nothing. I sighed.

'Do you think I'm happy about it? I lost my career over this. My life is in the toilet.'

He drained his glass and tilted his head to look at me.

'So you've got nothing to lose by taking him on.'

'There's always something. And if we take him on, we won't win.'

'So? You lose either way.'

'But I want to choose the terrain. You should understand that.'

He nodded.

'You mean you want to live to fight another

day?'

'That's the appropriate cliché, yes.'

He kept his eyes on me. Those pale, unblinking eyes.

'I'm not giving up,' I said. 'I'll get him some other day. Just not today.'

The couple stood facing the sea, the waves slapping slowly against the shingle. I looked back at my friend. He raised his glass.

'To that other day.'

EPILOGUE

June 1934

He was sitting in his suit in a corner of the room when she came home. *City of Dreadful Night* lay open in his lap. His father, a sunless man, had given him the bleak Victorian poem for his twelfth birthday. The gas jets were lit and the one behind his head cast his elongated shadow across the room.

'You startled me,' she said, her mouth somewhere between a smile and something more nervous. 'I didn't expect to see you today.'

He was sitting, left leg crossed over right, trousers on the left leg pulled up to avoid bagging at the knees, a narrow band of lardy, hairless leg between turn-up and sock.

'Where have you been?' he said.

'To Hove – to that doctor we heard about. It's all set for next week.'

He knew his temper scared her. He saw she was avoiding looking at his face, her eyes fixed instead on that narrow band of bare leg. Her eyes were still focused there when he stood. She looked up and saw his face. He moved towards her.

He felt he was in a cathedral or some vast

building where the silence buzzed. That strange susurrus of sound that pressed on his ears. Then he realized the dim roar was inside, not outside, his ears. His blood pumped through him in sharp surges. He checked his pulse with a finger on his wrist. His heart was beating quickly but not as rapidly as he expected.

He looked around him. Everything neat and in its place. He glanced down at his suit. He saw a dark spot on his waistcoat. He took his handkerchief from his pocket and rubbed at the spot. It didn't budge, although there was a blossom of pink on the white cloth.

He needed to still his ears. He walked to the radiogram and turned it on. The bulb glowed red. He recognized the music that grew louder as the radio warmed up. Ketèlbey's *In a Monastery Garden*.

He picked up the packet of Rothmans on the table beside the sofa. He smoked two cigarettes, listening to the music, looking everywhere but at her. She lay face down on the floor, blood in a spreading halo around her head.

He should have felt regret. He knew that. But long ago, in Flanders, his emotions had been cauterized. He had returned unable to feel. Besides, the carcass lying splayed on the carpet was not the woman he had desired and, in his way, loved.

For him the life had gone out of her weeks before he'd killed her. It had drained away the day she said:

'There's something I have to tell you. It will come as a surprise to you – as it did to me.'

He knew she didn't know about him. How could she? And so when she told him, she saw the immediate change in him but misunderstood the cause.

He'd explained the rules right at the start of their relationship. It was just a bit of fun. He would never leave his wife. He said things, of course. The things women liked to hear. But she knew – she must have known – that was just pillow talk.

He had been intoxicated by her. In bed there was nothing she wouldn't do. Things his wife would never contemplate. Soiling things. He was shocked by some of her suggestions – she could be coarse, using phrases he'd never heard before – but he had enjoyed what she did with him, there was no doubt about that.

He tolerated her wish to be seen in public with him. In the best places, places he would never take his wife. A part of him liked being seen with her – she was as beautiful as a movie star – whilst another part worried about being seen. Especially as she laughed in a ribald way. She was loud and vulgar. In private, he accepted it. In public, he was faintly embarrassed.

When she told him she was pregnant, his heart had hardened. She sensed it. She thought he was worried about a scandal. She promised to get rid of it but he could see she hoped to keep it.

It wasn't the scandal. She didn't know the reason. How could she? An abortion would make no difference.

He went to the kitchen and took her apron from behind the door. He put it on. He bent and opened the cupboard beneath the sink. He took out the toolbox. Removed the short saw.

He crossed to the window. He had a coppery taste in his mouth. All he'd asked of her in return for this flat, the money, the expensive meals was fidelity.

He knew the baby wasn't his. It couldn't be. His inability to give his wife a child had been a heavy burden for many years. It wasn't that he couldn't do the deed. It was that nothing ever came of it.

The day outside went on, unconcerned. Nothing in the street had changed. *In a Monastery Garden* was drawing to a close. It reminded him of the beautiful ruined frescoes he'd visited some months earlier in the churches on the South Downs whilst they were staying in Brighton.

He moved from the window to stand over her, the saw in his hand. The music stopped and there was silence. For a moment.

To be continued in *The Last King of Brighton...*

AUTHOR'S NOTE

A few things I need to explain about what's true and what isn't in this novel. First the Brighton Trunk Murder(s). The epilogue is my imagination, as is the diary. Everything else is factually correct, including anything in the diary to do with the police investigation of the actual case. The headquarters for the enquiry was transferred to the Royal Pavilion, but the files that are found there in this book are actually in the Sussex Records Office in Lewes along with the other files and photographs Kate Simpson looks at. Ditto the files at the National Archives, although they are much thicker than I suggest.

As far as the contemporary police story goes, I have invented a police region but tried to be accurate where certain police procedures are concerned. I have also been shamelessly inaccurate with other police procedures. (Peter James will be appalled.) Several of the disgusting cases thrown at Sarah Gilchrist (man dismembering friend, man pulling out girlfriend's teeth, raid on rotten meat warehouse) are, sadly, all too real.

I have taken a liberty with Brighton's geography in the creation of the troubled Milldean housing estate – which doesn't exist. And I've brought the old chain pier back into existence to sit alongside the West Pier and the Palace Pier because – well, because I can.